TWO ROADS FROM HERE

ALSO BY TEDDY STEINKELLNER

Trash Can Days: A Middle School Saga

Trash Can Nights: The Saga Continues

TWO ROADS FROM HERE

Teddy Steinkellner

SIMON & SCHUSTER BFYR

NEW YORK LONDON TORONTO SYDNEY NEW DELHI

SIMON & SCHUSTER BFYR
An imprint of Simon & Schuster Children's Publishing Division
1230 Avenue of the Americas, New York, New York 10020

Also available in a SIMON & SCHUSTER BFYR hardcover edition
Cover design by Krista Vossen
Interior design by Hilary Zarycky
The text for this book was set in New Caledonia.
Manufactured in the United States of America
First SIMON & SCHUSTER BFYR paperback edition July 2018
2 4 6 8 10 9 7 5 3 1
The Library of Congress has cataloged the hardcover edition as follows:
Names: Steinkellner, Teddy.
Title: Two roads from here / Teddy Steinkellner.
Description: First edition. | New York : SSBFYR, [2017] | Summary: "Five high school seniors face one life-changing decision and two very different roads"—Provided by publisher.
Identifiers: LCCN 2016028165| ISBN 9781481430616 (hardback) | ISBN 9781481430623 (pbk) | ISBN 9781481430630 (eBook)
Subjects: | CYAC: High schools—Fiction. | Schools—Fiction. | Choice—Fiction. | Decision making—Fiction. | Friendship—Fiction. | Love—Fiction. | BISAC: JUVENILE FICTION / Social Issues / Adolescence. | JUVENILE FICTION / Social Issues / Dating & Sex. | JUVENILE FICTION / Social Issues / Friendship.
Classification: LCC PZ7.S826432 Tw 2017 | DDC [Fic]—dc23
LC record available at https://lccn.loc.gov/2016028165

To Court,

Will you go out with me?

Yes ❑

No ❑

Maybe ❑

"The present is a battleground . . . where rival what-ifs compete to become the future what is."

—*The Thousand Autumns of Jacob de Zoet*, by David Mitchell

"BEWARE AND WARNING! . . . The adventures you take are a result of your choice. *You* are responsible because *you* choose! . . . Remember—you cannot go back! Think carefully before you make a move! One mistake can be your last . . . or it *may* lead to fame and fortune!"

—*Choose Your Own Adventure* series,
by R. A. Montgomery and Edward Packard

HOMECOMING WEEK

BRIAN MACK

I sat outside Coach's office with a feeling like my brain was about to give birth to a radioactive midget. The vibration was dull but intense, throbbing as hell and steady, too. *Whomp. Whomp. Whomp. Whomp.* The pounding was so hard I could almost hear it. It was like the little fetus was trying to speak. Like it wanted to tell me something.

I had to get my mind off my head before it drove me insane, so I stared at the stuff outside Coach Dent's door—the pennants, team pictures, and plastic trophies.

Mostly, the space is a shrine to Coach's golden boy and not-so-secret crush, the best quarterback in the state and the worst human being in the world: DeSean Weems.

There's a photo of DeSean leaping over a linebacker with his arms stretched out like he's Sexy Teenage Jesus. Here's one of him with some smoking-hot dance team chicks and some off-brand cheer babes. There's a pic of him slopping chowder at the old folks' home like a friggin' community service angel. Here's DeSean in the locker room, hoisting his league MVP trophy to the sky. You can see part of my ass cheek in that last shot.

There are other pics on the wall too, from way back in the day. These were the Dos Caminos teams that went all the way and won California state championships. The Bulldog glory years, my dad always says.

In the team photos from the eighties, everyone has hair down to their shoulders, back before those manes shriveled up into those skulls and those guys became assholes forever. Coach Dent is in the back row, pushing three bills and rocking about seven chins, which are stats even I can't dream of putting up. My pops is in the center, holding the team ball and wearing the grin of a dude who just got laid, probably by not-my-mom.

The last CIF title team is up there too, the miracle kids from ten years ago. My brother's squad. Kyle is kneeling in the front row, all rigid and robotlike, with the dopest diabolical Ivan Drago flattop that I tried in vain throughout my whole childhood to re-create until I realized my hairline was beginning to disappear at age thirteen.

There's no pic up from last year. I wasn't able to finish the season last year. No one likes to talk about last year. Not Coach Dent, not my dad, not Kyle, not DeSean. They're locked in on *now.* We all are. This is my senior season. This is my last chance.

My head hurt looking at the photos. And not just my

head. My stomach felt gurgly as crap, like Taco Tuesday meets the Tea Cups at Disneyland. My eyes stung from how burningly shiny everything was around me, I mean the glare was hella bright, like my-thighs-during-winter white. And my ears were still ringing. My temples were still thumping. The baby midget in my skull was screaming. It wanted to die.

"Big Mack!" Coach called out from behind the door. "Come on in, son."

I took one last look at the DeSean wall, flipped it off because why not, and got out of my chair. I felt the world spin for a moment, forced myself not to puke, and took a deep-ass big-boy breath. Then I did it. I walked right into Coach's office, right into my future, straight toward my date with density.

Wait.

No.

Destiny. That's the word I want. Destiny.

Well, considering the sheer girth of mine and Coach's asses combined, I guess density makes sense too.

Density, destiny, density, destiny, density, destiny, density, destiny.

Goddamn.

My head really hurt.

"Whose time is it?"

"OUR TIME!"

"Whose time is it?"

"OUR TIME!"

"Whose time is it?"

"OUR TIME!"

"GO SENIORS!"

"WOOF WOOF WOOF!"

"GO DAWGS!"

It was lunchtime. Five hours before Coach's office, way before my date with fatness. I was in the Greek Amphitheater, smack-dab in the middle of the stage. Everyone at school was surrounding me, cheering their heads off, losing their minds.

I was about to have the most badass moment of my life.

I bumped chests with Ernesto. I dominatrix-smacked Tua across the man titties for good luck. Then I turned to the crowd, and I gave them a freak show they'll never forget:

I slapped my thighs and did a couple of high stomps, like in one of Tua's Polynesian dances. I flexed my guns, which I'm guessing put some freshman honeys straight through puberty. Then I ripped off my "#69 MACK" football jersey, and when everyone saw what was underneath, they got ridiculously hype.

On my fat white belly, I'd had some rally girls paint a big-ass blue bulldog along with the words "SENIORS, BITCHES." It was our school logo, but way fiercer-looking, plus kinda sexy too, just like yours truly. And when everyone saw me take that dog for a walk, when they saw me jump up and down and side to side and jiggle that nasty tummy beast all around, they all went crazy, and they loved me. They loved me so hard.

It was time.

With the crowd still climaxing, I turned around and gazed up at it, all twenty-five feet of it. All twenty-five lathered-up, death-defying, legend-making feet of the object of my dreams:

The Grease Pole.

Dos Caminos is the only high school on the Central Coast—probably in all of California and maybe in all of America—that has the Grease Pole tradition. Basically there's this huge pole with a bell at the top. Every year in October, during every Homecoming Week in our school's history dating back to, like, farmers-doing-it-with-cows-because-they-were-so-bored-and-lonely times, the pole gets all smothered in Vaseline and crap. Then the whole school comes out to the Greek at lunch to watch as teams of three twelfth graders climb on to each other's shoulders to try to ring that bell.

No one's actually done it in a decade, not since my brother and his buddies made history back during his senior year. Every single year it's supposed to finally happen, and every year it doesn't. It's like the Messiah coming back, or Tua learning how to read.

But this was it. This was our time.

"Nesto," I said, "Remember, when you're up there, don't look down. And, Titties," I said to Tua, "when you're on my shoulders, keep your knees locked. I don't want your butt all in my face."

"Aww, yes, you do, cuz," Tua said.

"Only if we ring the bell," I said. "If we do that, you can put your butt wherever you want."

"Okay," Tua said, grinning. "In that case, I'm rubbing it up on Nikki Foxworth."

I mean-mugged him dirty. "You shut your obese, illiterate mouth," I said. "Nikki is *mine*."

Tua nodded and mouthed the words "my bad."

"Anyway," I finished. "Enough about your bloated ass. It's time to kick the *Grease Pole's* ass."

"Come on, boys!

"Let's get it, Dawgs!

"LET'S GOOOO!!!!!!"

With everyone in the whole school still shrieking like horny baboons, me, Ernesto, and Tua stepped across the safety padding and up to the pole.

The whistle blew and I got low. The three of us decided I'd be base since I'm slightly fatter than Tua, and also because bottom dude seems like the most important dude on the team, and look at me, just look at me, look at my effing belly dog—I'm the man, I'm the man, I'm the man.

Tua got on my shoulders and I held steady, even though

he's built like the most depressing Weight Watchers "before" picture ever. Then, using the pole for leverage, he slowly stood up straight, and while he did stumble for a sec, which blocked my entire field of vision and gave me a total eclipse of the moon-crack, I somehow kept my balance because I'm the patron saint of cool friggin' shit.

Ernesto had problems getting up too, but I kept barking orders at him, and he scrambled up my back, and eventually Tua's as well. I couldn't look up because I didn't want to strain my neck, but I knew he was close to the bell. I could hear everyone around me getting loud, like real loud, like louder than they got when we advanced to CIF semis last year, like louder than whenever DeSean flashes his fake asshole smile at a pep rally, like so loud it felt like time was slowing down, so loud I knew my life was about to change—

And I heard it! I heard that angelic sound. I heard the ring of that goddamned glorious bell, and I heard everyone going crazy, and I got the biggest life boner, and I felt like a gladiator superhero porn star *god*—

And in that moment, come on, I had to do it. I had to gaze out and see my people—

My backup linemen, Cody, Hector, and Ian—aka Grundle Boy, Chalupa, and Scrotum Face, aka Scrotes. They were all so into it, and Scrotes was humping the air for some reason, which is so Scrotes—

The rally girls, the cheerleaders and dance team chicks,

they were so stoked too, especially Mona Omidi—aka the Moaner—who was staring at me eyes all wide, mouth all open, ready to lick her lips and taste the Big Mack, but I'm not going anywhere near the Moaner as long as I have a chance with—

Nikki Foxworth, my personal rally girl, not to mention my special lady of the moment, who I didn't spot sitting with the other girls, which meant she was probs behind me, snapping pictures of my ass, which she called cute the other day—true story, haterzzz—

And speaking of haterz, where was DeSean Weems, because I had to peep the look on his face, I just had to, so I turned my head, more to the left this time, and I saw the back row of benches, and I didn't see him at first, but then I spotted him, but it was kind of annoying, since DeSean was turned away from me, because he had someone next to him—a girl, big shocker, a brunette I think, and he was getting kinda handsy with her, and it looked like—wait, punch me right in the diddle—was that—?

And that's all I remember for the next few minutes.

That's when five hundred pounds of offensive lineman came crashing on my head.

I must have spaced for a sec there, watching DeSean, and when I lost my focus, I guess my body just gave. I staggered backward, and that little hitch made Tua lose his balance, only instead of falling back, Tua fell forward, because all of Tua's weight is located in his tits, and so with

Nesto tumbling on top of him, Tua and his dirty pillows came crashing onto me, and as all that double fatness plummeted my way, Tua kneed me in the forehead.

I didn't wake up at first. Not for, like, ninety seconds. Nesto told me everyone held their breath the whole time, because what if I was dead—or worse, given the big game—injured.

And when I eventually came to, some rando adults made me answer basic math questions, like a special needs turtle from a stupid app for babies.

And in fifth and sixth period I couldn't pay attention, because everywhere I looked I saw fuzzy little stars, and I kept hearing this weird-ass rumbling, like God had tummy troubles.

And after school at practice, I missed five or six easy blocks, and I poured my Gatorade on my chin instead of in my mouth, and DeSean tattled to Coach Dent about how I'd done the Grease Pole without team permission, that goddamn glory boy snitch.

And that's the story of how I ended up in Coach's office this afternoon.

That's how my Concussion Baby was born.

"So . . . you think you can suit up Friday?"

"I dunno," I said. "I dunno."

"Well, how are you feeling?" Coach said. "Because that's the most important thing, son."

I shrugged. "I dunno. I—"

"But you know," Coach continued, adjusting his visor and leaning forward. "This here's a crucial game. Lagunita's only a game behind us in League, so we need this thing if we want a shot at CIF."

"I know," I said. "And—"

"And it's quite a moment for DeSean, too. He's going to have scouts there from USC, UCLA, and Oregon. You realize that? USC, UCLA, and Oregon. It'd sure be great if he had his Big Mack out there, protecting his blind side."

"Yeah," I said. "Yeah—"

"And you remember what happened last year, of course. You making that whole big deal out of one little hammy tweak. You choosing to sit out semis even though the doctors said you were good to go. I'm sure you, ah, remember how that went for us."

I didn't say anything. I just sat there in the office, surrounded by all that memorabilia, Coach staring lasers at me, my brain throbbing like a mofo, my mouth hanging open like a fool.

"So, what'll it be, son? Don't you want to redeem yourself?

"Don't you want to help your friend out?

"Don't you love the game of football?

"What'll it be, Big Mack?

"What'll it be, Brian?

"What'll it be?"

ALLEGRA REY

I felt unkind being so secretly judgmental toward everyone around me, but when I was sitting in the Greek at lunch today, I couldn't help but observe that all of the people were behaving exactly like little groups of animals as they gossiped and ate their food and waited for the Grease Pole competition to start. So I did what I always do when I'm waiting for Wiley to show up somewhere:

I composed a mental challenge for myself.

"A pride of lions.

"A herd of buffalo.

"A gaggle of geese.

"A murder of ravens.

"An implausibility of gnus."

"Are you okay?" Wiley said as he plopped his backpack down and took a seat next to me, proceeding to open up and simultaneously inhale his Nutter Butters and Fanta—

Oops, there it is. I'm judging again.

"I'm fine," I said. "I'm thinking of animal collectives. I'm attempting to see how many I can name."

"Oh . . . ," Wiley said. "Well, I don't know what animal whatevers are, but do you mean, like, um . . . a lameness of freshmen?"

"Ooh, that's a great idea!" I said. "I was actually thinking up real ones, but let's do that instead—let's invent high school collectives!"

"Okay," Wiley said, smiling.

"A glitter of theater kids," I said.

"A Hot Cheetos bag of stoners," Wiley said.

"An indifference of hipsters," I said.

"A vomiting of cheerleaders," Wiley said.

"A meat processing plant of football players," I said.

"An awesomeness of band geeks," Wiley said.

"A *super*-awesomeness of band geeks!" I elaborated.

"AN ORGY OF BAND GEEKS!!!" Wiley stood on the bench and bellowed, far more than a little too loudly.

Everybody within a ten-foot radius of our spot immediately turned around and shushed us, eyebrows arched in intense disdain. Apparently we'd out-animaled even the most bestial of high school animals, right as they were attempting to watch their primal phallic ritual. I felt so embarrassed.

"So sorry," I whispered to no one in particular. "Come on, Wiley. Let's go, before people shush us again."

"We're fine," he said. "No one cares."

"I care."

"But I wanna see Big Mack fall on his fat ass!"

"There'll be plenty of that on Friday night," I said. "Are you coming with me or not?"

"Sweeten the offer."

"What if I . . . let you pick our after-homework movie?"

Wiley snapped his fingers. "*Now* we're talking. I'm kind of in an eighties mood, so maybe *Teen Witch*? Or *Top Gun*? Oh, but you've never seen *Election*, right? You'd like it. It's about an overachiever who dominates everything in her path, not that you could relate. Hmm . . . I haven't watched a good puppet movie in a while. What are your thoughts on puppet sex?"

He regarded me very intently as he awaited my thoughts on puppet sex. I looked back at him like, you are too preposterous. Wiley took a final swig of his Fanta, the residue of which dyed his wispy pseudo-mustache a vivid shade of traffic-cone orange. I shook my head and grinned.

"Come on," I said. "And wipe your mouth."

The rest of the afternoon proceeded in typical fashion, with me checking items off my to-do list while Wiley tagged along. Before lunch ended, I stopped in with Cole Martin-Hammer to discuss Interact Club logistics and confirm this week's Philanthropy Friday at the retirement community.

I also made a cameo appearance at Math Club, where the mathletes acted snobbish toward Wiley and wouldn't allow him to have a slice of pi pie, which led to me giving Wiley my pi pie instead, which was too bad because I'd been looking forward to eating that.

Next I had AP Chem, in which Mr. Aspell did the sweetest thing by telling me what a pleasure it had been writing my letter of rec for my scholarship applications. I said thank you, and that I would be sure to keep in touch with him next year, hopefully from Stanford.

Finally, in Advanced Band, we had an extra-long practice in preparation for the homecoming game this Friday. It was mostly productive, except for the incident in which Wiley was exiled from the room for making fart noises with his tuba. After band, as he and I walked home, I warned him that if he kept getting in trouble, he might have his band citizenship grade lowered to a "Needs Improvement," which, combined with his declining grades, could potentially threaten his graduation status. Wiley responded by telling me to take my flute and stick it up my—

"WILEY!" I shouted, surprising myself with how vociferous I could be.

He staggered backward and did not speak for several moments.

"Um . . . ," he eventually said, rather weakly. "Thaaat's meeeee!"

I took a breath for myself as we left campus and made the right onto Calaveras to start the mile-long walk to our neighborhood.

"Why must you say things like that?"

"I'm sowwy, Awwegwa," Wiley said. "I was just being funny."

"You'll have to settle for me laughing at the other ninety-nine percent of your jokes. No more puerile comments about my flute, please. You know, I stopped going to band camp because of people like you."

Wiley paused midstep.

"I thought you stopped going to band camp because that's the summer your mom got sick and your family couldn't pay for it anymore."

Oh my goodness.

Was this boy born with a giant hairy foot in his mouth?

I walked away with brisk urgency, needing to get home for a little alone time.

"Allegra! Allegra, wait!"

I heard his footfalls as he scurried after me. I doubled my pace without looking back.

"I didn't know what I was saying, okay? I suck! I suck so much!"

I still would not turn around, not when he should have known better.

"I'm sorry!"

I halted for just a fraction of a second. I heard his heavy breathing as he approached me, then felt it on the back of my neck. I turned to face my friend.

"I'm sorry," Wiley repeated.

His face was pink all over. His eyes were half smiling, half distraught.

"I'm really sorry. I screwed up, you know? I can't explain my behavior. I don't know what's been up with me. Or, well, I do have one theory. Do you wanna hear it?"

I took him in for a moment: the erratic, still-orange patch of peach fuzz framing his upper lip; the shaggy, brown-blond hair that hangs below his ears, which he won't let me trim because he says it gives him Samson-like strength; the wolf T-shirt I bought for him as a joke two Christmases ago, a decision I have come to regret as he now owns twelve and wears them daily; the wide, toothy smile on his face as he leaned in toward me, a smile that was genuine to be sure, and even sort of adorable, but suddenly too close, unexpectedly centimeters from my face.

"Allie," Wiley whispered.

"Hold on," I said, grabbing my phone out of my bag. "I need to see something," I said as I unlocked the screen and pretended to check it.

"But—"

"Give me two seconds."

"Okay," Wiley said. "Whatever you want."

And that's when I saw it.

The e-mail that would change the course of my existence forever.

Dear Allegra,

Congratulations! It is with great pleasure we announce that you have been awarded a Bright Path Scholarship for your collegiate studies. This year, more than fifteen thousand of the highest-achieving, low-income high school students in the nation applied to become Bright Path Scholars, and only twenty-five were selected, making your accomplishment truly remarkable. In addition, we are pleased to inform you that through our College Match Program, you have been secured early admission to your top-choice college, Stanford University. As a Bright Path Scholar, you will be given a full-ride scholarship to Stanford, and

I blinked and read those words again. And again. And again. I read them until they weren't words anymore, just random squiggles. Random, life-altering squiggles.

I couldn't breathe. My phone dropped out of my hand. I put my hands to my face. I fell to the sidewalk.

"What?" Wiley said, crouching down next to me. I could barely hear him, my heart was pounding so loudly, my reality was shifting too quickly.

"What is it? Allie? Allie, is everything okay?"

"Oh, Wiley," I said. I threw my arms around him. "*I did it.* I did it, I did it, I did it! Wiley, I did it! *STANFORD!!!!!*"

I squeezed him tight, and I kissed him on the cheek, and I looked up at him and it was so wonderful because he looked so happy for me, so truly happy.

"I'm just . . . ," Wiley said, wiping the corner of his eye. "Oh my God, this is amazing. But how? What happened? You sure this isn't, like, Cole pranking you somehow?"

"You're right," I said through frenetic breaths. "This doesn't feel real. But remember that impossible scholarship I applied for this summer?"

I picked my phone off the ground, stood back up, and skimmed the e-mail.

"I guess I somehow . . . got it. And they're giving me a free ride . . . and they matched me with my first choice . . . and look, it says there's going to be a special reception at Stanford for Bright Path Scholars and other early-admitted students. . . . It's this December, over winter break. . . . I can't believe I'm going. . . . I really get to go. . . ."

I burst into tears, right then and there, only a minute

from my house. Wiley put his arm around me, and without saying anything, and without having to say anything, he walked me all the way to my house in blissful, teary silence.

"Okay," Wiley said. "Let's dry those eyes. You don't want to give the surprise away."

"Right," I said, dabbing my cheeks with my sleeve and cleaning off the leaky mascara.

"Hey," Wiley said. "Is it cool if I come in with you? I want to be there when you share the big news."

"Fine," I said. "But you're *not allowed* to give it away."

"Come on," Wiley said. "It's not like I have a big mouth or anything."

He made a tuba fart noise and grinned puckishly. I poked him in the chest and laughed.

"All right," I said. "I can't believe this is happening. Here we go."

I opened the front door, and the first thing I noticed was that my entire family—my mom, dad, Alejandro, Augusto, and my *abuela*—they were all together in the living room. They were sitting on the big couch in front of the TV, but the TV wasn't on. No one was talking. They were looking at me expectantly, like they'd been sitting there for an hour, waiting for me to walk in. Maybe they knew already. Maybe the scholarship people had sent my parents that joyous e-mail too.

"Hey, Reys," Wiley said. "Um, Allegra has some big—"

"Wiley," my dad said. "I'm sorry. We must talk to Allegra for a few minutes."

"Oh," Wiley said. "Should I . . . go home?"

My dad looked at my mom. She squeezed his hand.

"Yes," my dad said. "Allegra will see you tomorrow."

"O . . . kay," Wiley said.

He closed the door quickly, without saying good-bye.

"Dad?" I said. "What's going on?"

My dad didn't respond. He stared down at the ground. So did my *abuela* and my brothers. Only my mom could look me in the eye.

"*Mija*," my mom said. "I went to the doctor this morning, and she told me . . . they've found something in my ovaries again. I'm stage three, which means I could be fine, and there's a very good chance I'll be fine, but I'll have to start treatment again and . . . please don't cry."

I wasn't crying, so I wasn't sure why she said that, but she was looking at me like I was six years old, and I didn't know what to say. Actually, all of them were looking at me like that. My *abuela* even tried, I don't know, humming soothingly.

"Don't cry," she said in between hums, almost as if she were singing it. "It will be all right."

"I'm not crying," I said.

"You know what?" my dad said. "It's okay. This is a hard day. We can cry. It's okay."

"But I'm *not* crying," I said.

"Don't worry about it," my mom said. "Just let it happen."

"I'm *not* crying!" I screamed out. "I'm not *crying*! Look at me, people! I'm *not crying*!"

As soon as I said it, I caught my reflection in the front mirror. I saw my eyes, and I realized that I hadn't completely finished wiping them a few minutes earlier, when I'd learned about the scholarship, when I'd had the most euphoric moment of my life. My face was still completely covered in wet makeup. It was all blotchy and blue.

"These aren't tears, Mama," I said. "This is from before."

"What?" she said.

"Never mind."

I took a seat on the couch next to my mom, in between everybody else. Once I sat down, my mom tried to hold me, but I wouldn't let her. I held her instead, and she began to sob, which made everyone else do the same. They cried and cried and they cried so much that they sounded like animals, and they kept crying, and I kept holding on to my mom.

I couldn't cry. I wanted to, but I couldn't. I'd used up all my tears before, and now I couldn't cry with the rest of my family.

I don't want to go away anymore.

WILEY OTIS

In the first act of any great screenplay, the hero has a problem.

Indiana Jones has a bunch of precious stuff he wants to return to a museum. Luke Skywalker has an evil empire to worry about and some lingering daddy issues. Marty McFly has a mom who wants to incest him to the max.

And me, yeah, I've got my problem too. It might not be a Nazi- or mom-sex-level problem, but it's pretty big.

That's the other thing movie characters have, though. They all have a mentor or a best friend, someone they trust who can help them with their problem. Marty has Doc. Luke has Obi-Wan and fun robots. Indy has that kid with the hat who says, "Okey-dokey, Dr. Jones! Hold on to your POTATOES!"

But see, that's my other problem. My person who's the only person in the world I'd want to talk to about my problem, I mean, she's also my problem.

So how is my movie supposed to end?

I was thinking about these things—and everything that happened on the walk home from band yesterday—this afternoon during math. I was spacing out and doodling during class, because come on, how is algebra 2 supposed to help me in my future career as a filmmaker, when Ms. Valdez marched right up and tore my drawing off the desk.

"Wiley," she said. "This doesn't look like a parabola."

"It's not," I said. "It's a guy."

She held my paper closer to her face. Her eyes got all wide.

"Is that . . . a *swastika?*"

Everyone in class turned to look at me like I was the stupidest man boob in the world. Everyone always looks at me like I'm the stupidest man boob in the world.

"Well, yeah," I explained. "That's a Wehrmacht soldier. I was drawing that one part in *Raiders of the Lost Ark* where the dude gets his face melted off."

Ms. Valdez clucked her tongue. "This is a no-place-for-hate school. I'm assigning you a detention."

"It's not what you think—"

"No talking, not unless it's about parabolas."

"That Nazi is like a metaphor for my life!"

"Detention, Wiley. Sixth period. You know the drill."

I sat by myself in the library, wondering how Allegra's walk home was going without me, feeling like I'd just been given ten-to-fifteen in prison. I looked around the room, examining my fellow detainees. Maybe someone in here could help me.

There was a lameness of freshman girls, sitting on the couches and subtly sexting football players. But they weren't worth talking to. They were far too naive.

There was a Hot Cheetos bag of stoner boys at a side table, flipping through Where's Waldo? books and laughing their asses off. But there was no way I could approach them. Allegra would never let me near people who lack ambition like that. Plus, those guys would just laugh at me. They'd point at my awesome mustache. They'd call it gay.

And, of course, sitting at her desk, there was the Bear. The Bear is this terrifying librarian who is as burly and savage as a North American grizzly with a salmon in its mouth. She has always had a special hatred for me, even compared to other teachers. I couldn't go up to her, not unless I wanted to be drizzled in honey and devoured in a single bite.

So nope. No one could help me. No one was going to listen to my concerns and give me advice. Not here in detention, not anywhere ever. I was destined to be sad and lonely, for all of eternity. . . .

That is, until someone else walked through the front door. Until the universe opened up, and dropped the exact person I needed straight from the sky.

My guardian angel.

She was strikingly tall, like nearly six feet, with the longest, tannest limbs. She just moved here from Texas, where I heard her dad was a big-shot lawyer and her mom used to be a Dallas Cowboys cheerleader. She could be a sexy cowgirl right now if she wanted, or a lingerie model, or the lady who gets aroused while washing her hair in a shampoo commercial. Her hair was so shampoo commercial—all long and flowing, like a gushing brown river, which I realize sounds disgusting, but I mean, everything about this girl was intoxicating, from her lips to her lashes to her anime-size eyes to her delightfully shaped calves.

"Hi," the girl said to the Bear, the slightest twang in her voice. "I'm Nikki Foxworth. Sorry I'm late."

"Mfughh," the Bear grunted, and pointed Nikki to her detention spot.

Which, as fate would have it, was the chair right next to mine.

I'm still not sure what gave me the nerve to talk to Nikki this afternoon. It's very unlike me to make friends with anyone new. I can never convince people to find the decent guy buried deep inside this weird-smelling package.

But in all the best movies, and eighties movies especially—*Sixteen Candles*, *Weird Science*, *The Breakfast Club*—there's this thing, this recurring trope, where high school loser dorks have this weird, kinda magical ability to form special friendships with popular chicks. The geek will always have a scene with the hot cheerleader in which she gives him great advice, and then she'll kiss him on the cheek or something, and I know it seemed crazy, and that life isn't a teen movie, but I mean, for all the loser dorks out there, I had to try.

"Excuse me, Nikki? I'm Wiley. From your first period. I have a question. About the econ homework.

"I'm asking about school," I whisper-called up to the Bear, who flared her nostrils at me, but she didn't yell at me to stop talking.

"What's your question?" Nikki said without bothering to look my way. She was on her phone, secretly texting, clearly bored.

"It's . . ." I looked down for a moment. I caught sight of her tank top cleavage by mistake. I glanced back at her face. I looked down again.

"Oh," Nikki said. "So that's how it is."

She motioned to her chest.

"So you wanted to see my 'econ homework,' huh? I get it. Real classy. But not very original. No, sweetheart. No. I will not go to homecoming with you."

"Wait!" I said. My voice cracked as I said it. "No, I'm not attracted to you—well, okay, it's not that I don't find you attractive . . . I mean, objectively speaking, of course you're—but the reason—what I wanted to ask you was—I need your advice."

Nikki continued to glare at me with her pencil eyebrows arched up all super-judgy, but she didn't look back at her phone, and she didn't get up and leave, so I kept going.

"I'm in love. But not with you. I just want to make that clear. Although you do, uh, have very nice . . . econ homework."

This was the kind of blurt-out that usually earns me a detention from a teacher, or a talking-to on the walk home from school, but Nikki looked at me and almost smiled.

"You're funny," she said.

Her half smile turned into a genuine laugh as she pointed to the center of her cleavage, right to the middle of her—actually, you know what, probably not her boobs. Maybe it was more like her heart.

"We're in the same boat," she said. "That's why I'm sitting here right now. Because I'm in love and the world isn't fair. But that's another story, I suppose."

She tossed her head back and flipped her shiny L'Oréal hair over her bare shoulder.

"Anyway," she said. "Who are you crazy about, if I may ask?"

"I don't know if you know her," I said. "Allegra Rey?"

Nikki leaned toward me, her hand on her cheek. "Tell me about Allegra."

I've gone over the story so many times in my head, it came out basically all in one breath:

"I've known Allie for ten years. . . .

"I've been in love with her for all of them.

"Her family moved next door in second grade. I knew she was cute, even then. I also knew she was smart. So smart she could be president one day, or at the very least a marine biologist.

"In fourth grade I remember her twin brothers were born. That was the same year my dad moved out. Same month, now that I think about it.

"Seventh grade was when Allegra and I started walking home together, which was when we really became friends. One day I truly noticed her—her springy hair, her freckly nose, her weirdly small hands—and I realized that day she was the most beautiful girl I'd ever seen.

"Freshman year her mom got cancer. It was a really hard year. Allegra and I cooked dinner for her family most nights. She helped me learn algebra too, so I wouldn't have to repeat ninth grade. Even though she had to help her family. She helped me, too.

"These past few years, I've wanted more than anything to ask her out. I've even gotten close a couple times. Hell, I almost tried on our walk home yesterday. But at the last moment something always goes wrong, or I choke and chicken out.

"I know what my choice is. I know that by spilling my feelings, I risk losing the entire friendship, and that's the scariest thought. But you know, she just got into college far away, and her mom is sick again, so, like . . . if I don't tell her the truth . . . maybe I'll lose her anyway."

A chill ran down my back. I let out a massive exhale. "You're a girl. Tell me what to do."

Nikki nodded slowly. She brought her fingers to her chin. "Wiley," she said. "Wiley, Wiley, Wiley. You are such a good guy."

"Thanks," I said. "But, like, what do I do?"

She looked up at the ceiling, lost in thought for a second. "Lordy," she said. "You're in a bind. That friend zone is a rough place to be."

Then she did something that surprised me—she touched me. She lifted her hand and she touched her finger to my chest. To my heart, I guess.

"I do have one nugget of advice," Nikki said. "And it's this: If you decide to go after her, go hard. Don't pussyfoot around. You want her, so give her a reason to want you back, you know? This is your moment, Wiley. Grab the bull. Take the horns. Make the boldest play possible. It's what my boyfriend did with me, and we've been happy ever since."

"That makes sense," I said. "That makes sense."

I nodded at Nikki. She batted her Texas-size eyelashes back.

"Who is your boyfriend, anyway?" I asked. "The Big Mack, right?"

Nikki's eyes almost bulged out of her head. She's such a hot girl, but for a quick second there she reminded me more of a wacky dog from an old-timey cartoon.

"Oh no. No, no, no, no, no. I mean sure, when I first moved here I was assigned to be Brian's rally girl and all, but nothing ever happened . . . ew. Yech. No, no." Nikki let out one final shudder. She regained her composure and smiled. "No, I'm with DeSean now."

"Wow," I said. "Lucky you. Mr. USC, UCLA, and Oregon himself."

The conversation mostly faded after that. We sat in silence for a while. I thought about Allegra and what I might do to make myself worthy of her and all the ways I could fail, but all the reasons I need to try. At the same time, Nikki conducted an entire, possibly erotic, text chat with DeSean under the table. Popular girls are truly impressive sometimes.

Before detention ended, I did ask her one final thing:

The *Breakfast Club* question.

"Hey, Nikki?"

"Hmm?"

"I was wondering. After today . . . like, I'm gonna wanna update you on how the whole Allegra thing goes, but . . . but you know, you're cool and stuff. So, well, uh . . . am I ever going to talk to you again?"

Nikki put her finger to her lips. She furrowed her brow

slightly. "Honestly, sweets? I have no idea. I hope so, but who knows? Hmm . . . could really go either way."

I know what I have to do.

I know how my hero's journey ends.

It came to me after I left campus, after I passed by Nikki outside the library with her tongue down DeSean's throat. It came while I was at the mini-mart, grabbing Nutter Butter Bites and tapping my foot to the gas station radio, listening to two random guys talking about the big homecoming game and whether Big Mack was gonna suit up or let the team down.

It came all at once. The perfect idea.

I'm going to do it for freaking real. I'm going to reveal the entire truth to Allie, and in the boldest, most cinematic, most *me* way imaginable. I'm going to give her the happiest ever after.

And I'm going to do it Friday night.

NIKKI FOXWORTH

DeSean kissed me on the side of my neck, in my favorite place.

"You a bad girl?"

"I'm a bad girl."

"You a bad girl?"

"I'm a *bad* girl."

"You my naughty girl?"

"I'm your bad little thing."

"All right, bad girl," he said between kisses. "Why don't you prove it?"

My hand shot to my mouth.

"DeSeannnn."

I hadn't wanted to come to the Grease Pole thing to begin with. I'd wanted to do what DeSean and I have done every other lunch these past two weeks since we started seeing each other—sneak off in his car and make the heck out like it's five minutes till Judgment Day.

But D very much needed to witness the competition,

for personal reasons, he said. So he told me we could sit in the way back row, where no one would spy on us, where we could basically be alone, where we could get as intimate as we liked.

And he was right. None of the hundreds of people surrounding us were paying us any mind, because the whole time DeSean and I were canoodling—my arms around his neck, my legs across his lap, his hand between my thighs, his kisses all over my face—that entire time, Brian Mack was down on the stage, jelly-rolling and booby-shaking in the most desperate bid for attention I've ever seen. That poor boy.

I don't like thinking about Brian too much, so I looked back at DeSean. I pursed my lips and gave him a little smile.

"What do you mean, 'prove it'?"

"Well," he said. "It's like, you like me, and I like you—I love you, in fact—"

"I love you too," I said. I squeezed my thighs softly around his hand.

"So if we love each other," he continued. "Maybe we can, you know, do . . . certain stuff?"

"What do you mean?"

"I mean," DeSean added, in a low voice. "Let's take shit to the next level."

I giggled and shook my head. "Sweetheart, I told you before. I don't know if I'm ready."

He nodded. "You're nervous about your first time. Believe me, I was too. But there's nothing to be worried about. I'll be slow. And gentle. I'll treat you right."

He lifted his hips as he said it, pressing into me slightly. I felt him as he did it, all of him. It felt . . . well, golly, it felt amazing.

"What do you think?" DeSean said. "Today? After school? The spot?"

He said the words quickly, almost like he was panting. I looked up at him, my strong, sweet man. I made my eyes as big as I could.

"I really love you, D," I whispered. "And I want you. So bad. I want you to be the one to, you know . . . but I just don't think it's time. Not yet." I lifted my hands and placed each of them on his chest, one by one.

"Okay?" I said.

"Okay," he said, nodding.

"Okay," I said.

DeSean dropped his head. He grinned. "Damn, naughty girl," he said. "Stop acting so pure. You're killing me, baby."

He wiggled his fingers between my thighs. It tickled something fierce. I burst into laughter and tickled him back.

And right then, right at that very moment, that's the exact second we stopped thinking about sex.

That's when the bald boy got bopped on the head.

• • •

A few things happened right away.

First, and most important, Brian turned out to be fine. I breathed the biggest sigh of relief when he gave the crowd a big thumbs-up and did a happy little tushy dance. As weird a vibe as I sometimes get from Brian, I truly do wish the best for the kid. I'm glad he's all set to play this Friday—for his sake, for the good of the team, for DeSean.

D was furious, though. I've never seen him like that before. "I friggin' predicted this would happen," he kept on saying, and "fatass fool." I didn't want to have to defend Brian or whatever, but DeSean wasn't being fair, and he was showing a very ugly side of himself. I was about to say, hey, you know, if you're gonna get hateful like this, we might have to rethink this whole "taking it to the next level" thing, and that's—

That's when I got my detention.

"Foxworth! Off his lap. Hands on the bench. Feet on the ground. *Now.*"

It was Ms. Fawcett, the vice principal, the one with the pointy chin and the spiky hair. Back when I said nobody was watching us, apparently I was way off, because she had a look on her face like she had mentally recorded every one of our neck kisses, every twerk of our hips.

"No public displays of affection," she said to me and only me. "That's not the way to make an impression at your new school. I'm assigning you detention, Nikki, in the library, for the next two days."

She stared at me real hard and super-cold, like I was sixteen and pregnant or something.

Before she walked away, she said one more thing:

"Good luck this Friday, D."

I know I should be way more ticked off than I am. I know how unfair it is that I got two detentions and my boyfriend none, simply because he can't afford to be suspended for the big game. I know how harsh the double standard is, how insane it is that I should be treated like a witch getting stoned in the town square just for being cute on a bench with my guy. I know I have to walk the narrowest tightrope ever at this school, and I know that it's total bull.

But, true story, I don't even care that I had to do detention.

After all, the Lord tends to work in mysterious ways.

Detention is where I made my best memory of the year so far.

Wiley is beyond adorable. His passion for Allegra is like something out of a storybook. It's so amazingly inspiring. He's been waiting all these years for her, building up the bravery to make his gallant move. And now, with a little help from his fairy godmother, he's really going to do it. He's going to put it all on the line for love.

So honestly, I realized this afternoon, why can't I? Why should I spend the entire year worrying about being the new girl in town, about my reputation, about what people like the dance team captains or Ms. Fawcett think of me? Who cares? I've got to follow the same advice I gave Wiley. I've got to take action. DeSean is my dream. He's my future. I need to do what feels right.

"Okay, Mr. USC, UCLA, and Oregon," I said to D as he met me coming out of detention. "I have a proposition for you."

"What's that?" he said.

"This Friday. Homecoming game. If you guys win . . ."

"Yeah?"

"I'll be your reward."

DeSean's eyes got huge. He gulped. "And if we lose?"

I crinkled my nose at him. I gave him a secret smile. "I'll be your consolation prize."

He bit his fist. "You serious?" he said.

"Serious as cancer," I said flirtatiously.

"Yes!" DeSean whooped, jumping in the air and pumping his fist. "Yes! Yes! *YES*!"

When I got home, I snuck into my room through the back way. My dad's in Texas on business, so I wasn't worried about seeing him as I tiptoed in, but my mom—

My mom was sitting at the foot of my bed, a glass of red wine in her hand. On my bed, there was a big book open. She was flipping through the pages, looking at pictures.

"Freshman year," she said without looking up. "JV

Majorettes. Pep squad. Class social chair. Disney Club. You were so precious, sweet one. So precious."

"Why are you looking at my old yearbook?" I said. "What are you doing in my room?"

I half turned away from her as I said it, just in case there was anything incriminating on my neck.

"Your vice principal called," she said, still staring down at the book.

"Oh."

"She said she saw you at lunchtime."

"Yeah, but—"

"I thought we weren't going to be getting in any trouble."

"Yeah," I said. "But it wasn't fair, the double standard—"

"We made an agreement. You, me, and your father."

"I know, I know, but I don't think I did anything wrong—"

She repeated it, quieter this time. "We made an agreement."

She closed her eyes. She took a small sip of wine.

"Mom, I—"

"Do you have a boyfriend, Nicole?"

"What?" I tried to say. "Mom, I—what?"

I waited for her to look at me. She didn't. She flipped a page in the book. She sighed. She flipped another page.

I turned to face her. I covered the side of my neck as I did it.

"I'm sorry, Mom," I said. "I made a mistake."

My mother nodded and smiled. She closed the yearbook and placed the glass down. She stood up from my bed and walked over to me. She leaned in. She touched her forehead to mine. "Good," she said. "This is a new year."

I was a good girl in Dallas. I made good grades. I organized so many charity events through my youth group. I got mani-pedis with my mom every other Saturday and watched football and golf with my daddy most Sundays after church. And I told them everything. For a while.

And yes, I had boyfriends, but good girls are allowed to have boyfriends. There shouldn't be anything wrong with having a boyfriend.

I lost my virginity at the end of freshman year. His name was Garrett. He was a senior on the football team, and he was a real good linebacker, and he was going to be a walk-on at A&M. My parents still don't know about him.

There were other boys, too. Marcus. Luke. Bryce. Adrian. Lamar. Some I dated for a couple months, and some I saw just once or twice. None of them went to my school. A couple went to rival schools—football players, naturally. Some were my age, some a little bit older. All of them were gentlemen in their own way. I really do believe that.

And then, last year, there was someone else. I don't want to say his name. I can barely acknowledge his existence.

He was in my class. We started dating in December,

after football season ended. We became very close very fast, maybe because he was the first one to feel less like a glorified hookup and more like an actual boyfriend. I opened up to him in a way that I hadn't to the others. I trusted him. After a few months, I even told him about some of the others, because he seemed like he wanted to know. He was so sweet seeming about all of it. I really, really trusted him.

I had dance camp in Florida over spring break, and I was hooking up with him the night before I left. He said he was going to miss me during the week I was gone, and he hoped he'd have something to remember me by in the meantime. He asked if I wanted to make a movie. I thought it was a bad idea, but I have to admit, something about it excited me too. I asked him if we could delete it as soon as I got back. He said of course.

He used his phone to record us. That's all I remember, that he used his phone. I've blocked everything else out.

I was in the cafeteria at camp when my girlfriend texted me. That's when my world ended. Then my parents called, and my world ended again. I had to leave camp early. As soon as I got home, I called all my friends, but very few of them called me back. The ones who did told me he'd spread the video to his friends and that he'd spread rumors around too, the rumors about me and all of the other guys. Some of the rumors were made-up. Most of them were true. I never spoke to him again. I heard he got expelled, which sucks for him, I guess. But I bet he got to keep his friends. I'm sure he got to keep his life.

At first I appreciated the way my parents handled everything. My mom let me finish out eleventh grade doing my schoolwork from home. My dad secured a work transfer to his West Coast office so we could move to California this year, so I could start over again as a senior. The two of them promised me I would never have to dwell on this situation again. And in a way, they've made good on their word. Since the day we moved, neither of them has brought up the tape. Not a single time.

But they don't look me in the eyes anymore, either. They don't ask about my classes or dance practice. They don't invite me to mani-pedi Saturdays or daddy-daughter Sundays. Sometimes they ask if I have a boyfriend. That's all they ever ask me.

I desperately want what they want for me: for this to be a new year. All I want is to be a different person. Different activities, different friends—people like Wiley, good solid people like that—and, most importantly, no boyfriends. Absolutely no boyfriends. No godforsaken boyfriends.

And after all that, here I am. Baking brownies for the guys with my dance squad girls. Chasing another quarterback. Collecting hickeys after school. Lying about everything.

DeSean is different. I feel accepted by him and desired

in all the right ways. I love him, and I know that for certain. I want to give him what he wants, because I want it too.

But all the same, I'm terrified. I'm afraid of my parents. I'm afraid of the world. I don't want to want sex the way that I do. I'm afraid of being myself.

Bad girl. Bad girl. I really hate those words.

COLE MARTIN-HAMMER

And in 1912," Mr. Pargo droned on. "Frost's good friend, the poet Edward Thomas, whose long walks through the woods with Frost helped to inspire the poem in the first place, enlisted in World War I, citing the piece as his main inspiration. However, two years later Thomas was tragically killed in action, leaving us to wonder, somewhat ironically might I add, what might have happened had Robert Frost never written the poem at all. . . .

"All right, who's got some good analysis for me?"

Guh.

G to the mothereffin' uh.

GUH GUH GUH.

Why does high school have to be so.

Boring?

It didn't matter if I paid attention to the question. I'm going to get an A+ in AP English—same as I'm going to get an A+ in every damn class except stupid worthless math—without even trying. That's how brilliant I am and how remedial the rest of Dos Caminos is. I can afford to sit passively through every single period until June, ignoring the shit out of the teachers and focusing purely on what I love best.

Gossip, obviously.

So I sat in the classroom yesterday morning, and instead of studying "The Road Not Taken," I studied the faces of the people whose lives I will one day destroy.

Cody Shotwell was spacing out, scratching his ear with his pencil. I hope he scratches that shiz right off, that purple-nurpling, towel-butt-whipping, locker-room bully. I'll never forget the way he treated me in freshman year PE. And after I tell the whole school that his lady, the Moaner, has totally been cheating on him with Liam "Forehead Mole" Garner, well sheeeeit, he won't soon forget me either.

Arthur Mpare was lamely attempting to explain to Mr. Pargo that the poem is about hopes and dreams or some dog doo. I wish he would explain why last year he booted me from Black Student Union for "insubordination," even though he let mad undeserving white kids stay in the group. And I look forward to hearing how he explains the big drinking-and-gambling party he hosted last weekend, once I pass along an "anonymous tip" to the vice principal's office.

Thuy Nguyen got reprimanded by Pargo for falling asleep in class. Perhaps she's finally getting her comeuppance for the time she said there was a special place in hell for people like me and that I would never find love unless

I changed my "sinful ways." Speaking of sinful ways, maybe the reason homegirl is so tired is because rumor has it that she and her youth group leader have been sneaking into the bathroom and getting all Sodom and Gomorrah every night after Bible study.

Finally, and most irritatingly of all, there was Allegra Rey. Slouching in her dowdy red fleece. Frowning her frumpy frump mouth. Feeling all sorry for her friendless baby self. *Guh.* I wish just once I could expose that little goody two-shoes, teacher-you-forgot-to-give-us-homework, rodent-eyed, curly-fry-haired, weeble-wobble-shaped, British-people-mouthed, fake-nice bee-yotch for the fraudulent waste of humanity she really is.

Say, what was with that look on her face? Why *was* she frowning so hard, anyway?

Oh my Gerd. Wait.

Could it be?—could the gerd Lord be so great?—could she actually possibly have gotten *rejected* from—

"Cole?"

Pargo was standing directly above my desk, wearing a "caught you in the act, didn't I?" expression.

"Hey there, Cole. You with us?"

I glanced up. "Hmm?"

"What do you think the poem means?"

I buffed my nails on my chest like the laziest lion. I forced myself not to yawn.

"In my opinion, this notion that Frost's narrator so much as took 'the road less traveled by' is fundamentally fallacious. Sure, it may look in hindsight like moments in life amounted to a decision between two divergent paths, leading to two drastically different outcomes. Yet the truth remains that we can never know which was indeed the road less traveled, because in point of fact, we faced no choice at all. The pathways Frost presents are identical-looking, therefore the end points are opaque and arbitrary, ergo our futures are unknowable. Consequently, if you want to get all Greek philosopher about it, fate is leading each and every one of us to the exact same place, whether we like it or not. And I'm not saying death, but yeah, I'm saying death."

As I finished, I clasped my hands together and went full cheese on a big ol' smile.

The class looked back at me in still-faced silence.

Pargo nodded vigorously. He applauded exuberantly.

"Bravo, Cole," he said. "Excellent interpretation."

See?

I told y'all I'm a star.

"Mmkay, changeling," I said in the hallway after English, during nutrition break. "Whadja bring me?"

Everyone knows I despise everyone, but even a cold-hearted succubus like me can't help but adore Neil. He's my little sophomore baby. I call him my "changeling," like the

Indian changeling baby that Oberon and Titania fight over in *A Midsummer Night's Dream,* and not just because he's Indian, and not just because he has lustrous eyelashes like an American Girl doll, and not just because I'm saucy like Titania and king of the fairies like Oberon. No, Neil Bhansali is my changeling because I can get him to change into absolutely anything I want him to be: homework doer, math tutor, rehearsal partner, garbage digger, and of course, town gossip.

"I had a productive morning," Neil said. "I think you'll be pleased."

"Then go ahead and please me."

"Well," he said. "I was hiding in the men's room before first, and I heard J. P. Hamblen on the phone with his girlfriend. He sounded really freaked out. I think she missed her period."

"Damn," I said. "She pregz?"

"Perhaps," Neil said. "Or anorex."

"Or what if . . . ?" I lowered my voice. "Most scandalous of all . . . *she's in fifth grade.*"

Neil covered his mouth and convulsed. I love making him giggle at my inappropro ways.

"Dude," I said. "Did you hear about the AP Comp Sci cheating ring?"

"Yup. Three weeks with the Bear for each of them."

I rolled my eyes. "Can't believe they let themselves get caught. I *hate* when people cheat like idiots."

"Cheating is wrong," Neil said. "Whether one does it intelligently or not."

"Less moralizing, brah," I said. "More rumor-izing."

"Okay," Neil said. "Here's my best scoop of all. I don't know whose this is yet, but I found it in the recycling outside the ladies' locker room."

He unfolded a square of graph paper and handed it to me. I didn't have to read long before I came across such phrases as "ride me like a pony" and "make me quiver."

"*Jackpot*," I said, my eyes bugging out, my heart swelling with pride. I reached inside my pocket. "Sidekick, my boy, you da real MVP. You have definitely earned yourself one of these."

I pulled out the Slim Jim and tossed it to him. Neil caught the jerky stick and immediately began chowing down. Naturally, him being Indian and all, his parents don't allow beef products in the house, so every time he unearths an especially salacious piece of goss, I am able to reward him with cow meat in a cruel-but-generous way.

"We are going to do some obscene damage," I said.

"Yesh," Neil said, his mouth half full.

I dangled the sex note. "If anyone crosses us, they'll just have to deal with this."

"Sho good," Neil said.

"This must be what heroin feels like," I said. "Or getting into college."

As I said it, Neil nearly choked.

"Yo. You okay?"

He gulped down the Slim Jim. He lowered his eyes to the ground.

"Um," he said. "That reminds me."

"What reminds you?"

"I have . . . one more piece of info."

"What? Out with it. Spill."

"It, uh, concerns Allegra Rey. . . ."

"So . . ."

It was Philanthropy Friday, the afternoon before the homecoming game. I was standing next to Allegra at Casa de Maria, where old dementia people go to play bingo and die and where young overachievers go to scam their way into college. The frumpster and I were ladling Dumpster-smelling broth into mildewy bowls for cranky, unloved grandmas. I had my glorious mini-fro in a little hairnet. Allegra was wearing a sweater the same exact color as the soup.

"Heard you got some news the other day."

"Oh," Allegra said. She sounded all monotone and quiet. She stared into the soup. "I think she'll be okay, but no one knows for sure. I hope she can beat it, but I don't know. It's really hard."

"Lady," I said. "You ain't makin' none of the sense."

I took a breath and transformed my face into the fake-ass smile I normally reserve for talking to my mom when I want to make her feel bad.

"I was asking about Stanford—heard you might have gotten in? Congrats, chica!"

"Oh," Allegra said, still being a sad hobo. "Right. Stanford. It's definitely an honor. I don't know, though. With my mom being sick and everything, I might have to defer my acceptance, or even stay local for school."

I tilted my head so it went from "jaunty theater boy being fun" to "are you fa-reakin' kidding me?"

"I don't want to say 'gurl, please,'" I said, "but, gurl. *Please.* Look, I'm sorry to hear about your mom—so sorry, that's horrendous—but what the frick-and-frack are you saying right now? Don't you realize I'd give up my beautiful, symmetrical, award-winning face if I could guarantee a spot at Stanford? This is the dream right here—you got to snatch it."

Allegra didn't respond right away. She sighed and stirred. She did eventually look up at me, but she tossed her signature sloppy curls in front of her face as she did it, hiding herself behind a tangled thicket of frizz.

"Don't worry, Cole," she said. "I'm sure you'll get in too. You have so many of the same qualifications as me. You applied early, right?"

"Yes."

"But you're retaking the SAT to see if you can do better on math this time, right?"

"Um, *what*? Who told you that?"

"You did," Allegra said. "Last Philanthropy Friday."

I tilted my head from "OMG, who been talking mess about me?" to "You know what, frumpy butt? Let's change the subject."

"It's no big deal," I said. "You're totes right. I'll kill the SATs tomorrow morning, and we'll go off to Stanford together, and a year from now we'll be in the same freshman dorm, in the same coed bathroom, and we *still* won't be able to get this gosh-darn geezer smell out of our clothes. *Eau de* Depends, am I right? Lolz."

But Allegra did not lolz at that. She didn't even :) at that. And it's like, I'm sorry chica. I know your mom's not well, but you can at least pretend for one second to be fun.

"You know, Cole," she said. "If I could give you my spot right now, I absolutely would."

I placed my hand on her shoulder. I looked her square in the eye.

"And if you were stupid enough to give it to me, I'd absolutely take it."

Early this Saturday morning, on my way to the big test, I stopped at the gas station mini-mart, where I bought two things:

A pack of Parliaments. A bag of super-size Slim Jims.

I drove to campus and pulled into the student parking lot. I stepped out of the car, where I watched the other SAT takers as they walked down the hill, toward the cafeteria, right into the most important test of their lives.

I smoked as I watched them, filling my lungs with the same shit that's killing millions of people every single day—who knows, maybe even Allegra's mom.

It felt so good.

I thought about my plan one last time.

See, my problem the last two times I took the SAT was that I didn't have a plan. I thought I could handle the math, and I figured that since my dad is a statistics professor at the city college, that maybe he'd be able to help me raise my scores.

But I was wrong. None of that nonsense worked out.

But that's okay. Because now I have a plan.

And with it, I will dominate the world.

Over the summer, I "discovered" that I had "anxiety" and that I "couldn't focus." When I went to consult a therapist about it, the same woman who used to see my dad before he had to move up north, she referred me to a psychiatrist, who admired me for having the "bravery" to come into his office and who diagnosed me with ADHD.

A couple of months ago, I contacted the College Board, which administers the SAT. I told them about my newfound learning disability. And wouldn't you believe it, they responded by granting me *unlimited* time on all sections, plus my very own test room and proctor.

So today, once I identify the math questions I can't solve, I'll write them down on my scrap paper. Then, because I'll have unlimited time, I'll make numerous visits to the bathroom, and I'll bring my paper with me. The proctor won't notice, of course, because proctors are blind and stupid, like blind, stupid dolphins.

When I get to the bathroom, I'll pull a secret phone out of my shoe, and I'll text pictures of all the scrap paper problems that I can't solve over to my best friend, the boy whose trust I've been cultivating these past twelve months, the boy who owes me eternally for teaching him how to cease being a loser, the boy who just so happens to be our school's foremost math prodigy. Then, when I make another visit to the bathroom a few minutes later, Neil will have solved all of the problems I can't do for me.

And once I have my perfect math score, how can Stanford not say yes to me?

And once I've attended the top college in the world and made connections with all of the most powerful future leaders of the world, how will I not eventually dominate the world?

Climb on my knee, Planet Earth. And pull down your pants.

Daddy needs to give you a spanking.

. . .

As I sucked in my last cigarette, I watched the other test takers head into the caf, where their uncertain futures awaited them.

I wonder if cheating will make me a bad person. I can't quite shake this nagging feeling that I'll somehow regret it if I game the system, that it'll be a big fat slap in the face to those regular ol' kids walking down that hill, leading their regular ol' lives.

Then again, just look at those kids. Remember who they are. The baseball player, Nate Sullivan, who called me "faggot" in the third grade, back before I knew what that word meant, and again in ninth grade, when it cut me like a blade. The stoner, Woo Quian, who came up to me baked at lunch two weeks ago and asked what's with my family, why do I have such a crazy dad. The stress case, Sandra Allenby, who publicly accused me of cyberbullying last year, took her case straight to the principal's office, and damn near vaporized my chances at Stanford right then and there.

What if those people are just assholes? What if they deserve to be taken advantage of, to have gossip spread about them? What if they deserve to be squashed like snails by the likes of Almighty Me?

And at the end of the day, what if my decision to cheat doesn't even matter? After all, as strange as it feels to admit, my entire future might be preordained regardless. That's what I took from Robert Frost's moronic poem. Why should real life be any different? What if it's all one long, inevitable path, and there's no veering off course, even if you try?

What if I'm a bad person no matter what I do?

I stamped out my cigarette. I watched the students trudge into their testing room. I wriggled my toes in my sock, where the phone felt warm beneath my foot. I glanced back at my car, where the Slim Jims were sitting on the passenger seat.

Multiple-choice tests are just the worst.

ROAD ONE

FALL

1. WILEY OTIS

I don't give a crap about football, but it was a perfect night for football. The lights were bright. The cheerleaders were bronze. The air was chilly, but in that awesome way that makes you say screw it, I'm gonna cuddle up to the girl beside me. There was something so, I dunno, American about that night. It was like we were all being painted by Norman Rockwell while we shot automatic weapons at terrorists and pounded ice-cold Buds.

And not that I care about crap like this, but even the Bulldogs were winning. With a minute left in the first half, we were up by three touchdowns. This was kind of surprising, given that our star left tackle was sitting on the bench, wearing sweatpants, a hoodie, and the wacked-out expression of a three-year-old who just stuck his finger in a light socket.

"Poor guy," Allegra said, standing in front of me on the sideline. "This must be difficult for him, watching the team perform so well in his absence."

"Yeah," I said. "Sucks to be him."

I turned away from her.

"All right, boys," I whispered to the rest of the brass section. "You ready?"

J.P., Travis, Kevin, Pranav, and Fat Isaac all took their hands off their trumpets and trombones and gave me big thumbs-ups.

"Perfect," I said. "Sixty seconds until showtime."

Sixty seconds until she finally learned the truth.

Sixty seconds until the rest of my life.

As brilliant as Allegra is, and as wide-ranging as her intellectual interests may be, she's not exactly a cinema buff. Since she spends most of her time calculating complex equations and taking care of her mom and whatnot, it's only natural that when it comes to movies, she wants to take a break from thinking and soak up some lovey-dovey feelings goop. I mean, my number one film of all time is something like *Citizen Kane*, or *The Graduate*, or *Rashomon*, or *The Deer Hunter*. Allegra's favorite movie is *10 Things I Hate About You*.

Yet as questionable as that choice is, it also provided me with kind of the perfect opportunity.

Allie's favorite scene is the part where Heath Ledger confesses his love to the nerdy girl by having the whole marching band play a romantic song on the football field in front of the entire school. She watches that scene on YouTube over and over, and every time, she says something like wouldn't that be incredible, wouldn't that be the best.

So tonight, that was my goal. I was going to give her the best.

The band had to be on the field anyway as part of the homecoming halftime show. The principal was going to walk out and name the homecoming queen. The band was going to play "Isn't She Lovely" as she got crowned, and then we were supposed to step off the turf.

Only me and the brass boys, we weren't going anywhere. My plan was to grab the microphone and tell one very special flautist that I had an important announcement of my own. The brass section would then strike up a new song, the theme song from Allie's *other* favorite teen movie ever, and mine too, "Don't You (Forget About Me)" from *The Breakfast Club*, a song that happens to carry with it a maybe-not-so-subtle personal message. As we finished, I would ask Allegra to be my homecoming date, and my girlfriend also, and as I ripped off my sousaphone and let it drop to the ground, and as she jumped into my arms for a gigantic, last-shot-of-the-movie kiss, the brass guys would begin playing "All Right Now," which is the Stanford football fight song, and everything was really going to be all right now, because Allie and I were finally, happily, about to have the one thing that both of us so desperately need.

I glanced up at the game clock. Ten seconds left in the half. Ten years of waiting for this moment, and now just ten seconds more.

My heart was beating like a hummingbird on Red Bull.

Nine seconds . . .

My hands were dribbling sweat. I wiped them on my tuba and jacket.

Eight seconds . . .

Allegra looked radiant in the stadium lights. It was all I could do in that moment not to spill the freaking truth already.

Seven seconds . . . six seconds . . .

Our team was on the twenty-yard line, right in front of the band. DeSean dropped back for one last pass.

Five . . .

The Lagunita defensive dudes broke hard through the line. They came charging after DeSean. He scrambled around, trying to make a play.

Four . . .

He looked, looked, but no one was open. He hurried toward us, to the sideline, to try to get out of bounds—but he wasn't alone. There was a brawny beast of a pass rusher right behind him.

Three . . .

Just as DeSean was about to scoot out, the beast launched itself through the air. D didn't see it coming. He put the brakes on as he reached the sideline, but just as he stopped, that's when the blow landed. The creature threw its entire body onto its victim. The dude's knee made contact, right in the middle of DeSean's left leg.

Two . . .

I heard a crunch, like someone stomped on a bag of potato chips. DeSean went limp on the turf.

One . . .

The kids around me gasped. Some screamed. Allegra's hands shot over her eyes.

Halftime.

There was no homecoming halftime show. The mood in the stadium was so somber after DeSean's leg got destroyed that the school administrators made the decision to suspend the announcement of the queen until the following night. As the ambulance pulled onto the field, they ushered me and the rest of the band back up to the stands without letting us play. A few drunken dads and older brothers shouted insults at the Big Mack, screaming things like, "Why didn't you suit up?" and "How could you let DeSean get Theismanned like that?" A good chunk of the crowd began booing, even some of the kids in band. Allegra looked shell-shocked, like a guy from a Vietnam movie.

I didn't talk during the second half. No one did. Fat Isaac tapped me on the shoulder and looked at me like, yo, we practiced that dumb song all those times; we still need our money. I slipped him the hundred-and-fifty-dollar wad, the cash I'd been saving up to buy an HD video camera, the camera I'd been wanting so I could make high-quality films for my future girl. Allegra didn't say a word to me during the second half. Her mind seemed everywhere but the stadium. It became increasingly clear to me that I'd missed my chance at my big moment, maybe the best chance I'll ever have.

"So . . . ," I said a few minutes after the game, at the start of our walk home. "That was a barrel of laughs."

Allegra shook her head.

"Who do you think's hating life more right now, DeSean or Brian?"

"Wiley—"

"I mean D probably won't walk right for, like, a year, yeah? But the Big Mack's about to become such a loser, even we might outrank him on the coolness scale."

"Wiley, I don't want to talk about the game."

"Oh. Okay. That makes sense."

We walked in silence. Allegra coughed. I could see her breath. She seemed shivery, even in her heavy band jacket. I wanted to offer her mine, because that's what a boyfriend would do, but I knew she'd just say no.

"Let's shift gears," I said. "On to a funner note. We're not too far from my birthday, you know. I'm wondering how we might want to celebrate."

"Hmm," Allegra said. "Well, we'll have to do a film festival, of course."

"Eighteen movies for my eighteenth," I said. "The most ill-advised weekend ever."

Allie smiled. "What if we exclusively watched movies about growing up?" she said. "*Stand by Me. Boyhood. To Kill a Mockingbird.*"

"Or what if we went the other way?" I said. "Forty hours of wacky baby flicks and movies featuring talking animals who move their mouths."

Allie snorted. "You're a talking animal who moves its mouth."

"Or *wait!* Lightbulb! What if we *made* a movie?"

"Ooh, I like it. A Wiley Otis biopic?"

"*The Fart Heard 'Round the World: Wiley's Story.*"

"*The Boy Who Did His Math Homework: A Surrealist Fantasy.*"

"We could get one of your brothers to play young me."

"We could get one of the men at the home to play elderly you, looking back on a lifetime of regrets."

"*Sad Old Wiley: Same Nutter Butters, New Teeth.*"

"*Sad Old Wiley: Still Wearing That Blasted Wolf Shirt.*"

"*Sad Old Wiley: Having Future Sex with Robots.*"

I cracked myself up with that last one. I laughed until the mental image of a sexy robo-maid giving Alzheimer's me a sensual striptease-slash-lap-dance wasn't funny anymore, which took quite a while obviously. By the time I finally stopped, I realized Allegra wasn't laughing along with me.

"Shoot," she said. "Darn it. Can't believe I forgot."

"What?"

She put her palm to her forehead. "I am so sorry. It utterly slipped my mind."

"What?"

"Stanford sent me an e-mail," she said. "The special admit reception they've invited me to, it's in December, the same weekend as—I'll have to miss your birthday. I'm really sorry."

"Oh," I said.

"I feel dreadful," Allegra said.

"It's okay. Please don't worry about it."

"I could always skip the college weekend, or try and go to half—"

"Don't be insane," I said. "Of course you have to go."

We walked without talking for another block. I tried not to show what I was actually feeling. The wind picked up a little bit. I heard the sound of Allie's teeth chattering.

"Well, how about this?" I said. "Let's time-shift. Instead of waiting till winter break, let's have fun now. We could start our film festival tomorrow morning, or hey, here's a thought, even begin preproduction on *Sad Old Wiley.*"

Allegra lowered her eyes. She shook her head.

"I can't," she said. "Not tomorrow. We're taking my

mom to the hospital. She's starting round one of chemo."

"Oh," I said.

"Yeah," she said.

"Yeah," I said.

We didn't say much else until we reached our neighborhood. I think both of us felt pretty guilty, even though neither of us had done anything wrong. The world had just gotten in our way.

We stopped at Allie's house. I gave her a hug good night. She told me sorry again, then headed up the pathway to her door. She looked so adorable in her bright blue jacket, so small and defenseless, huddled against the wind.

"Hey," I said before she went inside.

"Yeah?" she said, looking over her shoulder.

"There's something I need to tell you."

"What is it?"

I took an epic, gigantic, potentially historic breath.

I still had the shot, if I wanted to take it. I still had the opening to make my bold move. I didn't have to let her walk through that door. Not without telling her everything first. Ten years' worth of stuff. Everything I told Nikki. Everything in my heart.

This could be my time.

"You're . . . um . . . doing a really good job. With this college thing and the mom stuff. It must be so stressful, but you're finding a way to handle it all. You're really keeping everyone in mind. You're a great daughter. You're a great friend."

"Well, goodness," Allie said. "Thank you for the kind words."

With that she waved good-bye, shut the door, and disappeared.

2. NIKKI FOXWORTH

As a little girl growing up in Texas, you don't ever imagine that you'll spend your senior homecoming inside a stuffy hospital room instead of out on the dance floor with your girls and your man. You never dream your beau will have his leg wrapped in a giant cast, fractured in two places. Or that he'll be operating on zero sleep and about a dozen different painkillers.

If you'd told little me that all those things were going to be in my future one day, well, gosh, I just might have burst into tears.

But sometimes real life is so much better than the fantasy.

DeSean was beyond broken the day after the game, basically lifeless as I stayed by his hospital bed in the hours following his surgery. That Saturday evening, he asked me when I was leaving him for the dance, and the way he asked it, his head lolling back, his voice flat and weak, oh, it darn near crushed my spirit for good.

But I had a surprise for him.

I left the room for a short spell, and when I returned, I was wearing my hair done up and my homecoming gown, a black midlength bodycon dress with strategically placed geometric cutouts along the sides, which may or may not have cost the better part of one of my daddy's paychecks. Plus I had a boutonniere, the most dashing oxblood lily, for my date. I pinned it on his chest and whispered that I wasn't going anywhere. Homecoming was coming here.

That's when the school called to say they'd just announced the results of the election for king and queen, and the winners were . . . us! Ms. Fawcett even stopped by with the crowns, and most of the football team and rally girls came in right behind her. DeSean couldn't get out of bed, of course, so he couldn't do the time-honored first dance with me, but someone played a slow song on their phone, and he smiled and shimmied in place, and I leaned over his bed and cuddle-danced with him for as long as he had the energy, and everyone took pictures of us, and it was heaven.

At the end of the night, after our friends left, I stayed back in the room. Not for inappropriate reasons, mind you, but just so I could massage my date's shoulders, simply so I could comfort him until he fell fast asleep. It really is true what my mother always said: There's nothing a girl loves more than nursing her man back to health.

So yes, I feel horrible about D's injury. Of course I do.

And I pray it doesn't impact his college career in any way. I pray that every night.

But all the same, there is that silver lining. This time he's had to spend away from football, it's bringing us closer as a couple, and I can't for one second regret that.

It's the imperfections, wouldn't you know, that make life pretty perfect after all.

"You look so hot in these pics," Brooklyn said.

"The absolute hottest," Channing said.

"I love this freaking dress," Brooklyn said.

"Hospital chic," Channing said.

Those girls are unbelievably sweet. Chan and Brook are the cocaptains of varsity dance, and even though I've only known them since I auditioned at the start of the year, they've basically already taken me in as their soul sister. Every single day since homecoming, so, like, dozens of times over the past few weeks, they've come to my house to give me compliments, do my nails, gossip about cheer, and just generally make life the funnest.

Last night they were over again, because now that it's late November and the football team's fallen short of the playoffs, we girls are in charge of planning out the boys' big end-of-year, thank-you-to-the-fans dance that they do every fall in the Greek. Obviously, though, when the three of us get together, there tends to be a bit more chitchat than choreo.

"And you know what else is hot, Nik?" Brooklyn said.

"Your decision to . . . Wait, you and D still haven't . . . have you?"

I bit my lower lip and shook my head. Probably blushed, too.

"Not yet," I said. "Partially because of the leg thing, and mostly because, well, I'm still not quite ready."

"God, I admire that," Channing said. "So much restraint."

"So much sexy courage," Brooklyn said.

"You know who would have done it with DeSean immediately, like, without even thinking?" Channing said.

"Let me guess . . . ," Brooklyn said. "Does her name rhyme with . . . 'loner?'"

"Yes," Channing said. "And every guy at our school has biblically known her."

"And back in old times we would have said 'let's stone her!'"

"For the crime of consuming one too many boners!"

"Who's the chick so diseased she can't be a blood donor?"

They shouted it at the same time, like perfectly synchronized cheer clones:

"THE MOANER!!!!!"

At that, they burst into fits. They giggled so hard they fell onto my bed and mussed up the sheets. I smiled too.

"Look, Foxworth," Brooklyn said. "I'm sure you know

this, but there's a right amount of time to wait before doing it, especially if it's gonna be your first time. Like, me and Conner, we were together for four solid months before we got there."

"And me and Dusty dated for two and a half," Channing said. "But, like, we've known each other since we were little, so it was okay."

Brooklyn nodded. "The point is," she said. "You don't wanna be like one of those cave-girl cheer sluts, giving it up to any football player who so much as sweats near them—"

"—So effing uncoordinated they can't even execute a basic kick ball change," Channing continued. "Which is why they didn't make it onto dance, which is why they have to do effing *cheer*—"

"—Which is why they have to stand there with those grandma-ass pom-poms and those chubbifying outfits, screeching at the top of their lungs like fat, unwanted mistake children," Brooklyn said.

"In conclusion," Channing said. "Screwww cheer. I hope they all get genital warts and . . .

"D-I-E!"

"D-I-E!"

"Get an S-T-D aaaaaand . . ."

"DIE!!!!!!!!!"

The girls high-tenned and tossed my pillows in the air. They cackled, looked at me expectantly, and cackled some more.

I felt my arm hairs stand on end, but I had to laugh with them. I had to.

"Yeah," I said. "Screw cheer. Stupid whores."

After a couple more hours of dance planning and name calling, Brook and Chan finally left my house around eleven. I waited for the sound of their car leaving before counting to a hundred by Mississippis. I walked down the hall and peeked inside my parents' room, where my mom was facedown snoring, a half-empty bottle of Lexapro at her bedside. My daddy was back in Dallas, so I texted him good night. I walked to my car.

I always feel vulnerable on the ride over, driving through the shadows like a girl in a horror movie right after everybody's agreed to split up. Luckily it's only a couple of minutes that I have to feel this way. I reach my hero before the monster ever gets me.

DeSean was waiting in his driveway, balancing on his crutches and clearly in pain but with a warm look in his eyes. I helped him into the front seat. I drove us back to my neighborhood.

I parked in our usual spot, in the corner of this big empty construction site that no one knows about, where no one can see us.

I slid gently into the backseat, taking care not to brush up against DeSean's cast. He took my hand in his and looked at me for a beat, mouthing the words "missed you." I whispered the same back to him. Then I leaned in and kissed him on the mouth. I was anything but gentle.

As we made out, DeSean put his hand all the places that I like. He ran it through my hair. Placed it on my cheek. Around my waist. Up my back. Eventually, he unclasped my bra.

"First try," I said, grinning.

"Mmm," DeSean said.

I peeled my top off. For a minute or so, I let him have some boy time and play around up there. Once he'd had his fill, I helped him get his shirt off too. I placed my hands on his museum statue pecs. I squeezed them and cooed, to show how much I was enjoying him. Then I pushed softly on his chest. I lowered him down to the seat.

"*Beeep, beeep, beeep*," DeSean said, like a truck backing up.

"Naughty boy," I said.

Next came the part I always want to draw out for longer, but who am I kidding? One second we were kissing like normal, and then, fast as you can say Jack Robinson, his shorts were off, and my panties, too, and I was grinding on him in perfect rhythm, by which I mean jackhammer-fast, and I could feel him down there, making his way urgently toward me, and my God, did it feel right—

And just like that, we were one.

I have no idea how long we went on for, because I never keep track of that stuff. It could have been two minutes or it could have been five hours. But what I know is that in that oneness I felt with D, I wasn't thinking about the other kids at school, or what the latest trashy rumors are, or who us dance girls are supposed to be mean to now. I wasn't thinking about my parents, or what they must think of me. I wasn't thinking about my future, what I'm supposed to do next year, who I'm supposed to be. And thank the good Lord Almighty, I certainly wasn't dwelling on the past.

All that stuff does seep back into the brain eventually. How could it not? Right after the high point happens, around the time you're cleaning up, when you're thinking how icky and silly sex really is, but how you just don't notice at the time, because that's how gosh-dang loopy the lovemaking makes you, I mean, that's also the moment when the brain clicks back on, when I realize I'm not just some pleasure-hungry animal acting on instinct, but a real human being, a girl with dozens of secrets and too many bad memories and absolutely zero solutions to any of my problems.

But oh, how I love forgetting.

Let me forget. Mmm, DeSean. Make me forget.

3. BRIAN MACK

ARE YOU READY FOR YOUR DAWGS?"

"YEAH!"

"I SAID, ARE YOU READY FOR YOUR DAWGS??"

"YEAH!!!"

"WE LOVE YOU, DESEAN!"

"I SEE YOU, SCROTES!"

"TUA, HAVE MY BABIES!!!"

The guys from the team were all together, up on the Greek stage. They were in a big huddle, wearing their blue and gold Bulldog jerseys. DeSean was in the center, barking at the rest of them, bouncing up and down on his crutches, rocking his fatty full-leg cast with the entire team's signatures.

I wasn't up there with the guys.

I mean, obviously.

The music started. The huddle broke. Each guy spun out, one by one, and struck a pose.

A ballet pose.

And yeah, every single dude up there—DeSean, Tua, Nesto, Hector, Cody, Scrotes, all of them—in addition to their jerseys, they were also wearing puffy pink tutus.

And at the sight of those meatheads in those froufrou skirts, the crowd in the Greek went even more monkeyshit than before.

I was sitting in the middle of the masses, watching my former teammates.

I was the only one not cheering.

The Male Ballet is a time-honored tradition. It's a crazy-ass, man-humping, motorboating riot. Next to maybe Grease Pole Day, it's probably my favorite day of the year.

Last year I was the star of the dance. There was this one part when the song "Santa Baby" started playing. I was wearing a Santa hat and a wifebeater so tight it barely covered my nips, and holding a giant, three-foot candy cane. The whole team got in a row and bent over, and I smacked each of them on the ass with the cane like I was the pledge master of a kinky Christmas frat. Then the music switched to that song "Dancing Queen," and someone put a feather boa around my neck, and I led all the boys in a choreographed disco dance. People were shocked by my surprisingly fluid moves, and everyone called it the best Male Ballet ever. Even my dad and brother had to admit it when they saw it on YouTube that night. "Fat Sexy Santa Punishes his Naughty List"—ten thousand hits and counting.

So that was last year. Some hilarious groovaliciousness from Mr. Big Mack. All-time life boner moment, for sure.

And this year . . . I guess I was the star of Male Ballet again.

The show kicked off with some fancy classical music. The guys pranced around in a circle on their tippy-toes. Everyone whooped and whistled for them, and I clapped too, because hey, those are my guys, and even if I let them down this season, I've got a lot of memories with those idiots. Anyway, then the music changed, and this super-ancient pop song started to play: "Who Let the Dogs Out?"

Enter Scrotes. He jumped out with his head shaved—which was crazy, I've never seen that ass weasel without his ass weasel bowl cut—and he ripped off his jersey, and he had something painted on his chubster tummy: a cartoon bulldog, and some words, too:

BIG MACK.

Oh, so this was how it was gonna be.

I stood up in my seat and waved my hands toward myself like, "All right, I can take it, bring it on, guys," but no one cared, because everyone's eyes were still glued on Scrotes, who jiggled his boobs around and pretended to suck on them—is that a thing that I do? Tua and Ernesto danced out, and the team surrounded them in a circle, and Tua climbed onto Scrotes's shoulders, and Nesto jumped onto both of them, and it made for a painfully familiar image.

That song "Bad Day" by that whiny loser guy started to play, and Ernesto and Tua pretended to fall off the dude pile and on to Scrotes's skull, and then Scrotes staggered around for a second, looking hella brain dead, completely concussed.

Then the music switched again, and that song about liking big butts came on. Scrotes turned his back to us and pulled his pants down, and he fully mooned the entire Greek. Written on his bare ass was LITTLE BITCH. He worked that hairy thing like he was grinding it up and down a strip club pole. A few kids in the crowd even flung dollar bills at me. Scrotes kept shaking, shaking, shaking, shaking, shaking that healthy butt until a bunch of teachers dragged him offstage, pants still below his cheeks, everyone at school still bouncing and shouting, pointing and laughing, laughing at me, same as they've been doing every friggin' day for the past six weeks. Only now they weren't doing it in secret. Now I was a school-wide meme wherever I went. The fatty who failed. The lonely oaf.

I had to get out of there.

Why the hell was I fool enough to subject myself to this? I should have gone off-campus for lunch, or eaten by myself in the bathroom, like I've done every other day lately. But at least I was smart enough to get out now, at least I could—

"Yo, BRIAN!" someone yelled.

I spun around to see who—

Dammit, dammit, dammit.

DeSean Weems was only a foot away from me, even though he'd been onstage, like, five seconds before, because hey, even with a compound fracture in his tibia and fibula, dude's apparently still the fastest QB in the state. My boys Ernesto and Tua were right behind D, their arms folded all nightclub-bouncer-style. Queen Nikki was at DeSean's side. She was literally perched on him, like a tiny bird. Some of her long wavy hair was draped over his shoulder, and she was looking up at him with those deep blue eyes of hers. Sweet middle-aged Jesus, that girl is beautiful.

"So . . . Big Mack," DeSean said, making the most of every syllable. "Just wanted to see how you liked your musical tribute. You like it, bro?"

"You know, whatever," I said, hoping I was smiling. "It's important to laugh, right? We've got to laugh at ourselves. Even if the season didn't quite go the way we wanted, you know?"

I tried to laugh as I said that. DeSean laughed too, but the way he did it was different. He laughed all over-the-top, like an old-school video-game boss.

"*Awesome*, buddy," he said. "Just the awesomest. Glad to see you have such a *healthy* perspective."

He put his fingers to his chin, like he was pretending to think, like he hadn't already scripted this entire scene in his mind, word for word.

"But *wait*. . . . Have you ever stopped to think about *why* our season didn't go as planned?"

"Hey," I said. "I should probably get going."

"*Maybe* because, just like last year, you were too pussy-ass to play through a little boo-boo. *Maybe* because your pussy-ass quitting ruined our O line, which put me in harm's way. *Maybe* because your decision to be a little bitch ruined both our season *and* my body, which means I've stopped getting recruiting letters from SC and started getting them from *Fresno State*."

I tried laughing again.

"Fresno State . . . At least you'll still get to be a Bulldog, eh?"

DeSean growled at me.

"Look, man," I tried. "I don't wanna focus on negative stuff. I just want to keep things light and fun."

"You're not supposed to have *fun*," DeSean snapped back. "You're supposed to be depressed. You're supposed to be *suicidal*, bro. Come on, asshole. You too developmentally challenged to figure that out? Earth to dumbshit: Everyone hates you. That was the whole goddamn point of Nikki's dance."

Huh?

I looked at Nikki. She wouldn't look back at me.

"Who else do you think choreographed that bad boy? Granted, the concept was pure DeSean. You like that ending? I thought 'little bitch' was a nice touch."

"Ha," I said. "Super-funny stuff." I gave him a little dap on the arm. "You know, man, I've actually gotta get somewhere before fifth."

"I heard a rumor," DeSean said, "that that's really what it says on your ass."

"Dude," I said. "I already told you and the guys so many times, I'm sorry for quitting. I didn't mean to eff up the season. I'm so sorry."

"*Duuude*," DeSean said, saying the word slowly and bringing Nikki closer to him at the same time, in a totally rehearsed way, because he'd definitely planned exactly what was coming next.

"*Fuuuhhh.*"

"*Kkkkkkk.*"

"*Yooouuu.*"

I wanted to reshatter his leg right then. I wanted to so hard. But at the same time, I had to save some dignity. I tried to leave, but as soon as I made a move, Ernesto and Tua blocked my way. I had no idea what they were doing, no clue what could possibly be more humiliating than everything that had come before. But then I found out, because each of them leaned in and grabbed a leg of my shorts, and before I could book it they just yanked and—

"NOPE!" DeSean shouted to all the people crowded around us in the Greek, pointing down at my shame. "LOOKS LIKE IT DOESN'T SAY 'LITTLE BITCH'

ON THERE LIKE WE THOUGHT! JUST SOME SKID MARKS ON HIS TIGHTY-WHITIES, THAT'S ALL!"

All those people are assholes.

DeSean. My ex-teammates. Everyone at school. Coach Dent. Hell, I'll throw my family in there too. And Nikki Foxworth, that two-faced whore. Can't forget her.

All those people are dead to me. They can burn in hell forever.

And me? What am I supposed to do now?

Well, it's simple, isn't it?

I've got to keep on dancing.

4. COLE MARTIN-HAMMER

Cole," Neil said. "Must you keep checking your phone?"

"One more time," I said, refreshing yet again.

Simultaneously, to satiate the changeling, I lobbed a Slim Jim chunk at him. Neil opened his mouth wide to catch it but missed, the beef tube bouncing off his forehead and onto the ground. He then picked it up and stuck it in his mouth all hurriedly. Gerd, I love that little guy.

"Find anyfing dis dime?" Neil said.

I shut my eyes and sighed.

"Still no word. These colleges say they'll e-mail with their decision Friday afternoon, but then Friday afternoon comes and it's like, where's my damn e-mail? Guh. I feel like murdering some exotic birds."

"I'm sure you're in good shape," Neil said. "What with your improvement and all."

I nodded. "You're right. Two hundred points. I should be golden."

Neither of us spoke for several seconds.

"By the way, Changeling, thank you again. You know, for everything."

"I told you," Neil said softly. "I'd rather not talk about it."

"Oh. Yeah. Totes. For sure."

Part of me still feels awkward about the whole SAT thing, even a weensy bit dirty. My head tells me I was only taking advantage of what was available to me and that there's nothing wrong with that. Yet the raw, churning ache I get in my stomach every time I try to discuss it with Neil suggests otherwise, to say nothing of the trouble I've had falling asleep.

But I'm just anxious about Stanford's decision—that's all that is. And I didn't hurt anyone else, not really. I mean, not to the extent that I already harm peeps via gossip anyway. And come on, Neil helped me execute my plan. He's, like, the most moral soul alive. He wouldn't have aided me in the service of genuine evil. I deserved my higher score. I outsmarted the system, fair and square. He believes that. I'm sure of it.

"Moving on," Neil said. "Should we get back to work?"

It was after school, halfway through December, the last Friday before winter break. The two of us were standing outside the theater, one pair of thespians among thirty or so others. The air was filled with that distinctly panicked callbacks energy.

I patted my diminutive friend on the head.

"If you say so. But look, sidekick, I can see into the future. I know exactly how this whole thing's gonna go. I'm a shoo-in for Cat in the Hat; there's no question about it. Most sheer talent, most charisma, and this is my senior musical—I've earned this. You've got a shot at Jojo if you play your cards right, but don't choke onstage or else Bayer's gonna cast you as a Who, or *shudder*, a Thing. I think Sofia would make a lovely Gertrude McFuzz, and Margot is like the dictionary definition of the Sour Kangaroo. And as far as Horton goes . . . I mean, I don't know. I'm not positive there's a Horton in our midst. It's like, think about it for a min: Who among us theater kids really has the girth and gravitas to convincingly portray a sad, lonely elephant . . . ?"

Then I saw him.

Just like that, there he was.

Plodding along, right toward us. Toward me. Gray hoodie, gray sweatpants, belly as big as a prize-winning pumpkin, shiny chrome scalp, and a frown on his face.

Horton the elephant.

People assume I was born this way.

They take it for granted that I up and sprang from my mama's womb fully formed, just as deviously bitchtastic as I am now.

People are idiots.

I was a shy, bitter, confused kid growing up. Shy because

I was the only black kid at my elementary and middle schools, and I wanted more than anything to fit in. Bitter because of stuff with my dad. Confused because I didn't know my sexuality for a long while, and especially confused because everyone else seemed to know it for me.

These were not ideal circumstances for a lonely lil' loser entering the ninth grade.

From day one, the assholes preyed on me mercilessly. The baseball players applied medieval torture to me every day in the PE locker room. DeSean's football goons invented sexually explicit slurs for me like they were J. R. R. Tolkien creating a new language. Even the wrestlers had the audacity to get in on the homophobia, and I mean, come on . . . wrestling.

Thank heavens there was theater.

Once I transferred out of PE and into Mr. Bayer's beginning acting class, everything changed, all at once. I changed. Being onstage gave me the confidence to say what I truly think and never hold back. The theater community gave me the pride to be who I am and to like who I like. Hanging out backstage and in the dressing room gave me the never-ending source of scandalous gossip that continues to serve as my lifeblood to this very day.

And, of course, theater gave me Brian.

When Bayer initially called the two of us onstage to do a scene together in beginning drama, I remember looking up at that squash-faced, scowly mouthed brute and thinking, *Oh no, what have I done to deserve this?*

Yet from the first-ever moment Brian wrapped me in one of his jelly roll hugs, it immediately hit me, like—well, too soon, I suppose—but like a big ol' *ka-thunk*, right on the noggin:

I realized I love this guy.

I loved how playful Brian and I could be together, making fun of the world on a mischief frequency only we could hear. I loved how nonjudgmental he was, how he never fabricated any BS tension over whether I found him attractive, which many of the other paranoid theater guys tended to do at the time. I loved his belly jiggles, his butt wiggles, his piggish giggles, and more than anything, I loved his talent.

Let's just say I've been out-acted only once in my entire career. Freshman year. The end-of-year showcase. The "tell me about the rabbits" scene from *Of Mice and Men.* I was, of course, my usual breathtaking self as George, but Brian's portrayal of Lennie, I mean . . . shit. Second best was good enough for me that day. A star knows a supernova when it sees one.

Sadly, like all beautiful things, Brian the actor died far too young. He told me that June that he wanted to try out for plays with me in tenth grade, but then his father, probably worried his son was being homo-fied by yours truly, forced Bri to enroll in weight-lifting period the following fall and focus on football full-time. And although Brian and I continued to joke around with each other in the halls every once in a while, it was clear that our connection, our practically best friend bond, was very much a relic of the past.

And yet here he was, all these years later, today at the *Seussical* callbacks. Here he was, standing before Neil and me, a glum and determined look on his face.

The prodigal porker returneth.

"Well, well, well," I said. "Slap my daddy and call him deranged. If it isn't Mr. Big."

Brian's forehead turned mildly pink.

"Hi, Cole. Sorry it's, you know, been a while. Can I . . . talk to you?"

I tilted my head toward Neil. I clapped my hands together twice.

"Changeling, my boy, be a precious gemstone and grab me some Horton sides, will you? And two Dasanis?"

Neil scurried off. I gave Brian a hard stare.

"I assume you're here to audition for the musical. You know, you would be ideal for the role of Horton. I'm already getting chills imagining you singing 'Alone in the Universe.'"

Brian scratched his chest. "Thanks? But I don't know. After lunch the other day, I don't think I want to be up in front of people anytime soon."

I raised a finger in the air. I jabbed it at him dramatically.

“Aha! I *knew* that’s why you were here! I’m sorry, Brian. That must have been really embarrassing for you, baring your ass in public for the five hundredth time.”

“Hey,” Brian said, grinning despite himself. “Come on, now.”

I let a smile spread across my face too. But not a gleeful twinkler like Big Bri’s. No, this one was more, shall we say . . . supervillainesque.

“I know real reason you come see me,” I said in an Eastern European vampire voice. “Eet ees because you desire . . . *revenge.*”

Brian’s mouth fell slightly open. “Well, yeah,” he said. “How’d you know?”

I made a scoffing sound. “Daddy, please! You’re hardly the first customer at the Ye Olde Gossip Shoppe. People love doing deals with this handsome devil. So what you looking for here, Biggie? Shameful family baggage? Adulterous online correspondences? Secret gay pics?”

“I don’t care,” Brian said without hesitation. “I just want to ruin his life.”

“Fair enough. And whose life, may I ask, will we be ruining?”

“DeSean Weems.”

I stepped back and whistled. “Damn, boy. *C’est impossible.* The kid is squeaky freaky clean. It’s like he’s been running for president his whole damn life. He attends church, seems to respect women okay, doesn't break any laws that I'm aware of. . . ."

"Just find something," Brian said. "Do what you do best. End him."

He said it with surprising authority. His voice was booming. His hands were in fists.

Then he added one more word:

"Please."

And sure, he may have been standing up tall, spine all straight, chest puffed out. But behind the facade, Brian seemed exhausted. Defeated. Borderline twitchy. It really was horrific what those assholes did to him in the Greek. I mean, not that I tend to treat folks any better, but you know, whatever.

"I'll do what I can," I said quietly. "But even with my many talents and the numerous resources at my disposal, there's no guarantee I'll be able to dig up any dirt."

Brian let out a huge breath. "Thank you," he said. "Holy balls, thank you so much. Okay, what'll this cost me?" He pulled out his wallet and began rummaging through.

I placed my hand on his and pushed it down. "Don't worry, old friend. It's on the house." I raised a finger in the air. "But . . . if I'm going to help you with this, there's just one thing you need to do for me. . . ."

Brian scratched his ear. "Huh?"

"Something you've owed me for a long, long time . . ."

"What?"

I winked at my scene partner.

"You have to audition for *Seussical*."

There was a momentary pause.

The smile spread like a blaze across his entire face.

"Hey, man," he said. "I was going to anyway."

Brian pulled me in for a hug, and I stepped in and let myself get some of that puff pastry lovin'. It was one of those perfect moments—my man Lennie, back from the grave, the two fearsome freshmen, best buds again—and if I could have hit pause on my life right there, I would have, and I'd have kept that feeling frozen for as long as I could.

But before I got too comfortable—

"Cole! Cole!! COLE!!!"

Neil was scampering toward us. He was hyperventilating.

"It's online! They've posted the decisions online!"

He pointed spastically at his phone.

"Check your e-mail! Check your e-mail! *Check your e-mail!*"

5. ALLEGRA REY

Stanford was awe-inspiring, almost overwhelming. The campus was enormous and impossibly diverse in its layout, a tribute to a prestigious past and an unimaginable future. There were endless red-tiled roofs, so reminiscent of the Mexico of my ancestors. Then, mere footsteps away, there would be sleek computer science buildings out of a science fiction novel, from another planet. Everywhere I looked, there were so many bright, beautiful, impressive *things*: palm trees all around, fountains, alcoves, bicycles, meditation spaces, frozen yogurt machines, totem poles—

And above all, there was happiness. Every person I observed on campus, be they a Frisbee-wielding grad student, an a cappella beatboxer giving a public performance, or a photo-snapping foreigner, and every person I spoke to during the early-admit reception at the Alumni Center—each and every one of them—seemed like the happiest person I'd ever met, and then, five minutes later, I'd meet a new happiest person.

Most of the other scholarship winners at the event had their parents with them. When they asked me where mine were, I lied and said, "Oh, they're tired from the drive up; they're back at the hotel." I'm not sure how many people really listened when I said those things. I suspect most of them just wanted to talk about what makes them happy.

I met a boy who informed me that he was the national under-eighteen Rubik's Cube champion. He proceeded to pull three cubes out of his pockets, and as a small crowd formed, he juggled them, twisting one in particular each time he caught it. Within about thirty seconds, he'd solved that Rubik's Cube without dropping any of the three. Everyone murmured appreciatively. The boy mentioned that he was also a competitive unicyclist.

There was a girl who remarked offhandedly that she'd recently published her third collection of poetry, the first to feature solely haiku. She asked if I would like for her to compose a haiku about me. I said sure.

Small, dull eyes belie

An inquisitive nature.

Welcome to your life.

A part of me wanted to ask if any of her haiku were about being nice, but then I realized that that would be very small and dull of me, so I smiled and told her how much my mother loves poetry.

The admit who left probably the strongest impression

on me was a boy wearing a T-shirt emblazoned with the phrase "AIDS FIGHTERS." When I asked him about the shirt, he told me he'd taken a gap year to start his own non-profit organization, AIDS Fighters, and that he was actually about to fly back to South Africa for a series of meetings with high-profile donors. He asked me if I wanted to see his tattoos. I said sure.

On his left triceps, there was an image from the cover of *The Giving Tree* by Shel Silverstein, in which the tree is dropping an apple for the little boy to eat. On the right triceps, there was an image from the end of the book, in which the little boy has become an old man who has used up all of the tree's resources and is now sitting on the tree's stump, weary and alone.

"I got these done to remind myself that there's people who take and there's people who give," the boy said. "And I don't want to take, right? I want to give back, you know? But we're at Stanford now. I'm sure everyone here feels that way."

"Absolutely," I said, nodding. "Absolutely."

You got this allie!! Wiley texted me while I was at the event. *Remember those other kids arent going thru what your going thru, so if you need to take a break or even come home early thats totally ok. I believe in you no matter what. I hope this weekend isnt too hard but if it is that makes sense. Just know i am always here for you!!*

I studied the text for several moments. It bothered me

for reasons I couldn't discern. Granted, I suppose it did speak to what I was feeling on some level. And true, Wiley has been quite considerate, albeit repeatedly awkward, regarding the recent stresses in my personal life. What's more, I knew I was supposed to text him back about something, something of at least mild importance.

And yet . . .

I didn't feel like talking to him. Simple as that.

Anyhow, I was standing in the middle of the reception, checking my phone, taking a brief refuge from the dazzling young scholars around me, from all the incessant happiness and limitless potential, when suddenly, I heard an extremely familiar voice.

"Hey you! Frumpy Butt! Where you been all my life?!"

I felt the hands come at me from behind, squeezing my arms without the slightest regard for my personal space.

"*Cole?* What the— Sorry, but what are you doing here?"

"Ooooh," he said, ripping my phone from my grasp. "Getting a lil' pep talk from the boy next door, eh? I've always wondered when that kid was gonna grow a penis and wiener his way out of the friend zone."

"Cole," I repeated. "You're here. At Stanford."

"Oh, don't furrow that brow," he said. "This ain't the dust bowl, honey. Cheer up."

Cole touched my forehead and attempted to smooth it out. I removed his hand from my face.

"Explain what you are doing here," I said. "Now. Please."

"Gurlll," he said. "Come on. I did just like I said I would back on Fogey Friday. I made the SAT math portion my personal sex slave, and I sent the scores straight to Stanny. And the other day at callbacks, wouldn't ya know it, I got the e-mail of my dreams, in which they invited me to this little ol' par-tay, which I bet you probably thought was only for winners of your Kids with Broken Dreams scholarship or whatever. But it's not. It's actually open to all of us new admit babies who could make the trip. So hey, looks like you're not as special as you thought you were."

"Oh," I said.

I could barely breathe. I didn't want to feel the way I did, because that felt judgmental and egocentric and wrong, so I tried my best to be polite. But I could barely breathe.

"Wow," I said. "Congrats."

The next day was worse.

I'd decided to go on an early-morning walking tour of campus to try to take Stanford in, to see if I could feel at home there, but I didn't make it two steps before Cole was texting to meet up with me, glomming on to my personal journey.

"Ooh, chica, you should live there next year," Cole said as we walked past Casa Zapata, Stanford's Latino-themed dorm. "The *hermanos y hermanas* in there could be, like, your surrogate *familia*. You know, since you're leaving your real *familia* behind.

"Oh my Gerd," Cole said as he and I walked past some medical school buildings. "You know, they have an amazing hospital here. My mom used to be a nurse there, back when my dad was a grad student, right before I was born. Maybe your mom could drive up for treatments? That way you'll be able to spend time with her, even after you ditch home.

"*Ay* gerd *mio*," Cole said as several tall, athletic guys who looked like football players jogged past us. "Who needs a scrawny Nutter Butter boy when you can munch on some beefcake, then slurp up some six-packs—am I right?"

"Cole," I said. "I think I might be ready to leave soon."

"Shut your *boca*," Cole said. "I told our friends from last night we'd meet them for fountain hopping."

Fountain hopping is a timeless Stanford tradition wherein students strip down to their underwear on a sunny day and play in the campus's innumerable fountains, going from swimming hole to swimming hole for the sheer delight of it. Now, on this particular day, I thought it was rather too chilly to bare my body, it being December and all, but Cole disagreed, and evidently everybody else did too.

"I can't believe this is our life now!" the Rubik's Cube boy said, preening atop a fountain statue shaped like a giant claw while I sat on a nearby bench and watched. "Who's got it better than us?"

"*Nooo-body!*" everyone else cheered at the same time. I do not know how they all knew this chant.

"I love all you guys! Let's be best friends forever! Stanford is my bliss!" the haiku girl shrieked in perfect five-seven-five structure while splashing about in merely her bra and panties.

"Cole, why won't your friend take off her sweater?" the tattoo boy shouted, flexing each of his *Giving Tree* images for the others to admire. "Doesn't she know how good the water feels?"

"I don't think she does!" Cole shouted back. He wasn't looking at me. He didn't even know where I was. "Homegirl's too afraid to have fun!

"Come on!" Cole said to the others, still not acknowledging my presence, not now that he was firmly ensconced in a brand-new group of brilliant, attractive, future-surgeon-and-senator-and-venture-capitalist friends. "Let's go swim in that red fountain that looks like a contraceptive device from the 1950s!"

"YEAH!!!" the others screamed in unison.

Within ten seconds they had all run off, skipping and yawping, just managing to remember their clothes and shoes and definitely forgetting to remember me.

Which, to be perfectly honest, was fine by me. I didn't need to spend any more time with those people. I'd really had my fill of college by then.

• • •

I've always had this image of myself as a college student, what I look like, who I am.

I'm considerably slimmer, because I actually have time to work out, because no one needs me to cook them dinner or teach them multiplication tables before bed. My hair is straightened, because I don't have Mama begging me to keep it natural, the way God intended. I'm wearing more makeup. I'm rocking fun jewelry. I'm dressed in bright colors, greens and golds and pinks. I'm undeniably cute.

In the late morning, I get out of my yoga or hip-hop class. I swing by Starbucks, where I meet a couple girlfriends. We scan our news feeds and laugh about reality TV and call each other "lady." I head off to class, where I study the side effects of stem cell transplants, or the economic development of postcolonial Latin America, or feminist jurisprudence, or sure, why not, haiku. I pursue whatever most excites me intellectually at the moment. I have no idea what I want to be, but my ambition has no ceiling.

After class ends, I head back to my dorm room, where my boyfriend is waiting for me. He kisses me on the forehead as I tell him about my day. He teases me about my busy schedule, but I don't mind. We lie down on the bed together, perhaps for a nap, perhaps for something else.

This is what I've been working toward all these years. It has always been my dream.

• • •

I didn't listen to the radio for the duration of my drive home. I eliminated all distractions. I stared ahead. For two hundred and fifty miles, I studied the road. I watched the freeway as it forked and converged again. I let my eyes linger on each off-ramp, every interchange, all of the innumerable twists and turns.

My choice remains right in front of me.

I can have it if I want. It's all still there. The scholarship. The friends. The new and improved me. The unfathomable future.

My day is coming. All I have to do is seize it.

And yet, deep down, I know my decision has already been made.

I can't go.

I need to support my family, and the best way for me to do that is to literally be there for them, through my mom's battle, through everything that follows. I cannot desert them. I can't be somewhere else, off having the time of my life or some such nonsense. I am not, nor will I ever be, a taker.

So I made my decision. Two roads diverged on the 101, and I chose my course. Stanford was on the left, and my family was on the right, and I took the road less traveled by, right off the freeway and straight toward home, and I was content with my choice. I was ready to face all of the consequences.

Yet right before I reached my house, just as I was all set to convince my parents of my no-college plan, I encountered something most unexpected.

Life, as it so often does, threw a detour in my path.

As I drove past the Dos Caminos campus, I saw something curious.

Someone, to be precise.

Someone about whom I wanted to learn more. Someone with a story to tell.

A boy.

ROAD TWO

FALL

1. WILEY OTIS

"Fat Isaac," I whispered. "It's time."

He nodded and gestured to the rest of the guys. As the fans in the stands continued to roar, and as the rest of the band marched back to the sideline, the brass section stayed out on the field, right there with me.

"Hey!" some AV kid said when I snuck up behind him and yoinked a microphone from his cart.

"Sorry," I said. "Gotta do this."

I switched the thing on. I took a step forward, the mic at my lips. I surveyed the stadium. I cleared my throat.

"People of Dos Caminos," I announced. "Let us take another moment to congratulate Miss Nikki Foxworth. What an honor!"

The crowd showered Nikki with a massive wave of applause. She princess-waved back to them, her crown balancing on her hair like a shiny star atop a Christmas tree.

"Now, if you'll excuse me for just a moment . . . there's something I want to say to a very special lady of my own."

Nikki glanced over her shoulder, back at me. Her eyes were sparkling. She was the only non-brass dude with any earthly idea what was about to happen.

After all, the plan had basically been hers.

"A-one! A-two! A-one, two, three, four!"

The guys and I have never made such badass music together. J.P. and Isaac on the trumpet, Travis and Pranav on their trombones, Kevin on the French horn, and me, of course, bringing it home on my Jabba the Hutt–size sousaphone. We blasted the ever-loving crap out of "Don't You (Forget About Me)," and as we jammed, my brain just overflowed with happy memories.

The middle school afternoons she and I used to spend playing Risk and Diplomacy, when we'd put on crazy historical hats and she'd refer to me as Wileyam the Conqueror and to herself as Allegrander the Great, and she'd dominate me every single game, and then she'd weep because she had no worlds left to destroy.

The times we used to comfort each other when one of us got real low. The silly crossword puzzles and word searches she used to create for me whenever my dad came home and acted like a jerk. The wacky movies I made on my phone the year her mom got sick.

The Disney movie marathons we used to have when we were kids, which over the years became scary movie marathons, which over the years became romantic movie marathons, not that I ever tried to get cuddly during those, not that I ever staged a romantic movie moment of my own—

Until now.

I didn't look Allie's way the entire time we played. It wasn't because I was scared or anything. I wasn't at all nervous how she'd react. Honestly, I just didn't want to spoil the moment.

But at last it came, the time I'd earned. The guys and I crescendoed together, and we took a bow, smiling with our instruments. The people in the crowd all paused, holding their breath, wondering what was next. I climbed out of my tuba and picked the mic up off the turf. I finally laid eyes on my girl, so unbelievably cute in her oversized jacket, standing all alone on the sideline.

She was clutching her flute with both her hands. She was blinking slowly. She had no idea what was coming.

"Allegra Rey," I said, and it was strange to hear my voice echoing all around the field, but good strange, the kind of strange you want to relive over and over.

"Come on . . .

"Whaddya say . . .

"Will you go to homecoming with me?"

Then came the longest wait of all time.

But after what felt like an eternity, she nodded yes.

The crowd went berserk, and the cheerleaders hopped

up and down, skirts and pom-poms flying, and the brass dudes struck up the Stanford fight song, which they weren't supposed to play until I did my second speech and asked Allie to be my girlfriend, but not a big deal, not a problem at all, because everyone was so pumped for me, so unbelievably supportive. I hustled over to the sideline, and I got a clap on the back from Ms. Fawcett on the way, and I high-pawed the guy in the bulldog suit. I caught a glimpse of Nikki too, and she was looking on with so much affection, such sisterly pride. I flung myself onto Allie and hugged her, I hugged her so hard I could have crushed a rib, but I loved her so much I would have given her mine. And for so long the two of us just stayed there, squished together in our perfect embrace, out under the lights for everyone to see, but truly there for no one else, nobody but ourselves.

I spent the first few minutes of the third quarter collecting congratulations from my band buds.

"Damn, Wiles. Never thought I'd actually see the day . . ."

"Wow, mister, someone sure punched above his weight, if you know what I'm saying. . . ."

"Dude, I always thought it was gonna be one of those things where you turn forty, you're both unmarried, and Allegra was too addicted to her career as a neurosurgeon to find love or whatever, and Wiley, you, like, lead a drum circle or something, and then finally you get together, but it's, like, really random and kind of unsatisfying."

"Um . . . thanks, Fat Isaac," I said.

I slipped him his money and waved him off.

"So," I said, turning to face my brand-new homecoming date plus hey, who-knows-what-else. "How does it feel?"

Allegra stared ahead, focused on the game. Our team was on offense, driving up the field right in front of where we were sitting.

"Uh, Earth to Allegra . . .

"Allie, do you copy?

"Yo! Since when do you care about football?"

"Oh," she said, still looking off. "Sorry."

"Hey," I tried again. "Everything okay? The whole school's congratulating us, and you're off in your own little world. What's wrong?"

She still wasn't responding, so I put my hand in front of her face. I had to get her attention, so I snapped my fingers, right in her eyes.

"Stop it."

"Stop what?"

"You're embarrassing me."

"You're right," I said. "That was rude. And I'm sorry, I didn't mean to embarrass you just now, but—"

She shook her head. "I'm not even talking about now. I'm referring to before."

"I . . . ," I started to say. "What?"

"At halftime," she said, her eyes distant. "When you asked me what you asked me, when you did it in that way. You put me in a compromising position. Either I say no, and I look like a sociopath and I humiliate you for all to see. Or alternatively, I say yes, but I do so without genuinely getting to mull the matter over, and I say yes for everyone in this stadium except myself."

She shook a few curls of hair in front of her face. "So, of course I said yes.

"But it's a two-way street, Wiley. Just as I was considerate of your needs, so must you understand my perspective. Surely you'd agree that right now is singularly the worst time to ask me what you asked me, and indeed to ask me anything. And not just because we're out here in public, being watched by thousands, like Christians in the Colosseum, but also because of the nature of what I'm going through at the moment. Think about my college decision. Think about my mom. Do I really have the bandwidth to be contemplating something as frivolous as a high school dance right now? Do you really think it's justifiable to put me in that emotional position?"

"I . . . ," I said.

I rubbed my eyes. I tried to make contact with hers. She was full gaze ahead, still zeroed in on the game, like nothing else mattered to her.

"I'm sorry," I said. "I was just trying to be bold. And fun. Of course I would never want to humiliate you. But I don't see why this is that hard. To me it's an easy thing, you know? I like you, okay? I like you, Allie. It's as simple as that, and—"

That's as far as I got.

"OH MY GOD."

I didn't see it happen. I heard it. The jarring clang and ringing reverb from the helmet crashing into the metal bench. The dozens of "what just happeneds" and "oh God, nos" being uttered all around me. The wail of the ambulance siren. The quiet prayers all around the stadium. Allegra's shallow, frantic breaths.

But I didn't see what happened to Brian Mack. All I saw was a huge, sprawled-out, motionless mass that the EMTs were attempting to somehow load onto the stretcher. I saw players from both teams in a circle at midfield, heads bowed, helmets off, all on one knee. I saw Allie beside me, her eyes finally somewhere besides the game, buried in her hands.

I wanted so bad to zoom past the whole scene. I wanted it to be way freaking later in the movie, after all the stupid weird sad crap.

"So . . . ," I said after several minutes of silence, trying to lighten the mood. "Going back to tomorrow for a sec . . . you wanna go straight from your house to homecoming, or should we grab a schmancy dinner first?"

Allegra winced. "Not right now."

"I'm sure he'll be fine. I'm just wondering—"

"Not right now."

"Right. Totally. That makes sense. Okay, in that case, I'll call you in the morning—"

"Listen to me."

"No, yeah, I am, but all I'm saying—"

"Please."

"I know it's awkward timing, but hear me out—"

"Have some compassion, for God's sake."

"Would Italian be good? Sushi's always fun, but who wants to boogie on a belly full of raw fish, right? So awkward, you know what I . . .

"Hey, where are you going?"

Allegra stood up, reached for her flute case, and glanced down at me. She let out a lengthy sigh. And she left. Allie left the game.

But not before saying one final thing:

"I'm sorry, Wiley. You're my best friend. But you really shouldn't have asked me. I could never go to the dance with you."

2. COLE MARTIN-HAMMER

I almost stepped on him.

It was this time a year ago, fall semester of eleventh grade, just before Thanksgiving. It was after school, which meant I was—where else?— in the theater. The halls outside were packed with dozens of stressed-out auditioners, all practicing dance combos and the most 'einous cockney accents you will ever 'ear. I, however, had nothing to fear. Mr. Bayer had already confessed to me that he'd selected that year's spring musical purely so I could bring my jauntiness, my tricksiness, my ever-bewitching untrustworthiness to the villainous role of Fagin. Just before my quote-unquote-audition, I happened to be practicing my Fagin walk in the hallway—shoulders hunched, knees high, hands dangling from my wrists like marionettes—which is when I almost stepped on him.

"Sorry! I'm sorry, Cole! I'll move."

He was curled up against the lockers, hugging his knees, damn near in the fetal position. Honestly, he could have passed for one of the orphans from the show, begging for a crust of bread. He was the spitting image of Oliver Twist.

"Oi!" I said. "'Ello, gov'na!"

"Sorry," he said. "I'll move."

"What's yer name, then?"

He looked confused. ". . . Neil?"

"And what part be ye auditionin' fer?"

The moment I said it, Neil's face fell.

"I don't know," he said. "I don't know what I'm doing. I think I should go."

He reached for his backpack. His hands were shaking. I'm sure if I'd listened closely, I would have actually heard him whimpering.

This poor kid. He didn't just remind me of Oliver. He also happened to resemble someone else, another frightened young lad who'd gone out for theater once upon a time.

He looked like lil' me.

"Rubbish," I said. "You're not going anywhere." I raised my foot and placed it on his shoulder, like I was claiming a new piece of land. He made an effort to stand up, but I pressed my shoe down and lowered him back to the ground.

"What'd you do that for?"

"What's wrong?"

"You have to let me leave."

I shook my head nope. "What's wrong, Neil?"

"I don't know," he said. "I thought I wanted to act. I

come see all the plays. I see you in them, I see everyone having fun. I wanted to be part of this. But then I got here, and yeah, I don't know what I was thinking. I'm not cut out for this."

He made another move for the backpack. I kicked it out of his reach.

"Poppycock," I said. "I won't have any of your lies."

I squatted to the floor, directly across from him.

"I was literally you," I said, my voice low. "I feared the world. I doubted myself. I tried to bail. But then one day, I made a theater buddy, and everything changed. He gave me confidence. Life got amazing. *I* got amazing. So let's go. Stand up. You're my scene partner. We're auditioning together. And I promise you two things, right here, right now. One, you're going to have the best time of your life . . .

"And two, you're going to be Oliver."

As ever, I was correct. Neil crushed the audition, utilizing but not succumbing to his pathetic orphan persona in order to land the lead role. Moreover, from that day forward, he has absolutely been the real-life Oliver to my actual Fagin, the partner in crime I've been lacking ever since Brian. Only instead of teaching him how to pick a pocket or two, I've instructed Neil in the twenty-first-century version of the naughty arts: how to scour the Internet to uncover the most degrading baggage. How to cyberbully dumb-dumbs without getting caught. How to hack the big test when you can't do math and you have no other choice.

Mischief isn't Neil's native language, that's for sure. Sometimes he excels at the tutorials I give him. More often, he displays evidence of this annoying thing apparently called a conscience. This is when our friendship hits a snag. I'll come up with some awesomely hilarious bit of prankery, and he'll start acting like we're back in the hallway a year ago, like I'm trying to stomp on him all over again. It's the living worst when he does this, when he activates crybaby mode. I mean shit, it keeps me up at night.

I think Neil likes being my friend. Every now and then, though, I have my doubts. I wonder if he hangs out with me solely due to the circumstances of how we met. I fear that he stays by my side not because he truly wants to, but out of some reluctant sense of loyalty.

But I try not to think about that.

I almost cheated.

It was last month, the morning after the homecoming game. I was standing on that hill, about to take that test, watching those kids.

I wanted to beat them. I wanted to dismember them. I wanted to flog and flay and tar and feather their hater-iffic asses. I wanted to take those racist homophobic bully snitches, and I wanted to make them suck on my perfect score and choke on my Stanford diploma, and I needed to show them exactly what they deserved for never being friends with me these past four years, for dismissing me before they so much as gave me a chance.

But as I watched them all, those nervous silhouettes, wandering into that big, scary room, I found myself thinking about another kid:

The little boy by the lockers, hugging his knees.

Neil was never onboard with my SAT plan. He got squeamish when I suggested it to him, way more than usual.

"It's wrong," he told me. "Cheating is wrong."

"A thousand apologies," I said. "But I really must do this."

"It's so much worse than anything you've done before."

"It'll be the last bad thing, the last time ever, I swear."

"You'll wish you hadn't done it. You always will."

"Hey, orphan boy," I reminded him. "I made you, okay? You freaking owe me."

After waffling on it for days, for weeks, he finally agreed to help me, but essentially at a price. He'd never look at me the same way again, he said. Our friendship would have a permanent crack, running right through the middle.

Still, I wanted to cheat. I mean, Stanford! I was born at Stanford Hospital, for crying out loud. My entire life, my parents have raved about their years there, about the people they met. The geniuses. The dreamers. "The crazy ones," my dad used to say, quoting some speech. "The misfits, the rebels, the troublemakers . . ." That is to say, people just like me. And all those people, they would actually want to be with me. They'd let me in.

And yet.

Before I left my car early that morning, before I went into my testing room to do the irreversible deed, I found myself thinking about yet *another* kid. But not Neil. And not young me.

My old theater buddy.

It's unthinkable. What happened to him at the game the previous night. One false move. One gentle push in the wrong direction. One little bop on the head. Suddenly his life, as we all knew it, it's over.

Who knows how exactly this universe works? Who can say whether we're rewarded for our good acts, or punished for our sins? Who can be certain that morality matters at all?

But hell, who wants to risk it, you know? Who wants to take the chance?

That settled it. Right there, right that split second, right before the test. I couldn't cheat. For Neil, I had to try to do the right thing. For Brian, I had to play it safe. For myself, I had to have faith that everything would work out in the end.

Flash forward to today.

"All right," Mr. Bayer said from his seat in the way back of the house. "Mr. Fagin and Mr. Twist. Which roles will you be auditioning for this time around?"

Neil cleared his throat. "Well—," he said.

"I think it's rather obvious, don't you?" I said, winking at our director. "You could even typecast us, if you so desired. Since I am, after all, an omniscient troublemonger with phenomenal fashion sense, I believe I would be ideal as the Cat in the Hat. And I think you'll agree that our pal Neil here is a wide-eyed, whiny baby with much to learn. Ergo, Jojo."

Bayer laughed, as he always does at my jokes. Neil took the ribbing like a champ.

"So," my sidekick said. "This afternoon, we'll be performing the Cat and Jojo's bathtub dance sequence—"

Ding!

"What was that?" Neil said.

"Ooh," I said. "Methinks my phone chimed."

"Cole," Bayer said. "You've gotta keep that on silent."

"My B," I said, reaching for my pocket. "I know I'm not *that* big of a diva . . . yet at least, lolz."

And I would have ignored the notification. I swear I would have turned my phone off without a second thought, for reals.

But I saw the words, right there on my screen: *Your Stanford University Admissions Decision.*

"Okay, guys," Bayer said. "Show me what you got."

"Hold up," I said. "I really need to check this."

"What?" Bayer said. "Before your audition?"

"Cole," Neil said. "This isn't the time."

I blocked them both out. I had to read the e-mail, right then and there. I had no other choice.

> *Dear Cole,*
> *The Admissions Committee has carefully reviewed your application to Stanford University. After much consideration, we regret to inform you that we are not able to offer you a position in the class of—*

"Hey there," Bayer said. "You with us?"

"Huh?"

"What is it?" Neil said. "What's wrong?"

I jammed my phone back in my jeans. "Nothing," I said.

"You sure?" Bayer said.

"You're ready?" Neil said.

"Yes, goddammit," I said, completely blocking them out, not giving two shits about being onstage, still hung up on that e-mail, still recounting those words over and over, letting them haunt me, like I'm certain they will till the day I take my last nicotine-flavored breath.

"Yes, goddammit. Let's do this stupid audition."

I bombed. My singing was flat, but my voice cracked too, which I didn't even know was possible. I half assed my dance, forgetting most of the choreography. During my scene, I flubbed a bunch of lines, and I couldn't bring myself to make eye contact with Neil, not a single time.

Whatever. None of it matters. My audition was a formality anyway. Bayer picked the show with me in mind for the part of the Cat. Whatever. None of it matters. I pussed out on that Saturday morning back in October. I blew the biggest opportunity of my life. I'm not going to Stanford. Whatever. I don't care anymore. My future is dead.

I could have been smart. I could have found my people. I should have had everything I desired. But I did the "right" thing.

3. BRIAN MACK

I love football. . . .

That's what I said in his office. . . . I told Coach I love football. . . .

Everyone loved me. . . . Nikki made me brownies. . . . DeSean called me a soldier. . . . The brownies were the shape of footballs. . . . Kyle said, "Way to nut up. . . ." My dad's friends came to the game. . . . They all wore gold rings. . . . I love Friday nights. . . .

My head felt great. . . . The band played "Dancing Queen." I felt like a million bucks. . . . The dance girls looked smokin'. . . . The cheerleaders were okay. . . . I played so hard. . . . Nikki looked perfect. . . .

I had the game of my life . . . opened big-ass running lanes . . . pancake blocks for days . . . blocked a kick, too. At halftime Coach said thank you. . . . DeSean said, "How you feeling, bro?" I popped five Advils. . . . I said I was fine. . . . I ate another brownie. . . .

The second half was awesome. . . . Bulldogs were on the

move. . . . DeSean yelled, "Hike!". . . I protected him like always. . . . D broke free. . . . I ran with him. . . . The crowd screamed, "Big Mack. . . ." Shit got loud. . . . That's all I know. . . . That's all my brain remembers. . . . I wish I could remember. . . .

I don't know what comes next. . . .

"Mom.

"Mommmmmmm.

"MOM! MOM! MOM! MOM! MOM! MOM! MOM!"

"What is it, honey?"

"STROGANOFF."

"Did you do your morning things?"

"WHAT?"

"I said, 'Did you do your morning things,' Brian?"

"Oh. No."

"Do your morning things, hon. Then I'll make you breakfast. Okay?"

"Okay."

I got off the bed. I looked at the picture by my bed. The picture was me. It had a red "1" on it. The picture was me brushing my teeth. The picture said, BRUSH TEETH—TWO MINUTES. I went to my sink and brushed my teeth. I counted two minutes. Then I spat out. I walked back to bed.

There was another picture. It had a red "2" on it. The

picture said, PUT ON CLOTHES—THREE MINUTES. I took off my jammies and put them in the basket. I put on shorts and my blue Bulldogs shirt. No socks because I wear Crocs now. The Crocs are blue like my shirt. I put my clothes on in one minute. So fast.

"MOM!

"MOM!

"MOM!

"MOMMMMM!"

The doctors told me the next part. . . . They say I should've told someone. . . . They say I shouldn't have played. . . . It's my fault I'm like this. . . .

We were running together . . . me and D. . . . He got past the marker. . . . He got a first down. . . . We were near the out of bounds. . . .

I got my bell rung at Grease Pole. . . . Nesto fell off Tua. . . . Tua fell on me . . . crushed my head. . . . I didn't want them to know. . . . I lied in Coach's office. . . . I hate when people hate me. . . .

DeSean wanted me to play. . . . Coach let me lie. . . . USC, UCLA, Oregon . . . Nikki wanted me to play. . . . My team wanted to win. . . . My dad wanted another gold ring. . . . I wanted it. . . . I wanted to win. . . . I wanted to be a legend. . . . What if I never played . . . ?

I couldn't see it coming. . . . The guy was behind me. . . .

I got pushed in the back . . . tripped over my feet . . . I fell because I'm fat . . . I fell like a tree. . . .

I should have stayed on the bench. . . . I should have kept it safe. . . . I didn't want to play. . . . I never liked football anyway. . . .

My head hit like, wham bam . . . all over again. . . . My bell got rung. My bell got rung. . . . I wish I remembered. . . . My life went black. . . .

I went to the kitchen. Mom was there. She was standing up. Dad and Kyle were at the table. They were eating eggs.

"What would you like for breakfast, Brian?"

"Stroganoff."

"Stroganoff isn't a breakfast food."

"STROGANOFF, DAMMIT."

"Okay, okay. I'm sorry, honey. Don't worry. I'll make you stroganoff."

I farted really loud. "Good."

I sat by Dad. He was looking at his paper.

"Why are you reading that?"

"Oh, this is the sports section. I'm reading about your friends on the Bulldogs. Looks like they're not gonna qualify for CIF this season. They sure missed you out there, champ."

Mom walked fast over to me and Dad. She put her hands on my hand. "But we're really glad to have you at home, Brian."

Dad put his paper down. "Oh yeah, of course. We're so happy you're here, buddy."

Kyle held his fist for me to bump. I gave it a bump. We blew up our fists. "Love you, dude."

"We love you more than words."

"You're doing so great, Brian."

"We're so proud of you, big guy."

I looked at them. All of them were smiling. Big smiles. Big fat happy smiles.

"Okay . . . ," I said. "Time for school?"

Mom says I fell asleep. . . . My brain was all bleeding. . . . Dad says I slept two days. . . . He didn't sleep one bit. . . .

They cut my head with a saw . . . the doctors . . . The blood got stopped, they said . . . the flow, they said . . . "second-impact syndrome" . . . Everyone said prayers. . . . My brain swole up huge. . . . I basically was dead. . . .

Mom called the pastor. . . . They all thought Big Mack was gone. . . . At least they thought my brain was mush. . . . I wish I saw them missing me. . . . I kinda wish I went to heaven. . . .

But then it was so random. . . . I remember it all, clear as day. . . . I randomly woke up. . . . I was like, *Why am I in bed. . . ?* My parents were crying. . . . Kyle was crying. . . . The doctors were crying. . . .

I saw my scar. . . . I was like, *Why am I Frankenstein . . . ?* The doctors said I'm lucky. . . . The nurse said someone's watching . . . watching over me. . . . Dad said protecting my blind side . . . I wonder if that shit is true. . . .

I wonder if I'll get better . . . like better for real . . . like good at sports again . . . good at school . . . I wonder how long I have to be like this. . . . Will I always have this scar . . . ? Will I always trip and fall . . . ? Will I always talk all slow . . . ? Will Nikki make more brownies . . . ? Those were amazing. . . .

I remember the hospital.

I remember it crystal clear. Those are my first good memories since the game. I was there so long. I was at the hospital forever. My thing happened on homecoming and I didn't go home till after Thanksgiving. I liked the hospital a lot. Better than home. I miss it. I miss how everyone was so nice.

Sometimes my friends came to see me. For a long time my teammates used to visit a lot. It was freaking tight-ass shit.

"The Big Mack is big pimpin'!" my friend Ernesto said. He liked my nurses. He liked how I said thank you to them and how they smiled and said thank you back.

"Dude, I heard about this thing called Florence Nightingale syndrome," said my friend Tua. "You got to get *busy* with some of these honeys, dawg!"

"Or maybe just get the Moaner in here," said my friend

Scrotes. He was pushing the buttons on my bed and making it go up and down. "She could have some major fun on this thing. And she'd totally still do you, Big Mack. She got that fetish, yo."

My friends gave me a football they all signed with gold pen. They brought pictures of kids at school wearing my Bulldogs jersey with MACK 69 on the back. Also they gave me a bracelet. They said everyone at school was wearing the bracelet. It was Bulldog Blue and it said #PRAYERS4BRIAN. Right before the times they left my room, my friends all got super-serious. They touched their bracelets to my bracelet and said stuff, like "You got this, man" and "We'll never abandon you." I told them stop being so gay.

My other hospital friend was Nurse Wanda. She is a big black lady with curly hair. I used to do acting with her son, back at Dos Caminos. She watched movies with me. Lots of them. She showed me *Singin' in the Rain* and *The Wizard of Oz*, movies like that. She said those are her son's favorites. Sometimes when we watched them, we sang the songs.

"Wow, Brian, you have quite the stage presence," Nurse Wanda said to me one time after we sang the good morning song. She bumped my fist.

"Thank you, Nurse Wanda," I said.

"You know, one of these days, we've really got to get you back out in front of some folks."

"Thank you, Nurse Wanda."

I liked those memories. I liked them a lot. I liked seeing my friends from the team. I really liked singing with Nurse Wanda. Those were good times. Good times, bitches.

But they weren't my favorite memories. They weren't my best day.

The best day of my whole hospital time was when DeSean and Nikki came to be with me. It was so special. They brought me presents. I still have the presents. It was so fun.

But they never came back. They came to the hospital one time but no more times after that. They said they would see me again. They said they would come hang after school. But they didn't. I never saw them ever again. I wonder why.

"Mom.

"Mom.

"MOM!"

"Yes, Brian?"

"I wanna go to school."

"I know, honey."

"Home sucks. It's boring."

"Okay."

"Home sucks. It's gay."

"Don't say that, Brian."

"I wanna go to the hospital."

"Well, you're done with the hospital for now."

"I hate home. It's shitty."

"I know."

"Where are my friends?"

"I don't know, but how about this? Why don't we invite some of them over?"

"No."

"Why not?"

"I don't wanna *invite.* I want them to *come.*"

"Okay . . . well, you know, I actually heard that some of your teammates have been practicing the past few days, for the Male Ballet. Why don't we stop by the Greek and pay them a visit?"

"NO."

"What do you mean, 'no'?"

"I don't wanna *stop by.* I wanna *STAY.*"

"Brian, we're trying our best here—"

"No, you're not."

"Yes, we are—"

"No, you're not."

"Brian, we love you so much. All we want is for you to be happy—"

"I wanna go to school.

"I wanna go to school.

"I WANNA GO TO SCHOOL."

4. NIKKI FOXWORTH

"Come on, babe."

"No, thanks, I'm tired."

"Tired? What's that supposed to mean?"

"Just not right now."

"But *when?*"

"I don't know, not yet."

"But, baby—

"Sweetheart—

"*Baby—*"

This was how it went for weeks and weeks. After school, DeSean would pick me up from dance practice. We'd drive over to the spot. We'd mostly be quiet on the drive, not talk about football or friends or anything like that. As soon as we parked at the site, we'd start doing stuff—make out, touch each other all over, and some other stuff too. The one thing we never did, though, was go all the way. Over and over I told DeSean I'm not ready, I'm tired, I'm nervous, I'm still not ready.

"What's your deal? I thought you wanted to. You said it was all you wanted."

"When did I say that?"

"You don't remember? After you gave that slacker kid a pep talk. Before homecoming."

"Yeah, but then homecoming . . ."

"Dammit, not the Brian thing again—"

"Well, I can't stop thinking about him."

"And he has anything to do with us . . . why?"

"I feel guilty."

"Too guilty to do it with your boyfriend?"

"It sounds stupid when you put it like that."

"Well, if you feel so guilty, why don't we go back and visit him again?"

"No."

"Come on, babe, I don't understand—"

"No."

DeSean paused for a moment. He looked at me with soft eyes. He extended his hand. He placed it on my chest and massaged there, softly. And it felt nice, it did, but the way it felt, it also reminded me of—

"No."

I never wanted to visit Brian in the first place.

"Nik, we gotta say hi. It's been two weeks. All the other guys, they've already been."

DeSean and I were in the hospital waiting room. The nurse had just given us the go-ahead to walk on in. I didn't budge from my seat.

"I don't know," I told D.

"What's your problem?" he said. "Don't you care about Big Mack?"

Of course I cared. That was exactly the problem. I had this mental image of Brian—who he used to be, what he could have been. And I wanted him to stay that way. I couldn't bear the thought of him being any, well, different.

"Aw, screw it," DeSean said, grabbing the toy from the magazine table. "I'm showing love to my friend." He stood up and strode straight to the room.

I hurried after him, feeling like a coward.

"Brian," the nurse said, opening the door. "Your friends are here to see you. . . ."

I hadn't thought he would be allowed out of bed yet, but as soon as we walked in, *whoosh*, Brian came flying off the mattress, and *whomp*, he wrapped DeSean and me in a massive three-way hug, clutching us tighter than a pair of kittens in a snowstorm.

"Nikki! D! Nikki! D! Nikki!"

"Aw, yeah, it's us all right," DeSean said, stepping out of the hug and rubbing his hands together. "And guess what? We. Brought. *Presents.*"

Brian's mouth fell open. He shot both fists in the air. I

swear to God, I've never seen anyone so happy.

"Mine first," DeSean said, pulling the action figure out of his pocket. He handed it to Brian.

"It's a . . . what's that? A little naked guy? With a hat?"

DeSean grinned at me. He patted Brian on the back.

"That's Tommy Trojan. Do you know why I'm giving him to you?"

Brian was already playing with Tommy, making the figurine do baby steps up and down his left arm.

"He's the USC mascot. I just found out the other day that I have an offer to play football there next year. It's all I've wanted, my entire life, to wear that red jersey, to run through that Coliseum tunnel. And I never could have achieved it without you blocking for me all these years. So thank you, Big Bri. Thanks for everything, bro."

Brian wiggled the tiny, manly piece of plastic between his fingers.

"Wow," he said.

"And, ah, Nikki . . . she's got a present for you too."

DeSean looked at me. Brian looked at me. Nurse Wanda, standing by the door, she looked at me. I looked down. I felt it, between my hands, behind my back. The gift I definitely had to give Brian but that I desperately didn't want to. It made this whole thing way too real.

"Well," I said. "Okay . . ."

"Come on," DeSean said.

"I want it," Brian said.

"Okay," I said. "Okay."

I held it out and presented it. The golden crown.

Brian took it gingerly out of my hands, as if it were actually forged from precious metals. He studied the crown closely. He pressed it against his cheek.

"Whoaaa," he said under his breath.

"Brian, do you remember the homecoming dance?"

He locked eyes with me. He slowly shook his head.

"Well, I know you couldn't make it there because you, um, weren't feeling your best that night. But, you know, we were all thinking about you. The entire time. And at the end of the dance, something very special happened."

"What?"

"You were voted homecoming king, Brian, and it wasn't even close. Congratulations. And that's not all. Guess what else?"

"What else?"

DeSean handed me my crown, the glittery silver tiara. I put it on.

"The night before, at halftime of your game, I was named queen. And you know what that means?"

Brian scratched the back of his head. "No."

I flipped my hair. "It means you owe me a dance."

I removed Brian's crown from his grip. I placed it atop his head. DeSean pulled his phone out and tapped the screen. The song "I Don't Want to Miss a Thing" began to play. I took Brian's hands and brought them down to the small of my back. I placed my fingers up and around his neck. We began to sway back and forth to the music.

And it was lovely, really.

Brian was so gentle, so innocent with that smile of his, so cuddly and cute in that crown. As the two of us danced, I caught a glimpse of Nurse Wanda. She placed her palms together and *aww*ed. I peeked at DeSean, recording us on his phone. He put a sleeve to his glistening eye.

I stood on my tiptoes, reaching close to Brian's ear. I lowered my voice to a whisper. "We're all praying for you."

"Thanks," Brian whispered back. Then he added, "You look nice."

I felt safe in his arms. I honestly did. In that moment, he felt exactly like himself. If I closed my eyes and just focused on the way he felt—his big soft arms, his relaxed breathing, his teddy bear tummy—it was sort of like nothing had happened all.

Brian leaned down. He said something else. "You feel good."

And it did feel good. It felt really right being there, thinking, *Hey, awful things may happen, but maybe, just maybe, they don't have to ruin everything.* I mean it could be that accidents and mistakes present the clearest opportunity for you to see life as it really is. The bad times let you embrace who you are deep down and focus on what definitely matters, which is caring for others, whether you're slow dancing next to a hospital bed, or even making love to your partner, because maybe those kinds of connections are all we should value and everything else is just nonsense, and—

That's when my eyes shot open.

That's when I felt Brian Mack groping the bejesus out of my breasts.

"You feel good," he said, pawing at them like a clumsy beast, trying to grab ahold and squeeze. "Mmm, Nikki, you feel good."

"No!" I shouted, ducking away, covering up. "No, no! That's bad, Brian! That's *wrong*!"

"Yo!" DeSean screamed, throwing himself between us. "*The hell*, man?!"

"I'm sorry," Wanda said, dragging a confused Brian away, sitting him back on the bed. "I'm so sorry. He does that."

I yanked my crown off and shook out my hair. I reached for my sweatshirt and threw it on, zipping up to the top. DeSean said a quick good-bye and the two of us rushed out the door. We hopped in the car and I never looked back. I haven't told my friends about the incident. I told DeSean he's not allowed to bring it up either. I never want to think about it. I never want to dwell on that night again.

Needless to say, I haven't seen Brian since.

"What'd you do that for?" DeSean said at the spot this afternoon. He was staring at his hand, which I'd just removed from my shirt. I scooted slightly away from him.

"It's complicated."

"Actually, it's not," he said. "It's actually shocking how simple all this is."

"I'll be ready soon."

"You said that before homecoming. Almost two months ago!"

"Then why are you still dating me, if it's been such a bad two months?"

"Because I love you. And I want to *make* love to you."

"In that order?"

"Come on, babe."

"'Come on, babe,' what?"

"Come on, babe . . . I love you. I really love you. I always will."

He leaned in and kissed me on the neck. He stroked the side of my face. He called me beautiful like always, and he brought his big hand toward me, and I thought he was going to touch me—oh God, not my chest, please not again, so I flinched without thinking.

But he didn't do that. He touched my thigh. He gave it a light rub. And I'm sure it was harmless. But it felt wrong, somehow like trespassing. It made me feel violated—

"NO."

"Hey, I was just—"

"Not there."

"But what about—"

"Not there, either."

"Well, where *am* I supposed to touch you?"

"I don't know," I said. "I don't know."

"Okay, you're a virgin. And that's fine. I understand that. But damn, Nik, why you gotta be such a prude?"

"I don't know."

"Are you *still* freaking out over Brian?"

"I don't know."

"Are you ever gonna get over it?"

"I don't know."

"Are you gonna say 'I don't know' to every friggin' thing I say?!"

"I don't know."

DeSean exhaled, long and deep.

"Shit, Nikki. Maybe you're right. . . . What *are* we still doing together?"

I studied my boyfriend, sitting there in the driver's seat. I really took him in.

His red and gold college jacket with his name already

stitched on. His smooth, sweet skin. His enormous hands. His chiseled jawline. His chiseled arm muscles. His chiseled everything. His deep brown eyes, which wanted so badly to understand.

"I don't know."

5. ALLEGRA REY

My evening was, as all my evenings tend to be, chaotic. I was home and finishing my outline for a twenty-page AP Lit paper on *Moby-Dick,* while also making sure to carve out forty-five minutes for flute practice, while also sending out an e-mail rescheduling this week's Philanthropy Friday now that Cole has suddenly abdicated his position as copresident of Interact, while also triple-checking the packing list for my upcoming Stanford early-admitted students' reception.

Simultaneously, my brothers were squabbling over which book they wanted me to read them before bed. Concurrently, my dad was asking if I'd seen the article he'd printed out and left on my pillow. On top of all of this, Mama needed me to make her some tea.

"Wait! Allie! No!" Augusto hollered, bouncing on his bed. "I hate *Captain Underpants and the Perilous Plot of Professor Poopypants*! Do *Wrath of the Wicked Wedgie Woman!*"

"No!" Alejandro wailed, trying to sumo wrestle Augusto into the wall. "We did Gusto's book last time! Do *Professor Poopypants* or else you don't love me!"

"Wedgie Woman!"

"Poopypants!"

"Wedgie Woman!"

"Ow, my body!"

"Allegra," my dad said, ducking his head in the doorway. "Have you read the article yet? The *New York Times* said Stanford had its most selective early admissions ever. Under five percent!"

"Allegra," my *abuela* said, poking her head in underneath Dad's. "Where are my Goldfish crackers? Do you know who's taken my Goldfish crackers?"

"Allegra!" my mom called from her bedroom. "I am so sorry, but have you started my tea? *Gracias*, *mija*!"

At that exact moment, amid all the pandemonium, I heard the doorbell ring. It was clear and loud and it cut through the noise.

"I'll get it," I said.

I walked to the door, breathing a temporary sigh of relief. Thank goodness for neighbors. When Mama was first diagnosed back in October, the families next door came to our house bearing meals with incredible frequency. While they haven't been visiting as regularly in recent weeks, a few friends do stop by periodically with provisions, often enough so I'm not completely overloaded having to get groceries every other day. As I opened the door, I hoped the neighbor on the other side had brought a bag of Goldfish. I've been so addicted to those lately.

But when I saw who it was, I felt the opposite of hungry. My stomach dropped, like at the start of a roller coaster. I could have thrown up, right there on the spot.

I know Wiley's been trying his best. I don't blame him for his intentions, which I'm sure are noble. That said, he and I clearly haven't been on the same page these past few weeks. We've barely occupied the same solar system.

He obviously doesn't want me to attend Stanford. He forces a smile every time I talk about the admit reception, or choosing a major, but I can tell he's wishing for a miracle. I know he prays I'll stay.

He doesn't want me to have to deal with my family issues, either. He seems to pretend like my mom's cancer just doesn't exist. All he wants is for the two of us to stay our goofy, carefree selves, no matter how serious life becomes. And never was this clearer to me than during his bizarre behavior the night of the homecoming game.

I still don't know what to make of that night. We haven't discussed it since. Not once. Secretly, I'd been hoping we could put it off forever.

But now here he was, standing at my front door.

"What are you doing here?"

Wiley looked bewildered, all jittery and flushed. Within a second, though, he relaxed his expression. He chuckled and held up his hands.

"I don't know. I guess just visiting my best friend. You know, like a normal person. Can I come in for a sec?"

I took a beat. "Let's talk out here."

"Well, would you at least close the door?"

"I have a pot of tea."

Wiley shifted back and forth on his feet. "Okay."

His face appeared to slip into panic mode again, but he refreshed it with a quasi-grin.

"I haven't seen you much lately," he said. "Not as many walks home, no after-homework movies. And when we've talked, we haven't truly talked. Does that make sense?"

"I'm sorry," I said. "Things have been crazy."

"And obviously there was the game, which we seem to have left on a weird note."

"Right," I said. "The game."

Wiley smiled. He wouldn't stop smiling. It was borderline unsettling.

I folded my arms. "You're making me nervous, okay? Tell me. What are you doing here?"

He nodded, more to himself than to anything I'd just said. It was as if there were some sort of cryptic beat he was following, a piece of music only he could hear.

Then he looked at me. Straight at me.

"I came here to celebrate," he said, smiling. His teeth were faintly yellow, in a post-Fanta kind of way. "It's almost my birthday, you know."

His backpack was on the ground next to him. He hunched over to unzip it. He reached in and pulled something out. Something red.

"I felt pretty messed up about homecoming, how everything between us shook down. And I punished myself for it, you know, by spending less time around you. I assumed you'd rejected me.

"But then I realized . . . that wasn't what happened at all.

"The thing is, I just wasn't clear enough about my intentions.

"As someone very wise once told me . . . I need to give you a reason to want me back."

Wiley placed the red baseball cap on his head. There was an "S" in the center, with a green tree superimposed over it.

"Happy birthday to me," he said. "Look what I got myself."

"What . . . ," I said. "What is that?"

"Stanford, of course," Wiley said, shaking his head like I was the densest girl alive. "It's your future, Allie, and mine."

"What . . . do you mean?"

Wiley cleared his throat.

"I love you, Allegra Rey. I freaking love you. I have for

the past ten years, and I will for the next twenty, the next fifty, and beyond. But I don't want my love to block any opportunities for you.

"So how does this sound: Next year, I go to Stanford with you. Not the college, of course. I could never get in there, or any college, really. But I could live up north with you. I could go to community college there, or get a job. Work on my filmmaking, even, like I've always wanted. And I could get my own apartment, or I could live with you, in the dorms. I could tend to your needs.

"There you have it. That's my pitch, my birthday wish. Whaddya think, Allie? Whaddya say?"

My head began spinning, like I literally felt dizzy, like I might fall right to the ground. These words he was saying, on the one hand I could have never imagined them, and yet, in the deepest recesses of my mind, I've been anticipating them for years. I've been dreading them. The word "love," it jostled my skull. The words "up north," they nearly made me gag.

And as awful as I felt, Wiley looked worse.

His eyes were bloodshot. His face was moist. His chest was heaving. His hands were spastic.

Worst of all, he was still—somehow—smiling.

Just then I heard it.

Reeeeeeeeeeeee!!!

"You know," I said. "Perhaps this isn't a good time."

"It's never a good time," he said. "Unless it's the perfect time."

Reeeeeeeeeeeee!!!

"I've got tea."

"Someone else can get it."

Reeeeeeeeeeeee!!!

"But my mom."

"Someone else can help her."

Reeeeeeeeeeeee!!!

"Wiley," I said. "You're not hearing me."

"Yeah, yeah, I get it, I totally get it. I know this is kinda weird, kinda daring, maybe even a little dangerous if we're thinking about it in terms of, you know, like Luke Skywalker, like Indiana Jones, like my hero's journey, but just hear me out, okay? Let some light into your life. Just let yourself have this one extraordinary thing—"

Reeeeeeeeeeeee!!!

"I don't like you!"

Wiley didn't move. As soon as I blurted the truth, he became an absolute statue. The only sign that the entire universe hadn't completely short-circuited on me was the cacophony of the teakettle's incessant whine.

"I'm sorry," I said.

I took a step forward and attempted to hug, or at least touch him. He did not budge.

"I love having you as a friend. My best friend, in fact.

Really, my only friend. I think you're perfectly suited for that. I am so sorry. If I sent any of the wrong signals—"

Wiley took his hat and threw it at the ground. It landed at my feet.

"Wiley," I said.

"Get your tea," he said, still not responding in any tangible way.

"I am so sorry," I said. "I feel somehow responsible—"

"Go get your tea, you fucking cunt."

The rest of the evening passed without incident. I read both books to my brothers, cover to cover. I pinned the admissions article to my bulletin board and told my father how grateful I felt to have him thinking about me. I binged on Goldfish well after my *abuela* went to bed.

When I served my mother her tea, she asked who had been at the door. I said a Jehovah's Witness. I then told her that I've made the decision not to attend the admitted students' reception at Stanford this weekend. She pushed back on that, but I insisted that I could always visit campus any other time, or learn about Stanford online, and that I have all the way until May to send in my acceptance, but that I simply have too many other things on my plate right now, particularly family obligations. I don't want to leave anyone behind, I told her. I reminded her to get a good sleep, what with her appointment early the next morning. She hugged me close and told me not to worry.

I spent the remainder of the night in my room, completing my homework. From time to time, my mind turned to Wiley. How I could have dealt with him differently, what I could have said to let him down more kindly, how it could have been better between us, what might have been had he never used that vile, vulgar, friendship-ending word.

Every time those thoughts crept up, I pushed them from my mind. I turned to the next page.

I miss my neighbor. I miss him already. But I refuse to cry over him.

That's just the way things go sometimes.

ROAD ONE

WINTER

6. BRIAN MACK

I'm sorry," she said to me, back on that fateful day. "But are you okay?"

I wasn't, really. It was almost evening, the first Sunday of winter break. Things hadn't been going so hot at home. My mom had been making me my favorite dinner, which she's been doing a bunch lately to try to boost me up. Only it never helps, because eating beef stroganoff makes me feel like a plump Russian troll. That's when my pops and Kyle rolled into the kitchen to give me shit for quitting football, like a pussy, and joining theater, like a pansy. I got hella pissed at them and straight up peaced without saying a word. I walked half a mile to the one place where I knew no one would find me over break, the Dos Caminos campus. I was chilling there solo, sitting on the front lawn, plucking some grass, whistling this song I need to learn for the musical, "Alone in the Universe"—

When that car randomly drove up.

When that pretty girl with the curly hair pulled suddenly into my life.

"Brian," she said, leaning out the driver's window. "Are you okay?"

"What?" I said. "Who are you?"

"I'm—"

She was a quieter girl, so I had to get up and take a few steps to hear her better.

"What?"

"Allegra Rey. I'm your year. I'm fairly certain we had health together, back in ninth grade. I play flute at all of your games, and—"

She dropped her head. She shook it all fast, like she was trying to get dandruff out of her bangs, or water out of her ear.

"I'm sorry," she said. "I shouldn't have brought that up. Football, I mean. Beyond rude of me."

She looked down at her hands. She picked at a cuticle on her finger.

"You seemed lonely is all, sitting there. I hope you don't mind me saying that. I wanted to make sure everything was fine with you. That's it, I promise. I can leave now, if that's what you want."

I shook my head. "That's funny," I said.

"What's funny?"

"That you were worried about me."

"Why is that funny?"

I shrugged. I thought it was pretty obvious.

"Because you're the one who looks like you've been crying."

The second I said that, and without a moment's hesitation, Allegra covered her eyes. She rolled her car window all the way up. She pulled away from the curb, into the street, away from me.

So much for the pretty girl.

Five seconds later, the car's brake lights turned on, followed by the reverse lights. In a flash, quick as a virgin's load, she was exactly where she'd just been, at the curb two feet in front of me.

"I'm sorry, Brian," she said, looking down at her feet. "I'm being capricious."

I stepped forward, up to the car. I put my hands on the roof. I leaned into the open passenger window.

"Okay," I said. "Number one, I bombed the SAT, so I have no idea what that word means."

As I said it, I saw the corner of her mouth twitch up, just the tiniest bit.

"And number two, why do you keep saying sorry for stuff? You're apologizing more times than, like, a crappy butler."

At this Allegra actually smiled. She made a soft sound, like, "hmm."

That's when she looked at me, square in the eyes, for the very first time.

And . . . yeah.

Something changed in me. Something shifted when I saw them.

They're not the most beautiful eyes. Kinda tiny and gray. You could even say beady. You wouldn't sing a song about these eyes. You wouldn't write a love poem.

But they know something. Something you don't. Something sad. And scary. It's like the frozen look a rabbit gives you when you're in the car and it's in the middle of the road. It knows exactly what's coming, but it can't do a thing to protect itself. And you want to stop and save the poor thing's life, but you might just smush it into roadkill.

Allegra's eyes blinked at me. I blinked back.

"Would you like a ride home?" she said

"Hell yeah," I said.

We didn't talk for the first half of the drive. Sure, it's a short ride from DCHS to my house, maybe eight blocks if that, but still, it was awkward as old-people sex, taking that first big step together at the sidewalk, then just as quickly taking two steps back. And I mean, I got what was going on. I knew we were both facing struggles of different sorts, what with how, ever since I quit the team, the entire world has treated me like a van-driving toddler stealer who makes skin suits out of his victims and sells them on Craigslist, and Allegra with her . . . Wait, what *was* her deal? Why the dead bunny eyes? And who the hell was this chick, anyway? She seemed so familiar.

"Hold up," I said. "Aren't you that girl who got into Harvard or whatever?"

Her face changed, just barely. She continued to stare at the road ahead.

"Yes," she said. "I suppose I am 'that girl.' Stanford."

"You're BFFs with Nutter Butters, yeah? The wolf kid, with the pube 'stache. Wiley."

Allegra took a breath in. She let one out.

"Yes."

I kept going.

"Look, I don't mean to pry. But you acted all crazy pills when I said you looked sad. Which means there's definitely a reason you looked sad. And if you're allowed to worry about me, I'm allowed to ask about you. So, like . . . what's eating you?"

I fully expected her to drop her head again, to go all la-la-la-I'm-not-listening, and to push me out of the car, to send me rolling down the hill like the snow-white avalanche that I am.

But instead what she did was, well, it was awesome, actually.

She told me stuff.

"I'm not sure where to begin," she said. "There's really such a maelstrom of things right now. My mom just learned—my family has a lot on its plate at the moment. And I could leave them behind if I wanted, but I fear that'd be selfish. And

Stanford, well, it's an honor to get in, of course, but frankly, I'm not sure college is all it's cracked up to be. And Wiley . . ."

She trailed off.

"Wiley . . ."

She said his name with the flattest tone in her voice, the most distant look in her eye.

"He's . . . I don't know. Ever since homecoming, he's been acting so strange. . . ."

Just then we came up on my house, which I pointed out to her. At that same moment, right as she was about to pull over, it hit me. I realized exactly what was going on.

"*Ohhhh.* Dude. Say no more. I know what's up." I put my hand on her shoulder. I gave it a mini-squeeze. "So it's tough, because like, Wiley's your pal, but, like, secretly this whole time, he's been trying to bone you."

WHAM.

As soon as I said it, Allegra jammed on the brakes. She braked so hard I practically thumped my head on the dash. I mean I damn near got a second concussion, which would have legit turned me into—what's the fattest vegetable there is?—like, a cabbage or something.

"Get out."

"What?"

Allegra kept her eyes fixed on the street, refusing to meet mine.

"Look," I said. "I'm sorry, but—"

"Now."

Oof. That hurt. Like a helmet to the gut. I gulped. I nodded okay. I got ready to step out of the car. I glanced up at the rearview mirror, and—

"Shit!"

Allegra's head snapped. "What?"

"It's him!"

"What?"

"He's coming!"

"Who is?"

"*Wiley*!"

She threw her hands above her head. She collapsed in her seat all duck-and-cover style. Her breathing stopped. It was like we had Navy SEALs surrounding the perimeter or something, just waiting for the order to burst in and open fire on us. The poor girl was so freaked out, so scared crapless at the consequences of being seen together with me. It was only after a full sixty seconds that she lifted her head from her knees and peered out through her fingers. That's when she saw that I hadn't moved, not at all.

"Wha—why didn't you—"

My body gave it away before I could. My mouth corners twitched up against my will. My eyes practically filled with tears.

"Heh-heh-heh . . . *got you*!"

I died. I died laughing at the hilariousness of the

situation. Allegra scowled, and at first I thought she was going to scream at me for being an asshole, or quietly insist that I go to my house and leave her life forever.

Instead, though, what she did was, well, she surprised me all over again.

"You're right, aren't you? You're absolutely right."

"I am? About what?"

She paused, letting the reality fully sink in. "He really does . . . want to . . . bone me."

I smiled with my mouth closed. "I shouldn't have joked about it," I said. "Especially after you told me all that sensitive stuff. That wasn't kind of me. I'm sorry."

Allegra shook her head. "Dude," she said.

"What?" I said.

"Dude."

"What?"

"Dude." She tilted her head up and beamed at me. "Stop apologizing. You sound like a crappy butler."

Without any sort of warning, Allegra sat high in her seat, leaned all the way toward me, placed both of her hands on my sides, and planted the biggest, warmest kiss on my cheek.

"It's been a pleasure meeting you, Brian. I'm not sorry it happened at all."

"Hell yeah," I said.

Hell yeah.

The selfish bitch and the little bitch. Has a nice ring to it.

7. WILEY OTIS

"You should have just played her the song, man," Darius said. "Music is like the ultimate panty-dropper."

"Just ask Elvis," Berger said.

"Or Tupac," Darius said.

"Or famed concert cellist Yo-Yo Ma," Woo chimed in. "That dude must go through, like, two dozen condoms a day."

I punched at the headrest of the front seat, where Woo was sitting.

"Come on, guys," I said. "Stop trying to make me feel better. It's over. My chance was gone the second DeSean got crunched. Plus she's with her Neanderthal now."

"You should never give up," Berger said.

"Yo-Yo Ma would never quit in pursuit of that ass," Woo said.

"It's too late!" I shouted. "I can't play Allegra the song because she chose someone else, okay? And I quit band anyway. I quit to hang with you clowns."

There was a short while when no one spoke. Woo looked at Darius. Darius looked at Berger. Berger looked at Woo. Smirks spread across each of their faces. They all looked at me.

"Well . . . ," Darius said. "What if . . . we were your band?"

"What?"

"We've already got the instruments," Woo said. He reached inside the glove compartment and pulled out a small beanbag with a Jamaican flag pattern on it.

"Check it out," he said. "I play the Hacky Sack."

He shook the Hacky Sack in rhythm, like it was a maraca.

"He plays the Sack, and I play the snacks!" Darius said, grabbing an empty Hot Cheetos bag from the car floor, which he crinkled and uncrinkled to the beanbag beat.

"And I play . . . ," Berger said, looking all around the car. "I play . . ."

"I play the kazoo!"

Berger stuck his hand deep in his pants pocket and pulled out a red plastic kazoo.

"The hell?" I said. "You own a kazoo?"

"Brah," he said. "What sort of self-respecting G doesn't own a kazoo?"

The three of them played their "instruments" for several seconds. It gave me a headache, the guys making those same noises over and over. All they did was irritate me. All they did was make me think of Allegra more.

"Dammit," I said. "I need some of that shit you guys are on."

I took the weed pipe from Darius's free hand.

I lit the bowl. I took a big puff in.

I tried to forget.

I've known Darius, Woo, and Berger since elementary school. Each of them used to be somebody else. Darius was a star track and fielder until sophomore year, when he tore his ACL and traded hurdles in for blunts. Woo was a pre-med prodigy until his parents burned him out and he began medicating in a different way. And Berger . . . well, Berger was always a stoner, but when the three of them joined forces, he went from Padawan to Jedi Master.

I never thought I'd become friends with those guys. Back in the day, Allegra wouldn't have let me. She frowned upon their antics. She used to see them across the halls and refer dismissively to their "smelly little world."

Then again, Allegra's the same person who shut me out as soon as her mom got diagnosed. She stopped spending time after school with me. She never let me make her smile. She left me alone on my birthday. She forgot to text me on my birthday. And even after I was cool with all of that, even after I forgave her in my heart, she betrayed me. I'd been waiting to reveal my feelings. I wanted to wait until her family situation improved, until she was ready. I was trying to do the gentlemanly thing.

But before I had the chance to confess my love, she went and freaking kissed someone else. And not just anybody, but that balding, brainless, plus-size ogre. That's how much I meant to her. Ten years down the drain, just like that.

So maybe I didn't need her anymore. Maybe I needed to try some new smells.

"Hey, guys," I said to the trio on the first day back after winter break. I had walked up to their usual spot, in Darius's car, in the very last row of the student parking lot.

"I have a thing of Mother's Iced Oatmeal cookies, some honey barbecue twisty Fritos, a buttload of Fruit Roll-Ups, and a book of optical illusions. Can I hang out with you?"

"Wiley, my friend," Woo said. "We always knew this day would come."

"You have impeccable taste in random shit," Berger said.

"Climb into the hotboxmobile, sire," Darius said.

Since that day, we've had the most memorable times ever, even if I can't totally remember them. We've ditched school to smoke and play video games, and to smoke and climb trees, and to smoke and feed feral cats. We've snuck onto campus late at night and climbed to the very top of the big theater roof, where we've peed off the edge, and I always have the longest stream by far, so the guys all salute me and call me "Streammaster General," and it makes me laugh so hard I have to steady myself, so I don't join my pee in falling fifty feet off the roof.

And then, immediately after I'm done laughing, right after I've zipped back up, my thoughts can't help but turn to Allegra.

Every time. Still.

Her twisty Frito hair. Her licorice-red jacket. Her little gummy fingers. Her M&M eyes.

I've got to lay off the munchies, don't I?

And I've got to forget about her. She's out of my life. I have to have fun with the guys and that's it. But it's like, every time I'm with them, there comes a moment when I can't stop thinking about my past, about what could have been my future. No matter what I do, my stupid, stubborn heart stays obsessed with her.

All the time. Still.

"Come on," Woo said, flinging the car door open. "Let's practice Wiley's song!"

"Yeah!" Darius and Berger said, hopping into the parking lot with their pretend instruments. We'd been hotboxing for a while after school, like ninety minutes at least, so no other kids were around.

"I don't know," I said, still in my seat. "I might not be up for it."

"We're doing it *for* you," Berger said. "If you say no, that's like the Make-a-Wish kid who doesn't show up for his own leukemia day at SeaWorld."

"But I don't have an instrument."

"Wiley," Darius said to me. He had a dead serious look in his eye.

"You play the tuba. . . ." He put his hand on my shoulder. He paused for seemingly five minutes. "The anal tuba."

At that, the other guys burst into little-boy laughter. In that instant, I wanted to walk away, or say "piss off," or text Allegra, *Come get me, please. I'm sorry. Let's at least be friends again. I'll do anything. Please come and save me.*

Instead, I lifted the pipe to my mouth. I took another hit.

One second later, in between coughs, I was laughing my ass off too.

"Ladies and gentlemen!" Berger called out to the sea of empty parking spaces.

"We welcome you tonight to our benefit concert, honoring a great cause, the Wiley Otis Foundation for Broken Hearts and Blue Balls—"

"And now," Woo said, grabbing the invisible mic, "we present to you, our number one hit single . . . 'Allegra Rey, I Hate You and You're Fat!'"

I made cheering crowd sounds as my three friends began playing their music. Woo shook his Hacky Sack. Darius crumpled and decrumpled his plastic bag. Berger went ham on his kazoo.

"Allegra, you bitch," Darius sang. *"I hate your saggy bitch tits."*

"*Why were you such a bitch,*" Woo joined in, "*to Wiley and his twelve-inch dick?*"

"*I hate you so much,*" Berger sang. "*Because you're such a slut.*"

"*And Wiley hates you too,*" Woo added. "*Just listen to his butt. . . .*"

"Tuba solo!"

I toot-toot-tooted, and toot-toot-tooted some more, and just when it seemed like I was fresh out of ammo, I toot-toot-tooted all over again. Allegra hates how I can fart on command. She thinks it's the most disgusting and least impressive skill in the world, but hey, we can't all be college geniuses like her, and this is the only skill I've got. If she can't appreciate that, then she can't appreciate me, and so I kept farting, and the guys kept laughing and playing their instruments and cheering me on, and I've never had so much fun in all my life, fart, fart, fart, fart fart, fart, fart, fart, fart, fart, fart, fart—

"Hey!

"*HEY!*

"What the hell are you doing?"

In the awesomeness of our jam sesh, we never even noticed when the car pulled into the lot. It was a student driver car with a sophomore girl behind the wheel, but that wasn't the bad part. The bad part was who was in the passenger's seat. It was our school's football coach-slash-driver's ed teacher, Coach Dent. He looked goddamn psycho.

"You! Stay where you are! You stay *right* where you are!"

I don't know how the other guys did it. They must just be way better than me at this whole doing sneaky stuff behind grown-ups' backs thing. As soon as Coach Dent screamed, the three of them full-on booked it. Darius, Woo, and Berger raced off the lot, down the hill, and into the nearby neighborhoods. And since Coach doesn't know who they even are, they pulled it off. They got away with getting away.

As for me, I don't know if it's because I'd been so concentrated on playing my instrument, or because I'm newer to smoking so the effects of it hit me harder, or maybe because part of me still feels like I deserve this, like I'm supposed to get in trouble every time I do something bad. At any rate, by the time Coach walked up to me, I was still in my tuba solo spot. And at this point I thought I'd be fine, because it's not like we'd been doing anything actually bad, like we were just messing around—making gross sounds, yeah, but that's not a crime or whatever. We weren't hurting anyone, so I had nothing to worry about, nothing at all.

That's when I remembered there was still a weed pipe in my hand.

A fully lit, totally smellable, very much illegal weed pipe.

Shaped like a naked lady, no less.

So . . .

Welcome back to detention, me.

Welcome back to detention for a very, very long time.

Hey there, Bear.

Missed you, girl.

8. COLE MARTIN-HAMMER

Knock-knock-knock.

"Cole baby? Can I come in?"

"Not now, Wanda. I'm otherwise disposed."

"How much longer you gonna take?"

"Could be all night. This is the most homework I've had all year."

"Okay, baby. Let me know if you want some food."

"Thank you, Wanda."

"Good luck with your assignments."

"Thanks, Mom."

Footsteps, footsteps, footsteps.

All lies, of course.

What homework? Screw homework. I finish most of that trash during the day, during my other classes. Sometimes I don't do it at all. I mean, I'm a Stanford student now. I do what I want.

No, nighttime is my time. It's when I conduct my real work.

It's when I get in the lab and do some research.

I began tonight's mission in simple fashion, by hopping online and typing "DeSean Weems scandal." Nothing came up, of course, but this was to be expected. Like any of the finest creative arts, a proper life-ruining takes time.

My social-media deep dive didn't reveal too much either. A recruiting-website rumor about D injecting himself with horse DNA. A locker-room pic in which he seems to be touching Scrotes in a slightly special way. A blog post he wrote about how his compound fracture has brought him closer to Jesus.

In the grand scheme of things, approximately diddly.

As I continued to come up empty, I must admit, I felt almost relieved. I mean, I've never had much against DeSean personally. I've always felt a kindred connection to the smattering of fellow black kids on campus. His mom and my mom are best hat-lady friends at church. And that jawline . . . How could one ever resent such perfection?

And yet, the man is captain of the football team. The same football team that called me fag and cocksucker freshman year, and racial stuff when DeSean wasn't looking. The same team that beat my ass in the locker room every afternoon after PE and told me that I liked it. The same team that, up until the moment I transferred into theater, had me seriously contemplating transferring from Dos Caminos, switching over to home school, dropping out of society altogether.

The same team that broke my friend Brian.

DeSean may not be as bad as the rest of them, but as their quarterback, as their leader, he damn well better pay for all of their sins, which—hoo boy, lucky me—means I get to play the role of a lifetime: that of the spiteful and vindictive Old Testament God.

One biblical ass-whoopin', coming right up. Big Mack, old pal, you're welcome in advance.

Knock-knock-knock.

"Cole?" my mother called. "Can I come in now?"

"No. I'm busy. Why?"

"Something I need you to do."

"This is a bad time, Wanda."

"It'll only take a few minutes."

"This is *important.* Go *away.*"

Footsteps, footsteps, footsteps.

All right, so if I couldn't take DeSean down directly, I figured I'd take the more devious approach. In superhero flicks, the ingenious bad guy always puts the boring-sauce hero in his place not by going right after him, but by targeting those whom the hero loves. So what I had to do was find DeSean's Aunt May, his Alfred the butler, his Lois Lane.

Even then I found squat. There was some comments-section speculation about DeSean's pops being controlling and abusive, but that's just sad. There were shots of the rest of the football team skeezing in a hot tub with freshman cheer uggos, but those are just predictable. I found some photo shoots from one of D's ex-girlfriends in which she's basically wearing lingerie, but honestly, who doesn't like to get a little nake-nake these days.

Knock-knock-knock.

"Baby, I need to come in."

"No, you don't."

She barged in anyway. "One minute. You promised."

"No, I didn't."

"Yes, you did."

"Well, I take it back!"

"You're acting like a child."

"I should *get* to be a child!"

"It would make him so happy—"

"What about *me?*"

"I love you. So does he. That's why you need to—"

"No. I hate him. You can't make me."

She held the phone up. She stared at me like she had all night. The woman had the coldest look on her face.

"Cole," she said. "Call your father."

My old man and I have never been able to connect.

Part of it is we're extremely different people. He likes basketball and jazz. I like old movie musicals and horrible housewife shows. He wears Mr. Rogers cardigans and Seinfeld jeans. I rock animal prints and purple pants and fly-ass kicks and business-dick socks. He teaches college-level math. I . . . tend to avoid math, when I can.

And, of course, there is the small matter of me being gay, which I do think is difficult for him to truly wrap his head around. But actually, for the most part he's pretty good about that stuff. That's not remotely the reason we can't connect.

No, beyond all the superficialities, the overwhelming barrier between Earl and me is this:

We're too much the same.

We are pariahs, Pops and I. Neither of us has ever been able to blend in with the crowd. People see us, and they see something different from themselves. They judge us immediately, and they punish us disproportionately. We have each had to learn the very real truth that life is not fair, that not everybody gets a spot on the team.

And theoretically, these struggles, this loneliness, it should bring us together. We should be united, father and son.

But the thing is, we deal with our shared problem in very different ways.

I embrace my lack of friends. Dad dwells upon his.

I overwhelm my enemies. Dad invents them.

I have never understood him. I've tried every day of my life, and yet every time I see him break eye contact with someone, or slump his shoulders, or plod away, it just boils my blood. I want to scream, *Earl, don't be a loser; don't give up.* But I know he can't hear me.

And I know the polar opposite is true. I know he sees the way I manipulate, whether it's people in my way, or my score on a test, and I know he can't understand how he of all men created someone like that. I think he hates me for who I've become. I'm certain he hates himself for never being able to stop me.

The reason my father hasn't been living with my mom and me this year is because late last summer, he attempted suicide. It was the week before my eighteenth birthday. I was at rehearsal for a summer stock show, and my mom came home from work and found my dad unconscious. She still hasn't said which room she found him in, or how he tried to do it, but she rushed him back to the hospital where she works, and she saved his life. Even though he didn't want to be saved.

We don't have long-term psychiatric-care facilities in Dos Caminos, or any good ones in the farmer towns near here, so my mom got my dad to voluntarily commit himself to the psych ward up north at Stanford Hospital, where she used to work. She still had a connection there, and she was able to get him a rare open spot. Of course she felt conflicted about how committing him would affect me, like she didn't want to take him out of my life so completely, but I said hey, Mom, he just tried to take himself out of my life pretty damn completely. And even if he stays crazy forever, I told her, I'll be up at Stanford next year anyway, right?

I didn't stop in to see him when I was visiting campus last month. I promised Wanda I would, but I didn't. I couldn't. I was having one of the best weekends of my entire life. It wasn't his time to destroy.

I know his attempts have had nothing to do with me. I know his depression, and his refusals to take medication, and overall what's happened to his brain over the course of his life, I know none of that is my fault.

And yet.

I can't silence this voice in the back of my head. I can't shake this persistent, permanent feeling that maybe, just maybe, my father isn't the toxic one. Maybe it's me. Maybe I sent him over the edge. Maybe if I'd been different these past eighteen years—and I don't mean a little bit different that one time, or kind of different for a few days right before he tried to do it—but if I'd been way different for my entire life, things could have been better.

What my dad hates most in this world is lying, trickiness, deceit. He feels so wounded anytime anybody betrays him or anybody else. He'll never know how to cure himself of his crippling sensitivity. He bears every last scar.

And all I've done for the past eighteen years is stab people in the back.

There might have been times when I could have

changed, could have possibly evolved. There aren't that many, but there have been a few. The day I made Neil spread his first malicious rumor. The morning I walked into the SAT, against Neil's wishes, my phone beneath my toes. The weekend I could have visited Dad in the mental ward but said no way, not for me.

Each of those times, I could have shown mercy. Each and every time, I chose myself.

I'm eighteen now, basically an adult. I've reached my final form, and I show no signs of ever getting better. Even if I wanted to in the future, it's not like the world will let me. Not this same world that has bent and twisted me into what I've become. Not this hateful place that my father tried to abandon for good.

None of this shit matters, so get yours while you can.

"You're right, Mom," I said. "It's time."

She put her hand to my chin and said, "Good man." She squeezed my shoulders with her comforting nurse fingers. She gave me the landline. When I nodded, she left the room.

"Cole!" he said, when I got through to him. "It is so good to hear your voice."

He began to speak. He launched into some meandering monologue about what he had for breakfast that morning, the jazz records they let him listen to, and when he might possibly get the chance to have visitors, come back home for a weekend, or some shit along those lines.

I don't know. I wasn't paying attention.

She said I had to call him. She never said I had to listen.

As my pops blathered on, *wah-wah, wah-wah-wah,* like the grown-ups in *Charlie Brown*, I swiveled my chair around. I returned to my laptop. I resumed my research. I refused to stop. I was going to work on this damn thing all night if I had to, and every night to come.

No rest for the wicked.

9. ALLEGRA REY

My friend didn't look like himself. There was a listlessness to his gait as he trudged out of the library, a heaviness to his head. The ash-gray clouds that filled the sky this afternoon seemed to be for him and him alone. Even his almost-mustache wasn't its usual cheddar color, which made me oddly sad.

"Wiley!" I shouted.

He didn't turn around.

"Wiley!" I tried again. "Wiley Otis!"

If anything, he moped away faster.

"Sad Old Wiley!"

He paused midstep.

I hustled over to him, posthaste. "There you are," I said. "Finally."

"Yeah," Wiley muttered. "Things have been crazy."

"Wait, were you in detention just now?"

"Oh. Uh—"

"What for?"

"Doesn't matter," he said. "What are you still doing here? Didn't band end a while ago?"

"Yeah . . . well, I'm staying a few extra minutes. Waiting for *Seuss* rehearsal to let out."

Wiley didn't respond to that.

"I miss you," I added. "Where have you been lately? You know my mom's been asking about you. She keeps saying, 'Where's my Wiley? Where's my Wiley?'"

Wiley stuck his hands in his pockets.

"We should get together," I continued. "Have a game night, do a movie."

There was a burst of noise behind us. Hands clapping, a cappella singing. The theater kids had apparently been let out of their cage for the day.

At that precise moment, Wiley turned away from me.

"Come on," I said. "It would be fun. I owe you for your birthday."

"I don't know," he said, his back to my face. "I gotta go."

"We could even throw a party," I said. "Invite some people over. You know, I really want you to meet—"

Wiley took off. He hurried away from the library and down the terraces. He walked much more rapidly than before, far more sure of himself.

"Wiley!" I hollered.

He didn't spin around. He wouldn't give me that.

"An awesomeness of Wileys!

"A super-awesomeness of Wileys!

"A BACCHANALIAN, MASQUERADED, THE-PASSWORD-IS-'FIDELIO' ORGY OF WILEYS!!!"

Nothing from Wiley. Nothing from Wiley for the umpteenth time. I'm not sure what I keep doing wrong. Or, well, I suppose there is one thing I can think of, but that's not my fault, and it's none of Wiley's business. I get to make my own choices. My life belongs to me.

Goodness, though. I wish I knew what I could do to help my old friend. I miss the boy.

"Yo," Brian said seconds later, coming up behind me. "Is there a problem?"

"What?" I said. "Of course not."

He wrapped his arms around my sides. He snuggled up for his daily spoon.

"What were you shouting?" Brian said. "It sounded weird."

"Nothing," I said. "Don't worry about it."

"He wasn't bothering you, was he?"

"No," I said. "I'm fine."

"You sure he wasn't trying to bone you?"

"Don't be juvenile," I said. "No."

Brian nuzzled the back of my head. "Ready to go pick up your brothers?"

I turned around so I couldn't see Wiley anymore. I faced Brian chest to chest, still ensconced in his comfy chrysalis of a hug. I stood on my tiptoes. I kissed my boyfriend on the lips.

• • •

"All right, men."

Brian transferred the oblong ball from hand to hand. He beat his chest twice and grunted like a warlord.

"I'm going to teach you kids . . . *how to play football.*"

Alejandro and Augusto *ooh*ed and clapped. I stood a few feet off, on the sidewalk adjacent to the park, marveling at the little trio they made with Brian. My sweet guys.

There was an atmospheric rumbling. The clouds above, which had prior to this point been a lighter gray, immediately darkened to a charcoal shade. Within seconds it was raining, and heavily at that.

"Aw, no," Alejandro said. "Now we have to go home."

"Allegra never lets us play in the rain," Augusto said. "She hates washing mud out of our clothes."

"Oh," Brian said. "Huh." He scratched the back of his head with the football. "Well, what if I told you . . . *that I don't care?!*"

Brian scooped each of my brothers into his arms and proceeded to toss-slash-roll them, like two bowling balls, into an especially muddy stretch of grass. They scooted on their little eight-year-old tushes down nature's Slip'N Slide, exploding into giggles and giddy screams. Brian then joined them, sliding headfirst into the puddle himself, splattering their faces utterly and completely, sending my brothers into further hysterics.

"Sorry, Allie!" Brian called back to me as he rolled around in ovine fashion. "Looks like you're dating a third grader!"

I put my hands on my hips and shouted back, "I already knew that!"

Brian grinned. "Are you mad?"

"Furious!"

"Grossed out?"

"Nauseated!"

Brian took each of my brother's heads, dunking their hair in mud, little doughnuts into coffee. They squealed in delight and crawled all over him, the world's greatest babysitter and most magnificent jungle gym all in one.

I suddenly got an idea. "Hey, boys!" I yelled. "Guess what?"

"What?"

I scampered toward them, with abandon. *"I'm a third grader too!"*

I hollered "weeeeeee!" and cannonballed myself into the center of their love pile, completely staining my jeans and boots with brown goop but absolutely rolling right onto my brothers' good sides and straight into my boyfriend's heart.

Brian was even more impressive this evening. The first thing he did when we got back to my house was ask my dad if it was okay that we had taken the boys to play football.

"I appreciate you checking with me," Dad said. "You are a respectful young man. But one thing you must admit: You did not, as you say, play *futbol.*"

"We did," Brian said. "I taught them how to throw spirals."

My dad shook his head. "No, no. *Futbol*, real *futbol*, is a canvas for artists, a spectacle for magicians. What you call 'football' is a game of savagery, and smelly rhinoceros men."

Brian smiled. "I'm glad I quit the team, then."

My dad nodded. "I'm glad too."

Brian extended his hand for a shake. "You've got to teach me how to play *futbol* sometime."

Dad took Brian's hand in both of his. "It will be a pleasure."

Next we went into the kitchen, where my *abuela* was preparing *tortas* for dinner.

"Hey, Abuela," Brian said. "How can we help?"

"You know how to cook a Mexican dish?" she said.

"No," he admitted. "But I'm pretty good at eating them."

"My Esteban could eat five *tortas* in one night," Abuela said.

"Well," Brian said. "I guess I'll have to eat six, then. One for me and five for Esteban."

"*Mi gordito precioso*," Abuela said, pinching Brian on the forearm.

Finally, we went into my parents' bedroom. My mother

recently began another round of chemo, so she hasn't been coming out for dinner lately, or honestly leaving the bed much at all. Still, Brian makes sure to pay her a visit when he's over, every night.

"*Mija*," Mama said to me. "I'm surprised you weren't here earlier."

"What? Why?"

"With Wiley."

"Wiley was here?"

"This afternoon, with his mother."

"Oh," I said.

I glanced over at Brian. He looked up at the ceiling.

"Well, I'm here with Brian now. My boyfriend."

"Oh, yes," my mother said.

Her eyes were half closed. Her mouth was shaped in a loopy smile. "I love Brian. . . ."

That was the last thing she said before falling asleep.

I put my hand on Brian's lower back as we tiptoed out of the room.

"I hope that wasn't too awkward," I said.

He batted his hand. "Not a big deal."

"You're sure?"

"Oh, I'm damn sure. No worries at all."

He leaned in and whispered something: "Hey. Wanna get out of these dirty clothes?"

• • •

I legitimately can't recall the last night I got even a minute of time for myself. With my mom's condition worsening the way it has been, and the rest of my family's needs escalating as a result, free moments have become exceedingly scarce for me. I've got to pounce on them when I can.

Brian and I were in my room before dinner. We were both on my bed. We had each just showered. I was wearing a tank top and pajama pants. He was in one of my father's robes. My door was locked.

"Mmm," I said, interlocking my fingers between Brian's.

"Yeah," he said, shifting onto his side, laying himself down.

"Brian," I said as I lay down too, curling myself into him and kissing him on the cheek.

"Allie," he said as he ran his hand down the front of my body and gently placed it on my thigh.

I'm not certain where I stand on the subject of fate. Most of the time, the future feels too fickle, and frankly unfeeling, to be anything but preposterously random.

It is tempting to believe, however, that Brian Mack has mud-slid his way into my life for a reason. At this precise moment in time, just as Wiley has fled my friendship in private shame, just as college has let me down and shattered my hopes for my education and career prospects, just as my mom's cancer has left her clinging to life, has left me wondering if I will ever truly be whole again, it is right now of all times that Brian's world has, for whatever reason, converged with mine. That doesn't strike me as an accident. Truth be told, it feels more like a gift from God.

"Brian," I said as I tucked one hand into the chest area of his robe.

"Ahh," he said, wrapping his legs around mine.

"Brian," I said, my eyelashes brushing up against his.

"Brian."

"What?" he said, snapping out of his amorous daze.

I scooched in and kissed him on the cheek. "I think we should have sex."

Brian froze when I said it. He half sat up. He opened and closed his mouth a few times. It was like he had to turn off and reboot, all in an instant, to process the magnitude of what I'd just confessed.

"Now? Before dinner? Okay, I have a condom in my wallet. I stole it from Kyle's room, like, two years ago. It's 'Ribbed for Her Pleasure.'"

I covered my mouth to keep from laughing.

"It's orange," Brian added.

I shook my head playfully. "Maybe not *right* now," I said. "But soon." I leaned in for another idyllic kiss. "Very, very, soon."

Brian wrapped me in the tightest embrace. He kissed me several more times, each on a different part of my body, culminating in yet another heavenly meeting of the lips.

Finally, he leaned in and whispered something to me. Four words, to be specific. Four words that, to that point, he had never yet spoken: "I love you, Allie."

And if my brothers hadn't knocked on my door ten seconds later to come summon Brian and me to dinner, I'm sure I would have capitulated and slept with him that very instant.

"I love you too, Brian. My goodness, I love you."

10. NIKKI FOXWORTH

I walked into first period and found two dozen red roses waiting for me on my desk. There was a card with them too.

Happy Valentine's. Meet me after school. The spot. <3 D

I clapped my hands and did a little victory dance. Everyone around me took pictures. A bunch of people asked to smell my roses. All of my friends talked about DeSean and me going off to Fresno State together next year and how amazing it's going to be—him scoring touchdowns on the field, me shaking my booty on the sidelines. The king and queen, living happily ever after.

Around lunchtime, though, things got weird. There was a strange vibe on campus. People were on their phones, like, way more than usual. Boys, mostly. I'd walk past, and a whole group of guys would be staring at their screens, like they were having the very same message beamed to them by aliens. Some of the boys were howling with laughter. Others were making a great show of covering their faces.

The girls I saw didn't look quite so strange, but there was something uniting them too: None of them would look me in the eye. Normally, I'll admit, there's some curiosity as to which outfit I'm wearing or whose handbag I'm sporting, but not that day.

"What's going on?" I said to my friends during nutrition break. "Did someone die?"

"Sort of," Brooklyn said.

"We have to go," Channing said.

I didn't see DeSean once, all day, but I made sense of that in my head. I figured his absence was maybe because he had, I don't know, organized some sort of V-Day scavenger hunt for me, starting with the roses and ending with a surprise at the spot. Yes, there would be sex, but probably something else too. Jewelry? A promise for the future? Ooh, and maybe the reason everyone was acting so shifty around me all day, maybe D had told them to act that way, like, for some special reason?

Golly, I used to love surprises.

When I reached the construction site after school, I felt even more like I was living in some kind of alternate universe.

Because DeSean wasn't at the spot.

Scrotes was.

"Surprise, surprise," he said as I approached him.

"Where's DeSean?"

He didn't answer that. Instead, he held his phone up and pointed the screen at me. He pouted his lips. He shook his head.

I knew what it was before he even pressed play.

"*Turn that off, you little shit!*" I screamed, beating the phone out of his hand.

For some reason, Scrotes just smiled.

"It's nothing personal," he said all calmly. "But DeSean has an athletic career to worry about, not to mention a brand. Do you really think he can afford to be associated with you now, especially during his crucial rehab period? He told me to tell you he hopes you'll understand and that he wishes you the best as you try to recover from this, but, yeah . . . Sorry, girl. It's over."

When I got home, my parents weren't there. I bet they were at school. Meeting with the principal. Meeting about me. Whatever. I went to my room. I locked myself in. I went to my speakers. I cranked up the noise, so loud it could shatter glass. So loud it could make you deaf. I skipped my usual dance mix. My tween-girl pop, my white-girl hip-hop. I went straight for the nastiest tracks I could find. Hardcore rap. Gangsta shit. The kinds of songs where violence is power, where killing is winning, where women aren't women; they're hoes and tricks and bitches. I let those words dominate the room. I let them violate my ears.

I raged.

I threw my head back and flung it forward, like I might break my neck. I let my arms thrash. I didn't care what they knocked over. I stamped the floor, like some kind of animal. I let out a scream, like a made-up beast.

I shrieked in rhythm to the beat of the songs. I gritted my teeth and pumped my hips. I thrust them back and forth, faster and faster, back and forth, rougher and harder. I did it till my back ached. Till my knees shook. Till my mind went blank.

I punched the air. I slapped it. I spun around and roundhouse kicked. I spun and kept spinning past the point of exhaustion. I spun past nausea. I spun and stomped and spun and screamed. If I spun fast enough I could break free of this path, I could release myself from the past, I could make all my thoughts disappear if I killed myself to the music, if I kept spinning, spinning, spinning.

I spun so hard that I drenched my sweatshirt. I threw it off. I kept moving. I danced for so long that I soaked my tank top. I peeled it off and chucked it away. I punched and pirouetted and leaped and tumbled and roared for endless minutes, for infinite hateful songs, right until the moment when I caught sight of my reflection in the full-length mirror.

I couldn't help but stop and stare.

There I was, in my bra and not much else. My body was

dripping. My face was red. My hair was a joke. I was so out of breath. But still, I wanted more.

I know her, that person in the mirror. I know her very well. As a matter of fact, I'd seen her earlier that afternoon.

Everyone knows her. The girl from the video.

As soon as I recognized her flushed cheeks, her sweaty torso, her hungry expression, I felt this urge to squeeze my eyes shut, to turn away. To block the image out, the way I have these past several months. To do what my parents have done, what my friends did to me in Texas, what DeSean just did. I felt like I needed to wish her away, the bad girl, the animal, the slut.

But no.

I like the girl in the mirror. I think she's kind of amazing.

I smiled at her. She smiled back.

I like sex. That shouldn't be some crazy thing to admit. It's a pretty conventional thing to like, actually. Practically boring. Of course, I'm the only one who's judged for it. And of course it cuts me to the core, being reduced to that one aspect of myself. But it's who I am, so I may as well be up front: I really, truly love sex.

Honestly, I think that's part of why I like dancing so much, because it reminds me of sex. I get to move my body. I get to find a rhythm. My brain shuts off completely. I'm allowed to forget about the world.

The world, though, it doesn't look at the girl in the mirror the same way I do. It wants her to put on some clothes. It tells her to stop smiling. It thinks she should stop dancing.

That's what hurts so bad. Not that people know I have sex, or even that they saw my body in that vulnerable moment, but rather what they think of me afterward. Once they see that tape, I'm not Nikki anymore. I'm not their girlfriend, not their daughter, not their peer.

I tried smiling at my reflection, but it didn't last long. An empty stare took its place. Something was missing. The picture wasn't full.

I'm not saying I miss DeSean. Jesus, no. What that boy did to me is no better than what my ex did by making the tape in the first place. There's a special place in hell for a man who turns his back on a woman just because she's so-called damaged goods. I hate DeSean. I never want to think about him again. I don't miss him one bit.

I've got to be resilient. I need to be independent. I must stop caring what DeSean, what any guy, what the entire world thinks of me. But dammit, it's hard. When I look at the mirror and see only myself, it's hard to keep a smile on my face. I mean shit, I feel lonely.

The thing about dancing is, as fun as it can be on your own, it's always so much easier, so much better, when you have a partner. Someone to share the music with. Someone to lift you up in the air.

I miss it already, having that partner to love. Not someone

to grope in the dark mindlessly, nothing like that, but a person who knows how to connect in every way beyond sex. A person who, in intimate moments, can take sex and make it so much more than that, who can make it love. I'm ashamed to admit this, but I have to be real—I want a guy in my life. Even after all this, I long for Prince Charming. I still, somehow, pray he exists.

But who am I kidding? I'm not some little girl. I don't believe in damsels in distress, in saviors on white horses, in destiny. That person who's supposed to accept me unconditionally? That's just someone who hasn't seen the video yet. That person's a myth. That person's a fantasy.

ROAD TWO
WINTER

6. BRIAN MACK

Sometimes Mom and Dad talk in the TV room and they think I can't hear them, but I can hear them. Like last night. They did it last night.

"He's trying his best."

"Right. For all the good it does."

"He's improving, faster than they said he would."

"What about the shit fits he throws every morning?"

"Well, he wants to go to school."

"Yeah, but lately it's gotten beyond the pale."

"He's frustrated. He's always had moments of frustration. That's who he is."

"Who he *was*."

"What's that supposed to mean?"

"Honey . . ."

"Honey what?"

"You know . . ."

"No, I don't. What are you trying to say?"

"You know full well what I'm trying to say. . . ."

"No, I don't. Why don't you tell me?"

"Well, you know, maybe we should revisit special ed. . . ."

"*No.* God, no."

"Honey."

"He needs more time, that's all. What he's attempting, it's been done before."

"How many times?"

"Brian's a fighter."

"Brian can't *read.*"

"Our son will be fine."

"Are you so sure?"

"Aren't you?"

"I'm being realistic."

"He's going to be okay."

"He's declining."

"He's improving."

"He's re—"

"Don't say it."

"But he's re—"

"Don't you dare say it—"

"Come on, honey. Brian's re—"

"Don't say it."

Back when I was better, I exploded all the time. I heard guys talk crap about me, fools on the Bulldogs, and I went beast mode on them. I jammed them in a corner. I said, "Who you calling oaf, you bitch." I smacked their asses hard. They cried like little pussies. You mess with the Big Mack, you get the buns.

It was like that in the hospital too. And when I first got home. Like when gas touches a cigarette. I burned crazy all the time. I yelled at my mom and screamed cuss words at my dad and punched Kyle in the belly, and when my friends stopped coming to see me, I punched the pillow on my bed. I was an angry mofo. Dad says I missed playing football. I want to tell him that's not what I miss.

But last night was different. Hearing my parents gave me a new feeling. For the first time, I didn't feel like blowing up. I felt the other way. I wanted to melt. Like the witch in *The Wizard of Oz*. I wanted someone to dump a bucket on me so I could melt. Just go away.

When Dad said that thing, that last word, I got under the covers. I put my pillow over my head. I wouldn't let myself hear more words. I tried to go to sleep. I wanted to dream. I wanted to wake up somewhere new. Where my parents don't fight. Where I have friends like old times. Where I know things again. I wish I could go back to that place.

If I only had a brain.

This morning, Mom and Dad took me to the hospital for a checkup. I was still so bummed from yesterday. I didn't put new clothes on when I got up. I didn't brush my teeth. I said hell no to breakfast.

The doctor was mean. I don't know what he was saying, but the way he said it made Mom put her head down. It made Dad put his hand on Mom's back.

Then the doctor told me good news—I don't have to do another operation. And more good news—when it's the new semester, I get to go back to school.

"Why is it good news if my parents are sad?"

The doctor was quiet. I hate doctors.

After the checkup, Mom and Dad said we could go out for ice cream. I said no. They said we could call my friends, see what Scrotes is doing over Christmas. I said I want to go home. I hate home, but the good thing about home is I can be stupid by myself there. I don't have to be stupid in front of people.

So it was time to go.

But as we were leaving, I heard her. I heard a girl.

"Hello? Brian?"

I turned around. I wanted it to be Nikki. I miss Nikki.

It wasn't Nikki.

The girl had hair like a jellyfish. She was short and fat. Well, she wasn't really fat like me, but she was kind of fat. She was pretty though.

I pointed at her. "I don't know who you are."

"I go to your school," she said. "I go to Dos Caminos."

"Oh, yeah? Bulldogs?"

She smiled. "Yes, exactly. Go Bulldogs."

I walked up to her. "My name is Brian."

"I know," she said. "Pleasure to make your acquaintance, Brian."

"I don't know your name."

"Oh. My mistake. I don't know why I didn't lead with that. My name is Allegra."

"What?"

"Allegra," the girl said.

"*What?*"

"Ah-leg-ruh," she said.

"All—," I said.

"Allerg—," I said.

"Allega—," I said again, but I couldn't do it, because I don't know how to say things anymore, because I'm dumb. I'm such a dumbass—

"But you can call me Allie," the girl said. She had the nicest smile on her face.

"Hi, Allie," I said. I smiled too.

She held her hand out. Her hand had a #PRAYERS4BRIAN bracelet on it. I held my fist out and gave her a bump.

I turned back to Mom and Dad.

"I don't want to go home yet," I told them. "I'm talking to my friend Allie."

"We know, honey," Mom said. "Take as long as you want."

I turned back to Allie. I looked at her with a confused face. "Why are you here?"

Her smile went away. It made me feel bad. Then it kind of came back, but different from before.

"I'm actually here for my mom," Allie said. "My mom is sick."

"I'm sick."

"Oh, oh no, I wouldn't describe you as 'sick.'"

"Your mom's retarded?"

"No," she said. "She's not . . . uh, my mom has . . . Do you remember what cancer is, Brian?"

I put my hand on my mouth. "Oh shit," I said. "Your mom's gonna die."

Allie's smile went away again. This time it didn't come back to her face. I thought she was going to run away all fast and leave me all alone. But she didn't, which felt good.

"You know, I hope my mom doesn't pass away," Allie said. "And I don't think she will, not for a long time. Anyway, she's only here for a checkup."

"I came for a checkup," I said. "I almost died."

"I know," Allie said. "I remember."

She put her hand on her bracelet when she said it.

"I miss school," I said.

"I know," she said. "And you know what? I miss having you at school too."

I made a fart noise with my mouth. A big, loud, wet one.

Allie stepped backward. Her face was grossed out, like if I made a real fart, like with my ass.

"Sorry," she said. "But why did you just do that, Brian?"

"You're wrong. You don't miss me."

"Oh, sure I do."

"How can you *miss* me? You just *met* me. You don't miss me. Shut up."

Allie opened her mouth. She closed her mouth. She looked at me hard. "Well," she said. "Yes. I suppose you're right. I can't miss you if I don't know you."

"I'm going now," I said. "I'm not gonna miss you."

"Because we're not friends?" Allie said.

"Yeah," I said. "I only miss my friends."

"That makes sense," she said.

"I don't have friends," I said.

I turned the lights off in my room. Lights make my head hurt. Also I don't like looking at my things. My memory things. My football that my friends signed for me. Pictures of me and DeSean from the newspaper. My old feather boa from Male Ballet. My gold crown.

I think I had a nap, but the doorbell woke me up.

There was a knock outside my room. I put my head under my pillow.

"Hello," the voice said.

"Leave me alone."

The door opened.

"Hey, Mr. Vampire? Why is it so dark in here? Please don't suck my blood."

Huh?

I threw the pillow off. It was weird that someone besides a doctor or my mom would come visit me. It was hard to see who it was in the shadows.

But I recognized that nice smile. I would recognize it anywhere.

"Hi, Allie."

She turned on the light. "You know, Brian," she said. "I really would like to be your friend. I'd like it very much."

She was dragging something behind her. A bag. It looked big and heavy.

"What's in there?"

"Oh," she said, pulling them out. There were red ones, blue ones, big ones with pictures, even a couple soft ones you would bring in the bath. "Just a few of my favorite things in the world."

I shook my head. "I suck at reading."

She took some books in her hands and hopped up to where I was. She sat on the bed next to me. "I heard you were having trouble," she said. "So I thought I'd come practice with you."

I shook my head. I crossed my arms. I wasn't stupid. I wasn't some sad guy she needed to help.

Then, two seconds later, I burped in her face. I smiled real silly. "Okay," I said. "You can be my friend."

We read all night. Every book in the bag. We read about a principal of a school who gets turned into a superhero, and he's fat and bald like me, and he wears tighty-whities like me, and he's pretty slow like me. We read about this family of bears who live in a tree, and they have the dumbest names ever, and in one book Brother and Sister learn how strangers are like apples, and in another one Papa hates Asians. We read a thing where a pigeon says he should drive a bus and you have to tell it to eff off. We read a book where a dude wears hella hats on his head and these monkeys screw with his mind. And we read this one where Frog and Toad have sex with each other. Well, it doesn't say they have sex with each other, but deep down you know they have sex with each other. Allie says that's called subtext.

I love Allie. I love doing stories with her. I love spending time by her side. I don't care that my other friends don't come anymore. Even if they never see me again, I don't mind. Allie is the friend I'm supposed to have. She's the one.

7. COLE MARTIN-HAMMER

All right, gang," Mr. Bayer called from the director's chair. "Let's take places for the top of the show. Cat in the Hat, you're stage left."

I perked up. I hopped out of my seat and onto the stage. I made my way to the spot, and as I did so, I got inspired for a move the Cat could do. So I acted out the combo—pivot away from the audience, bend one knee, touch the brim of the hat Bob Fosse–style, booty tooch for two pulses, then spin around and hiss. It was a slinky, sultry piece of choreo. I must have been a burlesque dancer in a former life, or a legendarily fierce concubine.

"Cole, what are you doing?"

"Oh, I just had a vision, this sublime bit of feline choreography—"

"Okay, but you're not the choreographer, are you?"

"Well . . . no."

"And you're not the director, are you?"

"No."

"And you're not the Cat in the Hat, are you?"

"No, sir."

"Then wait offstage, with the rest of the cast. Your entrance isn't for another three pages. That's when Thing 1 comes in."

Yup. That's what happens when you audition for a show literally no seconds after receiving the most soul-destroying e-mail in human history. For my senior musical, my ultimate high school showcase, the definitive performance of my life to this point, I was cast as the most inconsequential part in the entire ensemble: that silent, servile, castrated left testicle known as Thing 1.

And honestly, that wasn't the worst part.

"Neil, nice key change.

"Love it, Neil. Great ad-libbing during the auction sequence.

"Neil, can you run back to the dressing room? The costumers need to measure your head size."

Seriously. That's who beat me out for the lead role. That's who stole the red-and-white dong-shaped hat that should have been mine. My underling. My changeling. My one-time baby slave.

Every afternoon, I have to sit there and watch as freaking Neil collects kudos after kudos from Bayer, as he asks understudies to run and grab him an Aquafina and they actually do it, as he stands there onstage with that subtle, smug smirk that never once makes its way toward me.

I want to give that kid a history lesson. I want to remind him how things used to be. I want to shove him up against a locker and scream, "You're the reason this happened, orphan boy. I never should have trusted you. It's your fault I'm like this. I'm the one who should be on top of the food chain. You should be back on the bottom of the ocean, like you used to be, bowing before me, begging for plankton, *bitch.*"

But that's all gone. My diva days are done. My director shafted me. College rejected me. I'm not what I used to be. I'm just a Thing, and nothing can change that.

And honestly, that's not the worst-worst part.

"Guys," Bayer said, gathering us around midway through today's rehearsal. "I have an exciting announcement. We have a new addition to our cast. This actor will be taking over the role of Thing 2. And since this is his first day back at school in quite some time, let's give him, ahem, a *whopper* of a welcome. Introducing . . ."

He came trundling into the room, a golden retriever's smile on his face. When they saw him, every person in the room lost their damn minds. It was like bat mitzvah girls at a boy-band concert, or Scientologists at one of their secret pep rallies. It was insane.

"BIG MACK! BIG MACK! BIG MACK! BIG MACK!"

Brian clambered onto the stage, where he busted out a couple dance moves—surprisingly competently, might I add—and threw his fists in the air. The masses roared for their mascot.

But I'm the one who had to spend the next ninety minutes dealing with him.

"Brian, stop zoning out," I had to say before the first entrance of Things 1 and 2.

"Brian, stop reaching under your shirt," I had to say during a down moment onstage.

"Brian, stop picking at your ass," I had to say when I was made to escort him to the bathroom.

It was indescribably irritating. Everyone kept treating him like a cross between a decorated war veteran and the class guinea pig. And look, I know I'm headed straight to Hades for saying this, but, like, Brian used to be considered something of an unredeemable ass. I mean, that's the main reason I became friends with him freshman year, because we totally bonded over being funny jerk people. But then, one October night, this unspeakably horrible thing happened to him, and now suddenly, miraculously, he's the toast of the town.

But, like, I'm an unredeemable ass, and a horrible thing happened to me—I mean this Stanford thing has categorically ruined me, not just with the casting, but, like, for my future, for goddamn decades—and it's not as if anyone cares about me. And yeah, it's wrong to compare maybe-permanent brain trauma to getting rejected early admission or whatever. But I mean, Brian's happy now. The universe did him a solid. Ignorance is effing bliss for him. He doesn't even need the extra love from peeps. But I do, you know? I for reals do.

And honestly, that wasn't even the worst-worst-*worst* part.

Big Bri wasn't alone.

As is common on theater and film sets, the large animal had a handler to watch over it.

And she wouldn't, for the life of her, shut up.

"Brian, great job on that jazz square.

"Brian, if you stay on your feet the rest of rehearsal, I'll tell your mom you've earned Polish sausage tonight.

"Brian, if you pay attention to Mr. Bayer for five more minutes, I'll read you an extra Berenstain Bears when we get home.

"No, Brian," she said, shaking her head and laughing. "I can't give you a cheek kiss, but let's celebrate a phenomenal first day by going out for some ice cream, shall we? Would you like to join us, Cole?"

I closed my mouth into a frigid smile. "Dear Ms. Rey, Cole University regrets to inform you that it cannot accept your offer. But best of luck in all your future endeavors."

Allegra put her arm around Brian's waist. "I apologize," she said. "It wasn't my intention to—"

"Cram it," I said. "Take your dowdy jacket and gag yourself with it, and take your boy toy and cast him aside, and run along to Stanny and leave the rest of us behind, and go ahead and have your perfect little frumpy-dump life, because rest assured, none of us want you in ours."

I couldn't take it anymore. To be a college reject, that was one thing. To deal with Neil stealing my spot in the high school caste system, that was two things. To have to watch Brian Mack pull his pants down at the urinal and reveal his notorious alabaster ass, that was three—really four if we account for each blubbery cheek. But the prospect of spending several hours each day in the proximity of gerdforsaken Allegra Rey—that cloying, fraudulent, egomaniacal, bizarrely-and-creepily-close-to-Brian-at-all-times, shit-eating-grinning, Stanford-degree-hogging, life-stealing succubus—I mean, I just couldn't take it anymore. I refused to live like this.

I twirled away from Allegra. I cheated out, facing the audience. I placed one hand on my diaphragm. I put the other to my mouth. I whistled. Everyone looked at me for the first time in eons.

"Mr. Bayer," I announced. "Fellow cast members. Techies. It is with a heavy heart and with deepest disappointment, that I hereby announce my departure from the company. It is time to take my talents far, far away. I positively cannot work under these conditions any longer. You all have obliterated my love of the theater forever.

"Quoth my spirit bitch, Elphaba, 'I hope you're happy. I hope you're happy now.'"

And with that, I did it. I raised my head high and I sashayed through the emergency exit door and out of the theater, straight out of the only real home I've had these past four years. No one rushed after me to say, *We need you, Cole*. No one came to say, *Please don't leave us. You're an essential part of this community. We need you to save the show.* Even if they had, I would have pimp-slapped them right in the jaw.

And so I bustled on out of there. I hurled off the yoke of my past, and I flung that mask hard to the ground. I lifted my eyes to tomorrow. I gazed upward, yonder, to the great sky above—

Whereupon I saw it, the image that immediately jolted me like a lightning bolt to the chest.

The thing. The shadow. The person.

The tiny silhouette, perched atop the theater roof, about to do God knows what.

8. NIKKI FOXWORTH

Channing faced me. She took my hands in hers. "You know you did the right thing, lady."

Brooklyn sat on the bench behind me. She was braiding my hair. "You do not need that pussy hound in your life."

Chan gave me a little shoulder squeeze. "Let him go impregnate some other slut."

"I mean, D was actually pretty decent about it," I said. "But yeah, I just don't think I'm ready."

"And that's okay," Brooklyn said. "Sex isn't for everybody."

"Sex isn't for everybody," Channing repeated.

"Sex isn't for everybody," they both said again.

I nodded. "Thanks."

The girls and I were in the locker room, changing out of our dance clothes. Our practices usually end the same time as the cheer squad's, so some of those girls were in there too. They were on the other end of the room, away from us, far removed from the whole Nikki-Foxworth-is-a-worthwhile-girl pep talk.

Brooklyn and Channing have given me some version of that same speech pretty much every day since DeSean and I broke up, but what with Valentine's coming up, and what with me being single, this time they were going extra hard on the sisterly love. I don't know if they necessarily made me feel any better about how things ended between DeSean and me, but I felt valued by my friends, which I guess is the next best thing.

Of course, it being Brook and Chan, they couldn't quite stick with being one hundred percent supportive. There had to be some nastiness too.

"Well, sex may not be for everybody," Channing said, leaning in close to me. "But it looks like sex *with* everybody *is* for somebody."

She not-so-subtly pointed across the room, where Mona Omidi was stepping out of the shower and drying her hair off with a towel.

"I heard she's nailing Liam Garner again," Brooklyn whispered.

"Nah, pretty sure she's nailing Cody Shotwell again," Channing whispered.

"Who are we kidding?" Brooklyn said, leaning in closer. "She's probably getting it from both of them."

"Not to mention," Brooklyn said. "Those rumors about her and Dusty."

"My Dusty," Channing said with a sad panda face.

"And that's not all," Brooklyn said. "Because I even think there's someone new."

"Do you know who it is, Nik?"

They both smiled at me, vicious smiles.

Scrotes, they mouthed at the same time.

Their faces were so close to mine. They were inches away from me. I felt all crowded. I couldn't breathe.

"Hey . . . maybe let's go home?"

Channing shook her head no. She raised an eyebrow at me.

Brooklyn shook her head no. She winked at me. "Hey, Moaner!" she shouted across the locker room.

"Yeah, Moaner! We're talking to you!"

"Get your head out of that towel!"

"Towel Head!"

"Harem Slut!"

"TERRORIST!"

Mona looked up, bug-eyed. She'd been chatting with a few girls, laughing and gossiping, but in a split second her entire group went silent. Without speaking, the cheer freshmen and sophomores who made up her circle backed away, leaving Mona by herself, defenseless.

"What were you doing with my Dusty?" Channing said, stalking across the room.

"What were you doing with everyone's everyone?" Brooklyn said, trailing right behind her predator-in-crime.

Within an eight count, they'd reached the other side. When they got to the lockers, Mona glanced away, down at the ground. She's a darker girl, but her skin looked fully pale. Her body was shivering. I don't think it was from the shower.

The one thing Mona didn't seem, though, was shocked. I mean, she'd had this nightmare before. Every girl has.

"Why are you so shitty at cheer?" Channing said.

"Why haven't they cut your ass like we did from dance?" Brooklyn said. "You can't even do the splits, for God's sake."

"How can you not do the splits?"

"How come you can only get your legs open when there's a dick involved?"

I watched this all happen. I felt my forehead get flushed. I couldn't feel my fingers. I still couldn't breathe.

I flashed back to that day in the car, at the spot, to D asking why I had to be such a prude, to him suggesting that if he couldn't do me, he wouldn't date me. Now here I was, watching this poor girl, seeing her get fed the exact opposite message. I just sat there on my hands as she received the Texas treatment. The mean girls were calling her the same names they used to call me. No matter what she did, Mona was stuck, a prisoner of her own reputation. Just like me. Just like all of us. Damned if we don't, damned if we do.

I couldn't take it. No more. I couldn't.

I flew across the room. Before they knew what was happening, I grabbed Channing from behind. I flung her at the lockers. Her body hit hard and her head whipped back. The ringing noise was loud and long, like a gong. It was so satisfying. Brooklyn turned to face me. As Mona dove for cover, I took Brook's platinum hair in my hands and I yanked as hard as I know how. She let out a holler like I haven't heard since I used to visit my cousin's ranch back in the day. I mean she wailed like a pig whose throat is being sliced open. I jerked her head back and forth, from one side to another, until she apologized, until she begged. Just as I was about to let go, Channing sprang off the ground. She took my face from behind. She dug her nails into my skin, scratching my forehead and drawing blood, but I didn't give a shit. I kicked back, right where she wasn't expecting. Down below, right in the only place those girls seem to care about. That was when the teachers barged in. They grabbed me. They separated us. But not before I did some serious damage. Not before I taught those hateful creatures a lesson about picking on a lady.

Since that little episode, some would say I've gotten what I deserved.

I'm obviously off dance. Not exactly a shock. Brook and

Chan texted me I wasn't welcome at any more practices or basketball games, and their parents did everything short of take a restraining order out on me. I've got to admit, though, that I don't exactly care. I couldn't stand being around those types of people any longer.

What's more concerning is how the school gave me a whole mess of detentions. Now, again, the detentions themselves I don't mind. It's just me sitting by myself for an hour, which honestly, I've been doing pretty much the whole past year anyway.

No, what really and truly rankles is something that happened a couple days ago while I was in the library. Someone I talked to. Something that someone said. Something that put me right back in that locker room head space all over again, that horrible place. That dark empty room with the two large doors, one marked TEASE and the other marked SLUT. And you've got to pick one; there's absolutely no other escape. And whichever door you choose, there's a mob waiting on the other side. There's a witch trial, torches and pitchforks and all. And they call you names, and they chant your past, and they smash your spirit, all the way till you panic and run away to another town, where the grass is greener, where the smiles are sweeter, where life seems peachy keen until the second you walk into a new room and realize it's locked. You realize you're stuck. You know you're trapped all over again, in the pitch-black place with the same two doors.

• • •

But I want to talk about something else.

I want to talk about how something good can come from something bad.

After all, even the fugliest dress can have a silver lining.

I've made a new best friend.

"Hey," Mona said, randomly coming up to me after school last Friday, shortly after the incident.

"Um," I said. "Hi."

"I have something for you."

"What? Why?"

I mean, if history has shown anything, it's that I'm not exactly the biggest fan of surprises.

She pulled something out from behind her back.

"What are you doing?"

They came at me fast, her hands. Right at my face. It's not that I thought she was being violent or whatever, not after what I'd done for her, but at the same time, I couldn't help but be on edge, just a tiny bit freaked. It's hard to trust anyone these days. I have my reasons.

But Mona didn't punch me. She didn't scratch me. She pressed something firm on my forehead, just above my left eye. Something sticky.

"Is that . . . a Band-Aid?"

She burst out laughing. "Of course it's a Band-Aid. Haven't you looked in the mirror lately? Your cut's pretty gnarly."

"Oh my Lord," I said, whipping out my phone, checking my scar in selfie mode. "I look hideous. I'm a monster."

Mona shook her head. "You're not a monster," she said. She licked her hand and smoothed out my bandage. "You're my knight in shining armor."

I didn't know what to say to that.

"Hey," Mona added. "After you finish your detention . . ." She hesitated, like she was nervous about asking. "You wanna come over to my house?"

I thought about it for a good second. I considered how it might be fun to get to know Mona, because she certainly seemed like an improvement over my old friends. At the same time, though, I also thought about the message it would send if I did hang out with "the Moaner," what it would say to girls like Brooklyn and Channing about what kind of values I have, what sort of impression it would leave on boys if I was seen spending time with the so-called biggest slut at school.

As soon as I had the thought, I hated myself immediately.

"I'd love to," I told Mona. I touched the spot above my eye. "Let's nurse me back to health."

9. WILEY OTIS

I got so messed up last week, I did something I never do.

"Hey," I said into the phone.

"Hey," my dad said, grunting like he'd just woken up from a nap. "What do you need?"

"Nothing," I said. "How's New Mexico?"

"Great. Better than Utah. How's your mother?"

"She's fine."

There was a long pause. There's always a long pause.

"If you're calling about the check," he said. "You can tell your mom I'll send it over, but for now—"

"No. Wait. Dad?"

"Yeah?"

"Actually I do need something."

"What?"

I closed my eyes. I just said it. "I got my heart broken by my best friend. What do I do?"

There was another silence, for the better part of a minute.

"Welp," he said. "Been down that road before. Like the

last time your mother let me live with you guys and I followed all the rules. I never came back late, and I stuck to the separate beds, and I threw the ball with you and all that. But then, wouldn't you know it, she *still* had the gall to send me packing, all because she had a 'change of heart,' all because of some bullshit about 'living out the consequences of a mistake,' whatever the hell *that's* supposed to mean. I mean the nerve to say something like that to your own husband, you know what I mean, to speak like that to the father of your child, the nerve on that bitch—"

"You know what?" I said. "Never mind."

I ended the call. I put my phone away. I reached for a bottle of orange soda and chugged it all the way down.

Life goes on.

All the usual things happened to me this week.

Ms. Fawcett pink slipped me into her office to tell me I'm not going to graduate on time, not unless I make "major lifestyle changes."

The band dudes wouldn't talk to me during passing periods, which is how they've been ever since I quit, probably on direct orders from Allegra.

I tried to hang out with the stoner guys in the parking lot at lunch, but they looked at me suspiciously, made crosses with their fingers, and called me an "emotional narc."

And this afternoon in math, Ms. Valdez caught me doing

what I always do, doodling a scene from a movie. In this case I was drawing the final shot of *Boogie Nights*, that part where Dirk Diggler is all depressed and stuff, and—spoiler alert—he looks in the mirror and just whips out his dick—

"Wiley!"

"What?"

"That's . . . not an asymptote."

"Um," I said. "Well, it does curve. . . ."

"That's a detention and you know it."

I shrugged. "Okay. Whatever."

Detention. More of the same. I got to the library and there they all were, the same lost souls as always, going through the motions of their same old existence. The three stoners saw me, mouthed the word "emotionarc," and did a high fifteen. The freshman cheer girls slaved away at a bunch of #PRAYERS4BRIAN posters that won't ever save the Big Mack but that definitely just killed a few trees. The Bear snarled at me when I walked in, but I bet she growled because she's just as lonely and looking for love as any of us.

And hey, look.

Look who it was, sitting by herself in the corner.

Maybe she could help me.

"Hey, stranger."

Nikki's eyes flicked up to meet mine. "Hey, Wiley."

"You in detention?"

"I am."

"Mind if I sit here?"

"Go ahead."

I took the chair next to her. And for a moment there, I couldn't really talk, because I was suddenly so struck by her—that long, lean body, that sun-goddess glow, that endless river of hair, those sky-at-sunrise eyes, those *calves*—

Then I realized I was being weird. So I said something, anything.

"What's with your eye?"

Nikki shook her head. Some hair fell over her forehead, hiding her cut. "I don't want to talk about it."

"Oh. Sorry I asked." I paused for a second. "Why are you in detention?"

Nikki glanced up at her scar, then at me. "Why do you think?"

"Whoops. Sorry again."

She looked away.

I paused for one second, two seconds, three seconds, four.

"Well, I think it looks sexy."

"Ew," Nikki said, pulling her head back. "Don't be gross."

"Just joking."

Several minutes went by. Nikki played with her phone. I tried not to stare at her body. I tried to pretend like I wasn't imagining the two of us somewhere else, doing other stuff, far away from here. I just wanted to be her friend. That was all.

"So I took your advice."

She looked back up. "Hmm?"

"Remember when we last spoke? Before homecoming? Remember, I told you about Allegra, and—"

Nikki nodded. She put her phone down. "Right. Of course. I remember, at the game. When you played your song. So amazing. I . . . can't believe it didn't work out."

"Yeah."

"I am so sorry, Wiley."

"Thanks." I attempted to smile. It didn't really take.

Then something surprising happened. Nikki put her hand on my knee. Like, on my jeans. She ran her nails gently over the denim. It felt good.

"Sorry for the bad advice."

"No, no. You pointed me in the right direction. I was just the wrong guy."

Nikki pressed her fingers in the littlest bit. It was under the table, so no else could see it. Only I could feel it.

"Anyway," I said. "I just wanted to thank you. For talking to me about girl stuff, way back when. You were looking out for me. If I had more people helping me like that now, I'd be in way better shape."

"Gosh. What a sweet thing to say. You're welcome."

I rested my head all the way on the table. I closed my eyes. Nikki kept her hand on my knee.

"All I wanted was to help Allie. Be there for her, you know? But she dropped me from her life, just like that. She didn't want my help. I wasn't good enough."

"Don't say that," Nikki said.

"It's fine," I said. "It's whatever. I'm failing school, and I don't have friends, and I'm not attractive, and I'm kind of an asshole, and I'm probably just my dad 2.0, and I totally get it. I know why she—why no one wants me."

"Don't say that," Nikki whispered again. "Don't listen to yourself. You're a great guy. Really, you are. Any girl would be lucky to have a guy like you."

I opened my eyes. "Really?"

"There's no doubt in my mind," she said, lifting her finger and pointing it at me. "Wiley, you are a total catch."

"So . . . ," I said. "Would you . . . ?"

I don't know what possessed me to say it.

"Would a girl like you . . . ?"

I guess I just needed to know.

"Ever sleep with a guy like me?"

Nikki's hand shot to her mouth. "Oh my Lord," she said in a muffled voice. "*Ew.*"

"I was joking!" I said, holding my hands up. "Just joking!"

"Get away from me."

"What? You can't handle one dumb joke from a screwed-up guy?"

"Leave."

"Seriously?"

"Now."

I reached out to touch her arm, to calm her down. Nikki flinched backward, throwing her hands up. She nearly whacked me in the face.

"Ms. Behrman!" Nikki whisper-shouted to the front of the library. "Ms. Behrman, please make him leave!"

"All detention-serving students must remain at their *own table*!"

"Jeez, Nikki, I'm sorry."

"Don't touch me."

"Come on, I'm damaged!"

"Go away."

"Just be a friend."

"Stop harassing me!!!"

I walked through campus. Past the Greek. Around the football field. Through the hallways. Past the principal's office. Past the gym. Past everything.

I walked by all those buildings, and I thought, *Damn, people actually made those.* And not just those buildings, but every building. People made every structure that exists in this world—the mansions, the museums, the skyscrapers, the pyramids. And people made everything else: every movie, every piece of art, every bit of technology, every story. I mean, you think about it and it really blows your mind. Actual human beings actually made all that stuff.

But not me. I'm a film nerd who's never made a film. I'm a high school student who won't even graduate. I'm a horndog who's never had sex. I haven't built anything. I haven't done shit. I probably never will.

I felt my feet take me all the way across campus and back around the edge, past the library, up to the big theater. I felt my hands and feet begin to climb up the costume storage shed that attaches to the theater. I managed to get up that, and I climbed again. I shimmied up this pole to the top of the building, and I crawled up the roof to a higher part of the roof. My hands and knees started hurting because the roof was covered with these sharp little rocks, but I didn't care. I kept on climbing. After a few feet, the surface flattened out. I realized I was crouched at the highest point of the roof, the highest point of the whole campus in fact. I could look out and see all the places I'd just walked past—the Greek, the classrooms, the library—and I could see off-campus too, a little into the neighborhoods, and I just managed to see all the way to my house, to Allegra's—

I stood up to get a better look. I walked to the very edge of the roof, to see how far I could see. I looked down, and it was a surprisingly long drop, I mean you don't think about it every day, just how many high-up things there are in this world, just how fragile our bodies are. I mean one simple mistake, one little tumble off the Grease Pole, it can change your whole life. And here I was now, way higher up than that, and I saw the ground below me, and my head went clear for a second, and I felt this funny calm, and—

"DON'T DO IT!"

What?

"WILEY!"

What the—?

"WILEY OTIS!

"HELLO, I'M TALKING TO YOU!

"DO!

"NOT!

"JUMP!!!"

10. ALLEGRA REY

"Brian," I said. "I have to go home. I need to say good night to my mom."

"No."

"What will it take for you to let me leave?"

Brian glanced up at the ceiling, lost in thought. "Um . . . ten more books."

"One more book."

"Five more books."

"One more book."

"Two more books."

"One more book."

"One more book."

"Deal."

I put my hand out for a shake. "You promise?"

"I promise."

"After this, you'll definitely let me go home?"

Brian spat in his hand. He shook mine. "A promise is a promise is a promise."

I grinned despite myself. I patted him on the back of the head. "Okay, okay. One more book."

I reached for my bag of stories and hoisted it onto Brian's bed.

"Let's see, we've got some of your old favorites: your Eric Carle, your Mercer Mayer, your Robert Munsch. Actually, do you think we might finally be ready to graduate to a chapter book?"

Brian reached in the bottom of the bag and pulled out a large green hardcover. "I want this one."

"Huh . . . are you sure?"

"Yes."

"It's kind of a peculiar note to end on. . . ."

Brian pointed at the author photo on the back cover. "I want the scary troll man."

"All right," I said. "As you wish. The final book of the night is . . . *The Giving Tree*, by Shel Silverstein."

I read the whole thing aloud to him, the story that I'm sure he encountered as a child, much like everyone else, but that he must have since forgotten. The classic-yet-vaguely-disturbing tale of the little boy and the maternal tree that cares for him, and who over the course of the boy's life gives more and more of herself to him: apples for selling, branches with which to build a house, and a trunk with which to construct a boat, and at the end of each vignette the narrator states that "the tree was happy." Each and every time we reached that line, I let Brian read it out loud: "and the tree was happy."

Of course, there is also the book's unforgettable and highly ambiguous ending, which, personally, I find too depressing for words.

"I liked that book," Brian said after sounding the final line out loud. "That's my favorite book."

"Really?" I said. "You don't find it to be a tad . . . reductive?"

"I don't know what that means," he said. "But I wish my mom was a tree. Then I could be a bush."

I contemplated, then nodded. "That's a valid point."

Brian scooted toward me on the bed. He wrapped me in a mighty embrace. "Thank you for reading to me. Even though you help your mom and also your brothers. Thank you for taking time to be my friend."

I may have blushed at that. "Oh. Well, wow. I really appreciate that. My goodness, what a kind thing to say."

He scratched his thigh. "And you'll still be my friend tomorrow?"

I nodded quickly.

"You promise?"

"Of course, Brian. I will always be your friend."

"Okay. You can go home now."

When I walked into my mother's room, she was right on the verge of nodding off.

"Oh, good," I said. "Glad I caught you. I wanted to say a quick good night."

Mama lifted her head two inches. She cracked open an eyelid. "Where were you all night?" she said. "Wiley's?"

"No," I said. "Brian's."

My mom didn't react. She just lay there, eyes maybe ten percent open, chest moving up and down in a proto-sleeping pattern.

"Okay," I said. "Love you. I'm going to my room, so—"

"*Wait.*"

"What is it?" I said, reaching for the door handle. "I have a ton of chem homework, not to mention my poetry anthology for AP Lit, and you should really be prioritizing your sleep, so—"

My mom said it softly and simply. "We need to talk about your college."

I'd been dreading this moment. Ever since Mama let me get away with not visiting Stanford over winter break, the two of us have barely discussed my future. I've known, however, that she's never stopped thinking about it. Every night when I see her, when I stop in to say hi after my time at Brian's, I can feel her wanting to ask me when I'll accept my offer. But she always keeps quiet, because she doesn't want to jinx anything, because I've been telling her for months that I have everything under control.

I sat at the foot of her bed.

"What about college?" I said.

"Well, *mija* . . . what are you thinking?"

I looked at where her feet were, tucked snugly underneath the blankets and sheets.

"Um, so what I know for sure is this: The moment I chose not to visit campus, over winter break, I felt this overwhelming sense of relief. So yeah, I've been trying to listen to that feeling."

"Okay," Mama said.

"And everyone at home needs me so much, and with how you've been doing lately, I mean . . . Well, I'm not sure I want to talk about it, to be honest."

"Tell me," Mama said.

I looked from her feet to her face. She was staring back at me. Her body was slumped and frail, but her eyes were sharp.

"Well . . . ," I tried to say. "Um, you see, to me, it feels like things with you can go one of two ways. Either you'll improve, gradually but steadily, in which case you'll need me to continue taking care of you . . . or, and I mean, I'm certain this won't happen, but you could, you know, it could get worse, like, much worse . . . and the family would need me to . . ."

I dropped my head. I blinked back any possible tears. I couldn't look weak in front of my mother, not right then. I had to stop acknowledging her for just that second.

I looked up and finished.

"So I was actually thinking I'd stay here in Dos Caminos for school, maybe enroll at DCCC, probably tutor part-time for extra money. And as for Stanford, I mean, I can defer for a year, or actually what I was thinking was, I could . . . you know, turn it down altogether."

My mom's expression didn't change. She didn't seem surprised. "The scholarship and everything?"

"The scholarship and everything."

Mama nodded. "And you are sure you're not just being scared?"

I pulled back. "What?"

She nodded again. She half smiled. "You say you'd be staying for me, for the family. But in your heart, Allegra, you know what this family wants. You know our story. Your grandmother never made it past grade school, her greatest regret to this day. Your father and I, we were not lucky enough to be able to attend college. We have made decent careers for ourselves, it is true, but it has also been a struggle—for money, for respect, for time to spend with you. And the light at the end of the tunnel has always been you, and your brothers. But in particular you, and the shining example you'd be setting for your brothers. You are their hero, you know.

"I acknowledge that we put too much pressure on you, especially these days. We give you responsibilities far beyond your years, and the moment you finish your commitments, we ask for more of your time. I am sorry for that. As your mother, I am so sorry. But this situation here, it is quite different. You must not think of it as added pressure. You must consider it permission, release. You get to leave, my angel. When you attend college, you will be doing it for me, for all of us. You will be living your family's dream."

She curled up further, into her pillows. She tilted her head back. "Do not be afraid," she said, her voice barely audible.

"Mama—"

She never gave me the chance to tell her what I think of her dream. The speech had taken too much out of her. She closed her eyes tight. She began breathing heavily. She shut out the world.

Before she fell asleep, she spoke one more time: "Do not be afraid to do the right thing."

In my room, I logged into the Stanford admitted students website. I clicked through the home screen, past the endless pictures of gleeful band members, past the focused scientists, past the proud cultural dancers. I got to the decision page. I eyed the three different options:

Yes, I accept my admission to Stanford University!

Yes, but I would like to defer my admission to Stanford by taking a gap year.

No, I will not be attending Stanford University.

Yes.

Yes, but.

No.

Yes, I would like to be selfish and leave everyone behind forever.

Yes, but I would like to leave those who depend on me dangling in anticipation for a year, before ultimately burying my mom and leaving everyone behind forever.

No, I would not like to be selfish. I would actually like to do the right thing.

I read the options. I read them again and again, until they didn't resemble words. Just squiggles. Cruel, merciless squiggles.

My finger hovered above the screen. I knew exactly what to do, but I still felt tortured, all the same.

I took a massive breath inward. I exhaled fully and completely.

I selected, *No, I will not be attending Stanford University.*

I pressed "submit."

ROAD ONE

SPRING

11. ALLEGRA REY

Last night was marked by two momentous events.

One, I informed Stanford University that I would not be joining them as a member of their next freshman class, while simultaneously mailing a check to Dos Caminos City College, ensuring my enrollment in an associate degree program this coming fall.

Two, I had a conversation with my mom.

"Mama?" I said, bringing her nightly cup of tea into her room.

"Yes? What is it?"

She was sitting up in bed. She was wearing her softest headscarf and her lavender pajamas, the ones with the tiny moons, the ones my brothers like best.

"I have something to tell you."

"Is it about college?"

"No. I've got that all taken care of."

"All right. What is it?"

My mother took a sip of tea. I waited for her to finish.

"Brian and I are going to sleep together."

Mama blinked. She took another, longer sip, nearly draining her cup. "You are sure?"

I sat down on the bed, beside her feet. "This is something I've thought a lot about. I want to do this, and I want to do it with Brian. I love him, I really do."

"And remind me. You have been together . . . how long?"

"Almost three months. Three months this Sunday."

"And this was his idea?"

I bit my lip to keep from grinning. "No, Mama. It actually came from me."

"And you trust him?"

"Absolutely."

"And you want to know what I think?"

"Yes," I said. "What you think is very important to me."

My mom slouched back, stretching her legs out. She closed her eyes. I swallowed, preparing for the worst. A few seconds later, my mom opened her eyes. She took me in.

"Well . . . I cannot pretend I am the most comfortable with it. For me, I'd prefer you wait some more time. I would not tell your father or Abuela, you know. They would not understand. And I insist that you be safe, see a doctor, be very informed. I will also tell you that I do not need to hear anything more about it, not after today, not unless there is an emergency. But . . . in the end, Allegra, it is your life. I trust you completely. Whatever you decide, that will be the right thing. You have my support in anything you do."

I couldn't help but tremble. I love my mama. I love her so much. Her faith in me, her unwavering trust in my ability to make the best decision, to be an adult, it's astounding. She will never know how much it means.

I leaned into her body. I held her and I couldn't help but wonder how many more of these moments the two of us would get to share. I pushed that thought from my mind. I held her for a very long time.

This afternoon I joined the rest of my bandmates in attending *Seussical* rehearsal. With the musical's opening a matter of days away, we're taking the time to get in sync with the actors before we accompany them in the orchestra pit during the actual shows. For me personally, the dress rehearsals have been an indispensable and delightful opportunity to watch Brian perform up close. Plus I get to see him in his Horton costume, in which he looks unbelievably cuddle-worthy.

All the same, it can be vexing. Brian tends to act a bit differently around his theater friends than he does when he's with just me. Today, for instance, during a five-minute tech break, Brian was off in a corner with Cole, and the two of them couldn't help but begin an impromptu "performance" of their own.

"Tell me about the rabbitth," Brian said in an exaggerated, frothy-mouthed lisp.

"Well, Lennie," Cole said, rubbing his back. "There's gonna be rabbits."

"Rabbitth?" Brian said.

"Yes," Cole said. "All different kinds of rabbits—"

"RED RABBITTH?" Brian said.

"Yes, Lennie, red rabbits, and—"

"RED RABBITTH AND BLUE RABBITTH AND GREEN RABBITH?"

Neither of them could keep it together by this point. By the time Brian shouted, "RABBITTH RABBITTH, RABBITTH, I'M A BIG FAT RABBIT," Cole was pulling out an invisible shotgun and pretending to shoot Brian in the back of the head, and by the time Brian keeled over in mock death, both of them were lost in delirious laughter.

"Hey," I said, hurrying over before others noticed. "Can we not? You're being offensive."

Brian, still lying on the ground, glanced up at me. Cole tilted his head at me. Brian was in his puffy gray elephant outfit, Cole in his black-and-white spandex catsuit.

"I'm sorry, Allie," Brian said. "We were just doing a bit. We got carried away."

"Damn, girl," Cole said. "Who died and made you Queen of the Re-Res?"

"Cole," I said, "please be more respectful. Brian? While you're on your break, can I talk with you? I want to nail down logistics for our anniversary."

Brian nodded okay and got off of the floor. Cole made an obnoxious whipping motion. I refused to let myself be affected by such a petty gesture, so I didn't comment on how rude to women that was, and Brian and I were just stepping away, when—

"Baby," Cole said as he literally inserted himself between us.

"Hey. Allie baby. Have you gotten your Stanford confirmashe e-mail yet? Have you given thought to which dorm you wanna live in? What about that roommate preference form? What's your attitude toward drinking? Are you gonna party in college, or are you gonna stay a judgy-mouthed, tight-sphinctered, granny-panty prude forever?"

I couldn't believe what he'd just said. I tried to formulate a response, but I lacked the words to shield myself against such causticity.

Cole inched closer to me.

"You *are* going to Stanford, right? You didn't *defer,* did you? Or *worse?* That's what your boyfriend told me, but I don't believe him. Please don't tell me you bitched out."

I felt my breaths getting shallower. I felt the walls of my chest closing in.

"Brian," I said. "Say something."

"You *didn't,*" Cole gasped, his eyes wide. "You *rejected* Stanny? You actually *turned down* dork paradise? All so you could stay here with your oafy boo and your *mamacita*? Oh. My. Gerd. Oh my Gerdness gracious . . ."

I looked at Brian. His eyes darted back and forth between Cole and me. He looked so conflicted. I had no idea why.

"He can't save you now, chica," Cole snapped. "You lead your own life. You're responsible for your own dumb-dumbs. If you go down the road idiotically traveled, that's not on Brian, and it's not on *tu madre*, and it's certainly not on me. Why, as a matter of fact, I do believe it's your *own* damn fault—"

"You're a bad person!" I shrieked. "What makes you think it's okay to be this way? How did your parents *raise* you? You talk about *me* living my own life? What about you? All you do is suck the blood of others, then use their humiliation to create more fear. What kind of pathetic existence is *that?* I may not be joining you at Stanford, but at least I accept who I am, you hear me? I'm not a terror like you. I'm not a coward. I'm not a monster. And I'd rather never succeed in my entire life than ever go to the same goddamn college as you."

A small crowd had formed around us at this point. I have to confess, as I finished my tirade, I felt rather proud. These were things I'd been dreaming of telling Cole for years, particularly since that fateful weekend at Stanford, at which he played no small role in extinguishing my college enthusiasm. And if Brian, for whatever reason, was going to shirk the duty of defending his girlfriend, then I was going to do it myself, even with an audience. Especially with an audience. And surely the things I was saying, surely these are the insecurities that must actually haunt Cole in his weaker moments, so right then I was expecting him to react accordingly. I was anticipating he might become defensive, or wrathful, or depressed.

Instead, he clapped his hands.

"Well, well, well," he said.

Cole's slow claps reverberated across the entire theater. His expression was gallingly indifferent.

I looked at Brian. Brian stared at a nail in the floor.

Cole scrunched his nose up and pawed at the air. He meowed, right in my face. "Kitty's got claws."

He turned to Brian. He placed an arm around my boyfriend's shoulder. "I don't know, Mr. Big," he said. "I'm thinking if your lady won't hush up, we might have to do her dirty, huh? We could show her exactly what happens to the sad souls who mess with us . . . I mean . . . remember the last one?"

"So . . . ," Brian said, much later that night, in my room. We were lying on my bed. "Three months, huh?"

He leaned over one of my arms and kissed it all the way down to the tips of my fingers. He did the same with my other arm. He took my underarm and gave it a big wet raspberry.

"I love you so much, Allie."

"I love you too, Brian."

I took my hand and let it play idly along the top of his head, a little spider taking a stroll.

"I was thinking," Brian said, kissing his way up to my shoulder. "It's only a couple days till our official anniversary. I know we were planning on waiting till then, but—"

"Brian?"

"I mean, I have my brother's—you know—in my wallet, and I could just bust it out, and if the coast is clear, we could, like—"

"Brian?"

I pressed my fingers into his scalp, not enough to cause pain, but enough to stop the train of thought right in its tracks.

"Yeah, baby?"

"This afternoon, at rehearsal . . . when Cole said those things, those cryptic things at the end . . ."

Brian made an effort to squirm out from under my hand. "Uh, I'm not sure I remember."

"Think harder, then."

He tried to wriggle his way off the mattress. I held him in place.

"When Cole made that remark," I continued. "That thing about 'see what happens' to people who mess with him and you . . ."

Brian shook his head. "Shut up," he said. "That didn't mean anything."

"Don't you dare tell me to shut up."

"I'm sorry—"

"Don't you bother apologizing."

I watched his scalp turn from pink to red. I felt it begin to collect sweat.

"Just give me a sec," he said. "I really gotta pee."

I dug my nails in deep, I sank them into my boyfriend's skin.

"Brian . . . what was he talking about?"

12. WILEY OTIS

"So according to your latest progress report, you're failing three classes: econ, bio, and algebra 2."

"Okay."

"Coupled with the marijuana incident, this is very troubling indeed, Wiley."

"Okay."

"If you receive an F in just one class, you won't be eligible to graduate this June. That means summer school at the very least, and potentially, you'll even have to repeat senior year."

"Okay."

"Tell me. What do you want to do with your future? What do you aspire to be?"

"I don't know. I guess a filmmaker."

"Well, even filmmakers have to pass econ, bio, and math."

"Really?"

"Yes."

"Okay."

"Say . . . aren't you good friends with Allegra Rey?"

"Uh—"

"Here's a thought: Why don't you get her to tutor you?"

Those meetings with the vice principal used to freak me out, but I'm numb to them by now. Ms. Fawcett tries to motivate me with the scary newsflash that I'm a failure, but I already know I'm a failure, so it doesn't work. She mentions Allegra, like I'm supposed to go next door and beg forgiveness from the girl who threw away ten years of best friendship to have sex with an albino gorilla asshole. Then I get sent to detention.

Detention is like purgatory. It's a dark, silent, impossibly boring realm, and you know you're going be stuck there forever. So you sit at your table and think about forever, like past high school and into next year, when you don't want to be in school anymore, because it's a total waste of time. You want to follow your passion; you want to start making films. But you can't tell good stories, because you don't have any life experience, because you've never taken a chance. And you don't have any money, because you gave it all to the brass guys. So you try to get a job, but you don't have a college degree, let alone a high school diploma. So you have to take the saddest, most boring job imaginable, like sitting all day in a drive-through window, or waiting all night in a parking lot booth, waiting for forever, sitting in limbo all over again, waiting for nothing in life but the chance to wait some more, waiting and waiting—

Until one afternoon, about three weeks ago. When the library door opened. And a girl walked into the room. And everything changed.

"Hey you. Mind if I sit here?"

Wow.

Look who came to visit me in purgatory.

My guardian angel.

She smiled widely at me. She looked like she belonged in a pamphlet for an orthodontist's office. Her smile was that perfect and gleaming white.

"It's nice to see you," Nikki said. "I'm glad our paths could cross again."

"Yeah," I said. "What's it been, five months?"

"Since homecoming," Nikki said. "But hey, here I am now."

I pumped my fist. "Best plot twist ever."

Nikki took the chair next to mine. As she sat, she flipped her flowy mane over her shoulder. It was like that part in *Fast Times at Ridgemont High*, when the bombshell brunette steps out of the pool. I felt like the guy in the bathroom, only slightly less perverted.

"I missed you," she said. "I missed you, Wiley."

My eyes bulged, like the bathroom guy. I did the biggest double take.

"What?" I said. "We barely know each other."

"Oh," she said. "Yeah."

Nikki slumped in her seat, just the tiniest bit. She stared into space. It gave me a weird feeling, seeing that. It's not very often you feel sorry for the popular girl.

"It sucks, you know," I said. "What happened to you. You deserve better than that."

Nikki smiled weakly at me. She went back to looking at nothing.

"For what it's worth," I added. "I never watched the video."

Nikki nodded. She opened her mouth like she was about to launch into a monologue. She closed it and went with one word instead. "Thanks."

"Yeah," I said.

I drummed my fingers on the table. Nikki folded her hands in her lap. I sniffled. I coughed.

"I'm sorry I never reached out after the tape leaked. I guess I didn't know if we were good enough friends to talk about it, or friends at all really. I didn't want to weird you out. Also, I dunno, I guess I've been going through stuff of my own."

"I know," Nikki said. "I heard about Allegra. And Brian Mack, of all people. That's awful, Wiley." She reached back and tucked a strand of hair behind her ear. "I'm sorry."

"Yeah," I said. "Thanks."

Nikki sighed.

I sighed too.

"You know what the worst part of this crap is? It's not everything that already happened. Like yeah, it hurt when Allie left me for literally a giant thumb with a face, but I can get over that. I can forget the past. It's tough but doable. But you know what's *really* gonna ruin me?"

"The future," Nikki said.

"Right. Like sure, I lost Allegra as my friend, but also I lost her as a math and science tutor. So now, because she's out of my life, I'm not even gonna graduate?"

"Exactly," Nikki said. "And with me it's, like, this video follows me around everywhere I go, so now my parents won't let me out of their sight. My dad said he'll only support me if I go to DCCC, which means next year I have to stay trapped at home instead of getting out and starting over like I want."

"I probably won't even go to college to begin with," I said. "And even if by some miracle I do, who cares. I'm not gonna make any friends. I'm such a loser I lost my nerd friend to a bully."

"Hey," Nikki said, rolling her eyes. "Better a loser than a porn star."

"Don't take this the wrong way," I said. "But I actually wouldn't mind being a porn star, you know? I'm looking to break into the film industry, and it might be a cool way to meet some cameramen and casting directors."

Nikki smiled. "Nah, I don't think you'd like working in porn. You have to be naked a lot, and I know you like wearing your wolf shirts."

"Yeah," I said. "But at least I'd get to make some new friends. You know, like the pizza delivery guy. And the electrician. And the dude in the bunny costume with the strategically placed hole."

"Yeah," Nikki said. "But listen. If you want to be a truly great porn star like me, you have to be willing to shave"—she pointed at my little mustache—"*everything.*"

We snickered at that, uncontrollably. The Bear stood on her hind legs and shushed us. We didn't care.

"Hey," I said, after a half minute or so of silence. "You're not a porn star, you know."

"You're not a loser," she said.

"You wanna know something?"

"I do."

"You know when we first met and you gave me advice about love?"

"Yeah."

"I think about that a lot."

"I do too, Wiley."

"I'm sorry how people have treated you," I said.

"I'm sorry you lost your friend," she said.

Her hand was resting right in front of her, on the table.

Without thinking, I reached out and touched it. And it was awesome. She squeezed mine back.

From that day on, every detention all the way until spring break, it's been the two of us. I'll sneak a thing of Nutter Butters or Funyuns into the library, and we'll split the bag. Nikki will bring a fashion magazine and we'll laugh at the ads, saying who looks like DeSean in a wig, who looks like Allegra but ten times hotter. Without the Bear noticing, I'll show Nikki film trailers on my phone, and I'll tell her about all of the movies I want to show her someday, especially the eighties teen flicks, my guilty pleasure slash personal favorite genre.

Mostly, I love just talking to Nik. We'll start on a topic, like parents or love or sex or whatever, and ninety minutes later, we'll still be going. And even after the Bear scares us out of detention, even when we go back to our separate houses, we never stop talking. We text, we chat, we continue to connect.

I know I'm pissing away my shot at graduating. I know detention time is when I'm supposed to be doing my homework. I know I'm on my last chance if I ever want to leave this place, if I ever want to have a future. But honestly, screw all that. I don't want to kill myself worrying about tomorrow. All I want is to love the now.

• • •

"Spring break . . . ," I said this afternoon, post-detention. "Spring break . . . spring break forever . . ."

Nikki lifted an eyebrow.

"Wow," she said in a flat voice. "Spring break. Amazing. I'm so excited to escape being called a whore at school so I can go be treated like one at home."

I leaned over. I gave her a side hug. "I'm sorry, dude. I hope it's okay. You know, you can call me anytime anything comes up."

"Sure," Nikki said. "Thanks."

"I'll see you in a week."

"Right," she said. "See you." She picked up her bag and began to walk away. Then, randomly, she spun to me instead.

"Hold on," she said, placing a hand on my chest. "Who says we can't hang out over break?"

"What? We . . . What?"

"Do you want to come over tonight? I think you'll be allowed, because no offense, but my parents would never in a zillion years mistake you for a boyfriend of mine."

I made a face pretending like my feelings were so hurt. Then I grinned instead, and Nikki did too. We high-fived, clasping our hands together and letting them stay there. And as we stood across from each other, as we held hands, right then I got the most brilliant beyond brilliant idea that a stupid man boob like me has ever had.

"I'll bring weed."

13. COLE MARTIN-HAMMER

"Oh, the thinks you can thiiiiink, when you think aboooout . . ."

"SEUSS!!!!!"

The curtain closed and opened again. The audience's applause was rapturous. One by one, the less talented and, frankly, less attractive members of the cast—Steph, Sofia, Liam, Neil, Brian, et cetera—took their bows. That whole time, I knew that all of their cheers were really for me.

Then it was time for the Cat in the mother-effing Hat. I pounced forward and struck a pose, my skintight suit showing off the streamlined contours of my elite bod. I pawed at the crowd and blew a kiss, displaying my trademark mix of childlike mischief and kinky sensuality. For the final time ever in my high school performing career, I bowed my head. At this point, the entire auditorium orgasmed in unison.

It was glorious.

I felt godlike.

• • •

After the show came the cast party, back at my place. My mom wasn't there. She'd wanted to make closing night, but she drew another midnight shift. My dad wasn't there either. I mean, obviously.

I was totes fine with the lack of parents, though, because that set the stage for a night of good old-fashioned, kegs-in-the-kitchen, who's-gonna-throw-up-in-the-bushes, who's-gonna-give-who-a-secret-hand-job-in-the-laundry-closet-type fun.

"Mr. Cat in the Hat," Liam Garner said to me halfway through the party, Rashan Mohammed right behind him. "The mayor of Whoville and Yertle the Turtle hereby challenge you to a game of beer pong!"

"Excellent," I said, tapping my fingers together. "On but one condition: no pictures. I'd hate for someone from Stanny admissions to see me on social media in such a debaucherous state."

"Dude," Rashan said, nudging me. "You're the only one I don't trust with a camera."

"Astute observation," I said, winking. "Let me go grab my partner."

"Hey, Horton?

"Lennie?

"Big Mack?

"Flabby Bald Burger with a side of Fat Sauce, hold the Hair?"

I finally found Brian sitting in the far corner of the living room, all by his lonesome. His phone was in his hand. He looked exhausted.

"Chubby Lumpkins," I said, approaching him. "Some lame-lames asked if we wanted to school them at BP. I said yes. Let's go."

Brian glanced down at his phone, then up at me. His head didn't move, just his eyes.

"Come on," I said. "We have to prove we have the biggest, most masculine penises by being the most accurate at throwing tiny balls into unsanitary cups."

Brian blinked. "Sorry. I can't."

I reached into my pocket and pulled out an imaginary revolver. I loaded the gun and mimed aiming it at my temple. "Please don't tell me this is about Allegra. *Please* don't still be hung up on that drippy butt stain."

"I'm texting to see if she's coming tonight. I don't wanna miss if she texts back."

I fired the gun. I picked invisible fragments of splattered brain off of Brian's shirt.

"Honey boy," I said. "You've got to stop doing this to yourself."

"There might be a chance—"

"Bull*shit* there's a chance. Look, *lo siento*, *muchacho*, but neither of us could have predicted that you would ever date Allegra in the first place, nor how she'd react when she found out that we were the ones who leaked that naughty video. And I'm sorry about what it did to your relationship, for realsies I am, but you've got to build a bridge and get over it."

"You shouldn't've been so obvious in front of her."

"I know, I know, and I told you before, a thousand apologies, homey, but this isn't my fault, okay? And it's not that big a deal."

As I said that, a chill seemed to run through Brian. He clutched his phone. He stared ahead grimly.

"I'm not blaming you," he said in a low voice. "You were only trying to help me. I know that. I appreciate it. But I can't be around you. Not if I want a shot at Allegra."

I tried to smile. "*Ah*," I said in my funny vampire voice. "I see how eet ees. You are pulling Count Blackula's leg. You are making heem very vorried for no reason. But eet ees just a ruse! For you vill play beer pong after all!"

Brian's forehead wrinkled. He shook his head subtly, almost imperceptibly. "I'm sorry," he said. "I don't think I can be friends with you."

I froze for a breath. I threw my head back and cackled. "*Ha!* As if. Get that folding chair out of your vagina. Talk to me when you're ready to be chill again, 'kay? Catch you on the flip, yo. Byeeeee!"

I walked away from him, taking in the party around me, watching everyone as they made timeless theater-kid memories: taking selfies, singing five-part harmonies, cracking each other up with Mr. Bayer impressions, reveling in the glory of their youthful selves.

I still needed a partner for beer pong.

"Neil?

"Changeling?

"Neil, you angel-faced, baby-cheeked boy genius, where are you?

"Neil, you feminine-eyelashed, Madame-Alexander-doll-mouthed, twink-bodied pastry puff, where are you?

"Neil, you naive, servile, malleable piece of shit! Get your baby dick in here, child!"

Minutes and minutes went by. Still he didn't show. Not even when I dangled a piece of jerky in the air. Not even when I threatened to call his parents and tell them about all the jerkies.

Finally, I had to throw up my hands and walk back to the BP table, cat tail between my legs.

"Sorry, gents. Strangest thing, but at the moment, I cannot seem to find a suitable partner. Looks like I'll have to take the two of you on . . . by my own damn self!"

A few hours later, well after my beer pong victory, the party died down. Brian slipped off without saying a word. Everyone else danced out the door, crooning Broadway jams into the wee hours.

This is when Neil finally showed his puny, adorable face.

"Changeling!" I said as he walked into my kitchen and up to me. "There's my widdle guy. Where you been all my life?"

Neil regarded me. His expression revealed nothing. This was strange. True, he's not typically the most emotive person, but what with my being his omniscient master and him being my orphan boy, I can usually read him pretty well. Not this time, though.

"Where you been all my life?" I repeated.

"I was in the laundry closet," Neil said.

I made a face. "Doing what? Washing your ceremonial sari?"

"No," Neil said.

I put my hand to my mouth.

"Oh. Mah. Gerd. Are you secretly hot for me? Have you been waiting all year to confess? Don't you think it was a bit on the nose to wait for hours inside a literal closet?"

"Stop it," Neil said. "No."

"Then what the Hello Kitty were you doing off the grid, child?"

He spoke without hesitation. "I have something to tell you, and I wasn't sure if I was ready, but now I think I am."

"Lay it on me," I said. "You're freaking me out."

"You're not going to Stanford next year."

I raised one eyebrow as high as it could go. I tilted my

head to the left, damn near ninety degrees. "Um . . . false. You know I just accepted the offer last week, right? Signed, sealed, delivered, I'm theirs."

"No," he said. "I'm sorry, Cole, but you're not going there."

"LOL. And what would you know about it? Go eat a sacred cow or something, mmkay, brah? Leave me alone."

"You're not going to Stanford," Neil said, his face still exactly the same, still so creepily calm. "Because I told them about the SAT."

What.

The.

What.

As soon as he said it, I felt crazy dizzy. I sat. I practically fell into the nearest chair. Neil stood over me.

"I hate how you think you're better than people. You're not better than people. You cheat and lie and spread negativity to get ahead. That's not superior; it's shameful. Allegra was right when she called you a coward. That's exactly what you are. I am so disappointed in myself for trusting you these past years, for believing you could be anything else.

"Several weeks ago, I contacted the College Board, as well as Stanford and the other colleges on your wish list: Northwestern. NYU. Yale. Brown. I detailed your entire plot to them, and I sent ample evidence of your scheme in the form of e-mails and screenshots. I told them you manipulated me into helping you cheat, which you did, and I swore you would do the same to others in college, which I'm certain you would have. So I was just informed that you are being banned from Stanford, and the other schools as well, and that your most recent SAT scores have been invalidated. You should be receiving official word soon, perhaps over spring break.

"I gave you many chances, Cole. I kept telling myself that you could not possibly be this depraved. I kept giving you chances all year. And then I heard how you spoke to Allegra about Stanford, the way you rubbed it in her face. And I watched the video of Nikki, who you've never even met. And I realized what you've done to me since the day you 'discovered' me, how you've used me for your purposes, who you've made me become. And I refuse to be that person any longer. I wash my hands of you, okay? I am not your little changeling anymore, and I never will be again, as long as I live."

Neil finished talking, and he made a little face, and now that I've had some time to reflect on it, his face was, well, it's hard to admit, but . . .

He was smirking. Neil smirked at me. He practically smiled, and he kept that look fixed on his mug as he dropped his final line:

"By the way, I am going to get a superb college essay out of this."

With that, he walked out of my kitchen. He exited my house. He left me all by myself, at two in the morning, to sit there and think. I took a cigarette out of my pocket. I lit it. I began to smoke.

I've been in a fog ever since.

14. BRIAN MACK

My pops grunted, picked at his butt, and flipped to the sports section. As he scanned the page, he grunted again.

"Hmm, a thing about DeSean. Looks like he's trying to throw again."

I scooped some scrambled egg with my fork.

"Says here he threw a fifty-yard bomb in spring practice. From a chair."

I speared a chunk of sausage.

"Quote from the Fresno State coach saying DeSean's his best recruit in years, maybe of his whole career. Another quote from the Oregon coach saying he would have agreed, but what with the injury . . ."

I swigged down half a glass of orange juice, hopefully quick enough to get out in time, hopefully before Dad could—

"Shame what happened to him, huh? Hey, Brian, now that you're done with that Dr. Seuss nonsense of yours, you oughta stop by practice and talk to him. You need to apologize to that boy."

Dammit.

I grabbed a fistful of bacon and flung it at the opposite wall, where it slid down, leaving a trail of rank juices. I took my plate and dropped it on the floor, where it exploded into pointy shards. I crop-dusted the room in loud, nasty, epically Brian Mack fashion. I peaced before my dad could say boo.

As much I hate the man, though, he was right.

Well, partially.

I did have some apologizing to do. But not to DeSean.

To her.

The room smelled like death. I took one step into the gigantic elderly diaper that is Casa de Maria, and right away I understood why grandkids never visit these places. I put my hand to my nose. I was just about to bounce.

But I couldn't turn around. I was on a mission. This was some Greek mythology shit. I had to journey into the Underworld if I was going to win my lady back.

Allegra was sitting at a card table with two wrinkle-faced women. One of the women had jowls like a basset hound. The other had less hair than I do.

"Inez," the bald one said. "Tell her about Duke. Tell her what Duke said to Estelle."

"Well," the doggish one said. "It was yesterday evening. After *Jeopardy!* before *Wheel.* We were sitting here, minding our business, playing our bridge, when in walks the Duke with that big ol' cowboy hat of his."

"And that big ol' grin."

"That's right, Maggie. So we're sitting there, us girls, and Duke struts up to Estelle, and it's been some time since his wife passed, you'll remember, and he comes right up to her, hands on his hips, and he says, 'I been lookin' for a companion, miss. And I think you'll do just fine.'"

"Oh my goodness," Allie said, her eyes all lit up, her hands clasped together. "And what did Estelle say to that?"

"Well," the jowly lady continued. "Estelle about fainted from shock, as you might expect, and she put her hand to her heart, and she said—"

I coughed right then.

The woman stopped talking. All three heads turned to look at me.

"What are you doing here?" Allegra said.

"Babe," I said. "Can we chat for a sec?"

Allegra frowned. "Please don't call me that."

"Is this him?" Inez said in old-person whisper. "From all your stories?"

"He's handsome," Maggie said. "Nice head of hair."

"I need a minute, Allie," I said. "That's all. Just a minute of your time."

Allegra turned to her geezer friends. "I am so sorry," she said. "I have to take care of this."

She got out of her seat and led me to a corner, over near the jigsaw-puzzle table. "What do you want?"

I smiled as big as the moon. "You," I said. "Look, I'm sorry about the video—"

"It's not just that."

"I'm sorry I trusted Cole—"

"It's not just that."

"I'm sorry I . . . Hey, it's not the sex stuff, is it? That's not important to me, not at all. We can take it super-slow."

Allegra took a quick peek over her shoulder and a small step in. The next thing she said, she said quietly. "Brian. I accept your apologies. I truly do."

"I'm not an asshole," I said.

"I know," she said, shaking her hair out, letting some curls fall. "There's nothing wrong with you. You're sensitive, and affectionate with my family, and you were considerate to give me space over spring break, and you're hilarious, and you're resilient, and Maggie is right, you know: You're very, very handsome."

I smiled at that final word. I took a step toward her. I stood over her now.

"Awesome," I said. "That's awesome. So, like, if you accept my apology, and it turns out you want me after all, then, like . . . will you go to prom with me?"

Allie tore away. She strode across the room, and the way she was leaving, so steady, so sure of herself, it was as if she was getting a do-over of the day we first met, back when she almost pulled away forever in her car. She was escaping, like the princess fleeing from Donkey Kong; she was disappearing to her castle, where she could be safe from the monkey forever. Goddammit, she was at the other end of the room now, back to the wrinkled ladies, and as she sat down, right before she blocked me out, right before she turned away for good, she said one final thing.

"I'm sorry, Brian. I am so sorry. Part of me will always love you . . . But you can't take me to the prom. I'm going with someone else."

Keep on dancing. Keep on dancing.

Allie still likes me. Of course she does. She's pissed about what Cole and I did, but time will take care of that. She just wants to own her power for a hot minute. I respect that. She was testing me that day, that's all. For sure there's no other prom date. That's some jealous-making nonsense. That's just mind games bullshit.

I have to stay the course. Remain positive. Keep on smiling. Fix the past.

I found Nikki after school today, outside the library. She was standing off by herself, wearing a gray DCCC sweatshirt with the hood all the way up.

"Um," I said. "Hey."

Nikki blinked, lots of times. I realized she wasn't going to say a word, not until I gave her some of the right ones.

"So I know this is awk. I know we haven't spoken in months. But can I have a sec? I promise I won't give you any more crap about that video, because you don't deserve that."

She paused for a moment. She flicked her head back, releasing her hood and throwing her wavy brown hair over her shoulder. "All right," she said.

"I'm just trying to reach out, make amends, be a better man than I've been before."

Nikki nodded. "That's sweet."

I cracked my knuckles on each of my hands. "Yeah, so I need to apologize. It was a dumbass thing I did. Like, yeah, I was pissed at you for choreographing that hurtful dance and for choosing DeSean over me. But we never should have gone after you, and you know, above all, I never should have signed off on it. I never should have said yes to Cole sending out that link—"

I wasn't prepared for it. Nikki's face, it just fell. Normal one moment, devastated the next. She was one of those flowers that wilts all fast in a nature movie. It was hard to watch.

"That," she struggled to say. "That. That was *you*?"

"Shit," I said. "I thought you knew."

"About Cole, yes. But not about *you.*"

"I'm sorry, dude. Big-time. I really am."

"Leave me alone."

"Come on, I'm trying to—"

"Now."

"I will, I will, but—"

"Stop harassing me."

It was my turn to slump.

I walked from the library to the front of campus, to the big green lawn. Everyone else had gone home by this point. I plopped down on the grass and sat there for hours.

I stared at the street in front of me. I watched the cars go by. For a minute I thought, *Hey, maybe it'll be like last time. Someone will come, someone unexpected, and they'll drive on over, and they'll say a friendly hello, and they'll pick me up, in more ways than one.*

But what am I, five? What a baby-ass thought. That kind of shit never happens. Not when you've made the dumbest possible choice at every turn. Not when no one likes you.

So I just sat there. I sat on the lawn till my butt went numb, just plucking grass, dumb as I ever was.

15. NIKKI FOXWORTH

All we did, all spring break long, was watch movies. Every night, Wiley would show up at my front door, bearing an armful of old DVDs. We'd go down to my basement, taking every unhealthy snack in my kitchen along with us. And we'd just go all night, binging on munchie after munchie, movie after movie. Wiley wanted to show me all of his favorites, which meant by the end of the week, I think we watched every film ever made.

Wiley wanted to show me his favorite face-switching movie, so we watched *Face/Off.* Then his favorite schoolchildren murdering each other movie, so we watched *Battle Royale.* Then his favorite sad orgy movie, so we watched *Eyes Wide Shut.* Then his favorite movie where hip-hop dancers have to band together in order to save their rec center from being turned into a shopping mall, all through the power of funk—*Breakin' 2: Electric Boogaloo.*

And then, this past weekend, Wiley had an epiphany. He figured that since I'm the "hottest girl at school," and since he's "some random loser dork," then why not cap off our marathon in appropriate style, with a series of exclusively hot girl and loser dork movies?

So we did. We watched *Clueless*, and *Heathers*, and *Mean Girls*, and *Bring It On.* And we watched *Weird Science*, and *Revenge of the Nerds*, and *Never Been Kissed*, and *Lucas*.

And last night, the final weekend night of break, we finally did it.

We watched Wiley's favorite film from his favorite genre. The greatest hot girl/nerdy guy movie in cinematic history . . .

The Breakfast Club.

Golly, that whole week with Wiley was so unbelievably sweet. So simple, so blissful, so innocent . . .

Well, fine. I'll admit.

It wasn't *that* innocent.

We did smoke about a million pounds of weed.

"Oh my Lord," I said. "That was amazing."

We were outside, in the middle of the construction site formerly known as the spot, sitting on a blanket, underneath the stars.

"My parents never let me watch *The Breakfast Club* growing up," I said. "They said it was sinful." I finished rolling my joint and licked the end to seal it. "Thank you, Wiley, for showing it to me."

"Of course," he said as he tossed his head back and took

a pull from the handle. Besides smoking, we were drinking vodka. It was like we wanted to be even more of a high school fantasy than the movie we'd just watched.

I lit the end of the jay. "Only one thing about the movie bothered me, though."

"What?"

I took a long hit. I exhaled a puff of smoke. "The ending."

Wiley squinted. "What do you mean?"

I reached for the Smirnoff to double-fist with my weed. I twisted it open and took a sip. It burned my brain in the nicest way.

"So it goes like this, yeah? The asshole bully gets to score with the queen bee girl. And the jock guy gets to hook up with the crazy dandruff girl, after she puts on mascara at least. But, like . . .what about Anthony Michael Hall?"

Wiley shook his head. "What about him?"

"Well," I said. "He doesn't get to hook up with anyone. He has to stay by himself and write the paper."

Wiley nodded. "Well," he said. "He's a loser."

"Right," I said. "He's a loser. But the appropriate way for the story to end would be with him becoming a winner. *He* should be the one to hook up with Molly Ringwald, not the bully."

Wiley laughed. "Why is that?"

"Because," I said, passing the joint to Wiley. "Everyone deserves a win sometimes."

He scoffed. "*Really*," he said. "Everyone deserves a win."

I placed my hand on his knee. "Yessir."

He took a hit from the jay. "Even losers?"

"Even losers."

He shook his head in disbelief. "Even *losers*?"

I tossed my hair back over my shoulder. I lowered my voice. "Yes, Wiley. *Especially* losers."

It happened so damn fast.

Wiley read my signal. He leaned across the blanket and planted a big-time kiss on me. His little peach fuzzies brushed against my face. I liked the way it felt. He tasted like a mix of alcohol and Swedish Fish. I liked the way he tasted.

He was an excellent kisser. Stunningly good considering I am five hundred percent positive he had never kissed a girl in his life before me. Maybe it's all those hours he's spent watching romantic movies, researching proper techniques. Or perhaps our kiss was some kind of destiny.

We took turns being in control. I lay on the blanket and Wiley kissed me from above. Then I straddled him and gave him kiss after kiss after kiss, some hard, some soft, all of them warm and caring.

Before anything crazy happened, I thought it'd be best if we went inside.

My parents were out all evening, drinking endlessly and avoiding thinking about me. Still, it was fun to pretend like we might get caught, so Wiley and I snuck down to the basement, holding our breath, snickering all the while.

As we kissed on the futon, our bodies all sprawled, we went faster than before, faster and harder, going purely off pleasure, like people in a movie. I don't want to say which kind of movie.

I made the first real move. I reached for the bottom of Wiley's wolf shirt and pulled it over his head. It was the cutest how he looked when I did it, all wide-eyed and confused. He got the idea, though, and unbuttoned my blouse.

Then we were in our pants, and then our underwear, and he was running his hands over my bare skin, and I loved the way it felt, and he told me I looked so hot, and he didn't look so bad himself, and we kept going, kept grinding, kept tasting.

And I rushed through the next part, like I always do. I asked if he had protection, and he shook his head no, but I said it's okay, I got you. I covered myself in a blanket and I grabbed a condom from my room. I came back, and he was covering his chest and stomach with his hands, looking shy. At the same time, though, I saw it in his eyes. He looked ready.

I positioned myself. I positioned him. I peeled off my bra and said, "Don't be nervous. I'll help you, sweets."

And before I knew it, he was doing it.

We were doing it.

And then one, two, fifteen seconds later—

We were done.

And then one, two, three seconds after that—

Wiley fell asleep.

And as I lay on the futon, with his arm draped across my torso, with his head resting where my breast meets my shoulder, as he mumbled in his sleep, as he snored and dribbled all over my body, as I went back over the past few minutes, over everything that had somehow just happened . . .

I really just wanted to hit rewind.

"Wha? What's going on?"

"It's six in the morning. Your mom just texted. You have to go home."

"*What?* What happened?"

"You fell asleep after the movie. I let you sleep through the night. That's all."

"Really? I could have sworn we—"

"Fine, we kissed a little bit, but it was a mistake. It won't happen again."

"Oh."

"Come on, Wiley. Let's get up."

"Wait—"

"Rise and shine. I have church."

"Wait . . ."

Wiley glanced around the basement, his eyes empty. "We kissed?"

I nodded. I tried to smile. "It was an accident."

He rubbed his eyes. "Oh."

I nudged him off the couch. I helped put his shoes and socks on. I prodded his body up the stairs. He lurched forward step by step. He moved like molasses. Still, we were almost at the top. He was almost out the door, nearly gone for good.

"Hold up . . . Why is my shirt on backward?"

A chill shot through my chest. He couldn't know.

"Wiley, it was like that the entire time. I promise."

He put his fingers to his wispy mustache. He thought for a moment. Then he nodded. "Oh."

It was only as he got farther from my front door, as he got closer to his car. That's when I noticed it.

That's when I spotted the wolf.

That face. That ridiculous face that was supposed to be on the front of his shirt. As Wiley walked away, it stared back at me. Fangs bared, tongue dripping with blood, eyes glowing bright. Those yellow eyes with the tiny black centers. They had something to say:

I know what you are.

I know where you've been.

And wherever you go . . .

Whatever you do . . .

Whoever you thought you could become . . .

It doesn't matter.

I know what you did.

ROAD TWO

SPRING

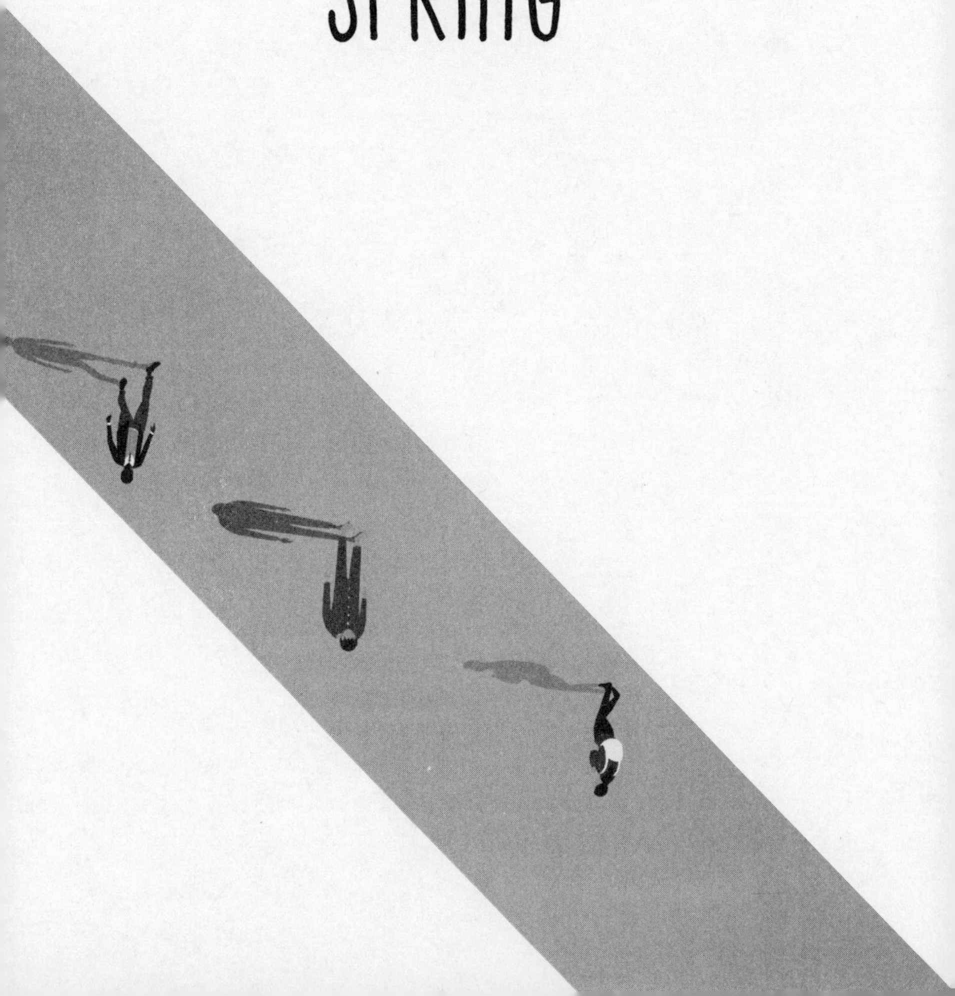

11. WILEY OTIS

"WILEY!

"WILEY OTIS!

"DO!

"NOT!

"JUMP!!!"

I teetered at the edge of the roof. The wind was howling. My hands were wobbling. The campus buildings and neighborhood houses below me looked so small, like Lego bricks. The tiny people milling about, they were like ants, completely unaware of the story unfolding above them.

I heard the footsteps behind me, rushing toward me. I spun around. Cole was there, completely out of breath. There was a heroic glint in his eye.

"Wiley," he said. "Wiley, my boy. Don't do this to yourself. You have so much . . . to *live* for!"

He extended a hand in slow motion. He stared deep into my eyes.

And he winked.

Nope. Too cheesy.

"Cut!" I shouted, unpressing the record button and putting down my phone.

"Hey, man," I said. "I like the effort, but a little heavy on the melodrama, yeah? Maybe next take, don't gun so hard for the Oscar."

"But I'm so deserving of the award," Cole said. "I've gone full method and shed seventy-five pounds in order to truly inhabit the role of Cole Martin-Hammer."

"Let's try again. This time, go for subtlety."

Cole tilted his head. "Subtly . . . erotic?"

I rolled my eyes. "Actors."

"Okay, okay. Quiet on the set. Rolling, aaand . . . action!"

For the past two months, since the day Cole stormed out of rehearsal and spotted me on the roof—when, like, obviously I wasn't trying to do anything; I mean, come on; I mean, seriously—ever since that day, we've been the thickest of thieves. Come to think of it, maybe that's the real reason my hands and feet decided to take me to the top of the theater that afternoon. The universe must have wanted me to meet Cole.

Throughout the first three-plus years of high school, he and I never had much to do with each other. Aside from the fact that we both gave Allegra the occasional migraine, we had nothing uniting us. But since fate or whatever has brought us together, we've discovered that we actually have a shocking amount in common. We're both completely over caring about schoolwork. We're both cool with never discussing our family situations at all. We both love watching movies—him with his musicals, me with my eighties flicks, my black-and-white classics, my Japanese experimental cinema, and my puppet porn. We'll plow through three, four films in a single sitting after school, and the only time it gets even the least bit awkward is during a boring scene, when Cole occasionally tries to bring up his gossip stuff and I have to tell him not right now. I don't want to talk crap about people. I don't like talking about Nikki. I don't like thinking about Allegra. I just want to watch the movie.

Luckily, things don't stay weird between us for long. Or they do, but in a good way. Things get really, really weird.

It was my idea to make a movie. I figured since I'm a filmmaker and Cole's an actor, we could combine our powers to pull off something really badass. Then Cole had the even more brilliant idea to make not just any movie, but a biopic—a film about ourselves, a dramatization of the way we became friends, a post-modern meta-commentary on our own lives, starring us as us.

It's been hilarious. I made the early request that we not film any scenes featuring the characters of Nikki or Allegra—I mean, why go there?—which has resulted in us tinkering with the narrative a bit. In the new plot, instead of getting rejected by Allegra, I turn down the sexual advances of Fat Isaac, played by Cole with pillows stuffed in his shirt. Instead of being called a pervert by Nikki, I get scolded in detention by the Bear, played by Cole as a furry. Cole also lends his acting talents to the roles of Miss Fawcett, Coach Dent, Scrotes, Neil, and the voice of my shirt wolf, who sings a soulful ballad to close the second act, "Hungry for a Friend."

Today we were up on the roof, filming the pivotal scene, the one where Cole saves my life, in which he and I finally become best pals after circling each other for years. Naturally, we took our usual creative liberties. Everything we shot was a bit more, well, dramatic than what actually happened.

"Wiley! Don't jump! I've fallen for you, my mustachioed prince!"

"Cut. Try again. I thought we said *less* erotic this time."

"Wiley! Don't do it! The insurance policy, it's not worth it!"

"Cut. Cole, I thought we rewrote that plotline."

"Wiley! Stop! The stone people, you're the only one who can defeat them!"

"Cut. *What?*"

"Wiley! Noooo! Your dad . . . I'm sorry he didn't make it to the big game."

"CUT! Hey, I thought we were deleting any reference to him."

"I just wanted to inject some emotional stakes."

"Trust me, you're doing plenty of that with your eyebrow acting alone."

"Well, come on, Wiles, what real stuff *are* we allowed to delve into?"

"You'll know when I tell you."

"Shouldn't I get a say?"

"No. You're the talent. I'm the *auteur.*"

"You kidding me, homey?"

"This is my story. It's not for you to tell."

"I'm just trying to help you."

"What do you mean? I don't need any help."

Cole stared me down. He lowered his voice. "You sure about that?"

"What do you mean?"

He gave me a look like I had the IQ of Forrest Gump.

"Wiley," he said. "That day . . . when I saw you on the roof . . ."

"Dammit," I said. "Stop trying to accuse me of being depressed. I'm *not depressed.*"

Cole nodded quickly. "Okay," he said. "Fair enough. But, like, everything we've done these past couple months, all the laughs we've had, from that day until now . . . is any of it helping?"

I held up my hands. "I don't know. . . . I guess yeah, doing the movie is fun. But, like, I don't know, man. I don't know."

Cole paused for a moment. A gust of chilly wind blew right as he said the next thing.

"What if I told you there's a better way?"

"What?"

"I know what you've been going through," he said. "I've got my ear to the ground. I know why you won't talk about them. I know Nikki made you feel like an abusive sex dog. I know Allie dumped you in order to hang out with a giant anthropomorphized egg with another, smaller egg on top that serves as a head. And jokey jokes aside, I know your pain, Wiley. I've been there before."

"No, you haven't," I said.

"Sure I have. I've been excluded too. My whole life."

"How?"

"Let's see. My dream school rejected me. The theater community, none of them fought for me. I don't have any friends, not a one, besides you. And my father? You know that guy you've suspiciously never met? Spoiler alert: He tried to take his own life rather than spend another single second with me."

My mouth fell open. "Oh my God."

"That's right," Cole said. "He left me. Just like yours did."

"Oh God," I said. "I had no idea. I am so sorr—"

Cole held up a finger. "But you don't see me crying about it, do you?"

"Um . . . no?"

"That's right," Cole said. "We don't cry. We never leak weakness. Whining is for bitches. There's something else we can do. Something far more effective. And it ain't making movies, but you'll still be needing that thing."

He pointed at my hands. He held up his. I tossed him my phone.

"We have a weapon at our disposal. The ultimate weapon. It's how we turn the tables, how we get our lives back on track."

He clicked into my phone and opened the Internet. He closed his eyes, and it was like he was choosing between two options; he mumbled a silent *eeny-meeny-miny-moe*.

"Wiley, my boy," he said. "If you remember just one thing in this life, remember this: Don't get sad. Get even."

He tapped on a search browser and typed in three words: "Nikki Foxworth scandal."

I tried to tell him that maybe the Nikki thing was my fault. Maybe I deserved the humiliation she gave me. Maybe this isn't right. But Cole shushed me. He convinced me. Nikki sent me down the path I'm on now, he reminded me. She could have saved me, but she shamed me instead.

We didn't work on the movie the rest of the afternoon. We're suspending the shoot indefinitely. That was all fun and games, but it's real life we're concerned with now. It's research we must do. Cole is absolutely right. We need to get even. It's the only way. It's our only chance to make things fair.

We remained atop the theater, glued to our phones, well into the night. We stayed there, through the wind and the cold, for hours and hours, until we were the only souls left on campus.

Before we left, we did one final thing:

We peed off the roof.

12. BRIAN MACK

I wish I never came back to school.

It's boring. Special class is boring. The kids are dumb as rocks. Nico eats his hands. Austin throws things. Madison cries and runs outside. It's, like, baby stuff. I mean we're doing reading. It's like kindergarten.

I feel bad for the kids in special class. They've been like this since they were little. I remember Madison in elementary school, having recess with a grown-up when we had normal recess. I remember Austin and Nico throwing sticks at each other in their special PE. Those kids have always been different. This is the only school they've been in. Cookies and stickers is all they know.

I'm too smart for this shit. I'm too smart for these kids. They've been in stupid school their whole lives. But I used to be regular. I used to have buddies. I used to have fans. Nikki wanted to bang me. I used to be awesome.

The doctors say I might be okay. At my last checkup they said I could get better. Like better for real. Not a lot of people have what I have. "Second-impact syndrome," they said. It's when football players get their bell rung twice. High school kids with brains that are still growing. Two concussions right in a row, wham bam. No one knows what happens next. You could get all the way healthy. You could be frozen forever. The doctors smile when they tell me the news. I could still get better.

But the way the doctors say it, it makes my parents cry.

Screw the doctors. I'm not some freaking idiot like the kids in my class. I still know stuff. I remember what I was. I know what I am. And I'm not dumb about the future. I know why my parents cry. I know what I'll never be.

I'll never be the Big Mack again.

I'm Brian now. Just Brian.

Too smart for special ed.

Too slow for the real world.

"All right, gang. First dress run. Let's make it count!

"Places for the top of 'Oh, the Thinks You Can Think.' Here we go.

"Margot, cheat out.

"Neil, great energy.

"Hey, pause for a sec . . .

"Where's Brian?

"Has anyone seen Brian?

"Someone check backstage for Brian!"

I totally blanked.

I was sitting by myself, like on the side, and I was waiting. I was waiting for when Neil snaps his fingers, because that's when Thing 2 runs on. I was by myself because Allie wasn't there. She was at the hospital, helping her mom. She said she would try to meet me after rehearsal. And I'm stupid without her. I forget things, so I forgot to run onstage. Then I remembered, but way too late. I jumped off my butt and I ran to my spot. But my new costume is slippery, the footie part, so I got to the stage, but I was running too fast, too fast for my body. So I fell. Everyone was watching me and I fell friggin' hard. I slipped off my feet and crashed to the stage like *WHOMP.*

"Brian?"

"Oh my gosh, is he all right?"

"His head—what about his head?"

"Is this the third time, or the fourth, or . . . ?"

"Oh no."

"Oh God."

"Someone text his parents."

"Someone call an ambulance!"

I heard them. I heard all of it. All their words.

My head was ringing like it got thumped by a hammer. The world was all blurry. I could only see colors and shapes. The blood was drip-dripping out of my nose, making a puddle on the ground, like someone squeezed a big-ass strawberry.

But I didn't care about any of that shit. I cared about the words.

And I couldn't take it anymore.

So I exploded.

"I'M FINE! I'M FINE, DAMMIT! DON'T CALL MY PARENTS. DON'T CALL A DOCTOR. I'M FINE! YOU'RE ALL ASSHOLES. YOU'RE ALL IDIOTS. I'M GOOD AND I'M FINE! GODDAMMIT, GODDAMMIT, I'M FINE! CAN'T YOU SEE THAT I'M GREAT? CAN'T YOU SEE THAT I'M HAPPY? SHUT UP, YOU DUMBSHITS! GO TO HELL! LET ME BE! I'M FINE!"

"Are you okay?"

This was after I ran out the theater. Way after. I was sitting at school, in the very front, alone on my fat-guy lawn.

"Brian," she said from inside her car. "I heard what happened. I'm so sorry."

"Leave me alone," I said. "I'm fine."

Allie opened the door. She waved her hand, like, *come in*.

"I'm sorry I wasn't there," she said.

"No, you're not," I said. "You don't care."

"What? Of course I do."

"You just want to feel good about yourself."

"That's ludicrous."

"I don't know what that means."

"I'm sorry they babied you—"

"No, you're not."

"I'm sorry no one understands what you're going through—"

"No, you're not."

"I'm sorry the world is so unfair—"

"No, you're not."

"*Fine!* I'm sorry . . . I'm sorry you're . . ."

She made a face, like she couldn't say it. She wouldn't say it. She wouldn't let anyone in the whole wide world say the truth out loud.

"I'm sorry you're . . . retarded."

I froze.

I stared at Allie. She stared back.

"Okay," I said.

I got in the car.

We didn't talk at first. Allie drove past the houses to my house. I bet she was thinking about the thing she just said. I wonder if she had regrets.

"How does it feel?" Allie said halfway through the drive. "You know . . . being in your brain?"

I looked around the car. I scratched my head.

"Do you feel sad, like, in a vacuum? That is to say, on your own? Or is it that everyone else makes you feel sad, the way they act toward you?"

I let it be quiet for a little longer. "Both."

I waited, then added, "But mostly everyone else."

Allie nodded. "Do they make you feel like you're not good enough? Like it doesn't matter if you try to get better? Because it's as if they already don't expect anything of you anyway?"

I put my finger on my nose. My nose was still a little bloody. My finger got red. "Yeah," I said. "That."

Allie pulled her car to the side. I looked out the window. We weren't at my house yet. I wondered why she stopped. I wondered what she was about to say. Maybe it was important.

"What if I told you . . . that there's nothing wrong with you?"

I shook my head. "No," I said. "Everyone says that. But everyone's lying."

"There's nothing wrong with you."

"Shut up."

"There's nothing wrong with you."

"I'm stupid."

"Well, I think you're smart, Mr. Big Mack. And kind. And resilient. And very, very cute."

She said that with her momish smile, and it made me feel good, and I was just thinking how nice she was, and how pretty she looked, how much I liked her pretty gray eyes and her squishy little face, and I was thinking how much I liked all those things together when all randomly she shut her eyes hard, and she twisted her face weird, and she started making crazy monkey noises, and there were tears in her eyes.

"Oh my goodness," she said. "Oh my goodness."

"Allie," I said. "Allie, are you crying?"

She put her hand over her face. Her whole body was shaking like a grandma's hand.

"No," she said. "I'm—I'm laughing! I'm laughing!"

I felt funny in my forehead. I scratched my chin. "Why?"

"I just . . . I just realized . . . you're . . . you're still in your onesie!"

I looked down at myself. She was right. I was still wearing my outfit, my big red Thing 2 costume. Red pajamas with footies and a butt flap. A curly blue Afro wig. My body looked like the Kool-Aid Man. My hair looked like the Cookie Monster's pubes.

I grinned like a mofo too. "You're right," I said. "It is pretty funny."

We laughed for the longest time, till our bodies hurt. At the end of our laugh, Allie put her hand on my back. She touched it like a massage for a while. She brought her fingers under my wig, to my head. She touched there forever too. It felt amazing. Like nothing I've ever felt before. It made me feel so awesome. So stoked to be alive. Goddamn. What a woman.

13. NIKKI FOXWORTH

Ugh," Mona said late last night.

It was the final night of spring break. We were sitting and snacking on her bed. Mona's mom had just taken the standard motherly five minutes to reprimand her daughter for her outfit choices, her recent grades, and her diet, and she'd taken all the good food out of the room with her, so we had to pull an emergency stash from the back of Mon's closet.

"Every day she treats me like this. Every day. And she wonders why I don't want to be a mom."

"Plus you have to have sex in order to be a mom," I said. "Is she aware of that?"

"No," Mona said, dunking a peanut butter pretzel into hummus. "My mom thinks you get pregnant by closing your eyes and whispering the word 'baby.'"

I shook my head. "I am so sorry, sweets."

Mona eyed me. "How do you deal?"

"What do you mean?"

She washed her food down with a sip of secret, under-the-bed Lime-a-Rita. "You never let the judgment faze you. How?"

I lifted an eyebrow. "You mean like in the locker room, when I was so chill under pressure I turned into a homicidal lunatic and almost got myself expelled?"

Mona laughed. She handed me a Red Vine. "You know what I mean," she said. "People come at you, wanting to bring you down, but you always hold it together."

I thought about what I've dealt with this whole past year, from being dumped by DeSean, to being groped by Brian, to being propositioned and practically stalked by Wiley. I couldn't believe Mona was right. But honestly, she kind of was.

"Well," I said. "I guess you have to find a way to tune out the haters. Even if they call you things at school. Even if they live in your house. You've got to ignore all the BS and hold your head up high."

"But other people listen to those haters. Everyone believes the bad stuff about me."

"What about you, though?"

"Huh?"

"Do you believe the bad stuff?"

"Oh . . . I don't know."

"What do you mean, you don't know? It's a simple question. Do you believe you're a worthless sex monster or not?"

Mona shrugged her shoulders. She looked down at her hands. "I don't know," she said.

"You can't give them that power," I said. "You can't let yourself care."

"I know."

"You look like you don't trust me."

"I want to."

"But it's easier to believe the bad stuff, isn't it?"

"Yeah."

"Yeah," I said. I thought about DeSean, about Brian, about Wiley, about Brooklyn and Channing in the locker room, about my mom every night at home.

"You are so awesome," I started to say, but Mona flinched. I closed my mouth. She shook her head. She truly is amazing, but it's like nothing in the world can convince her.

I looked around the room. I noticed Mona's old spelling and music trophies. I noticed her cello case, another artifact from another time, back when her mother was proud of her. I saw a pair of pom-poms. A pair of toe shoes. An enormous, frilly tutu. I took a big bite of licorice.

It hit me.

"Well," I said. "There is one *other* thing I do when I get low. . . ."

"What's that?"

I flashed the jazziest hands I know how. "I *dance*."

I hopped off the bed and over to Mona's speakers. I plugged in my phone and pressed play on the first song I saw.

"Dancing Queen."

"Woooooooooooo!!!" I shouted, gyrating my hips, rocking out with an invisible Hula-Hoop.

"Yeah, lady! Get down with it!" Mona said, grooving on the bed.

"Show me them high kicks, girl!" I hollered back at her. Mona blushed. I prodded her with my foot. She stood and did a couple of the Rockette kicks she's famous for on cheer.

"Okay, let's see that booty!" she shouted back at me. I shook my butt up, down, and around, like I was washing a car in a rap video.

"Grapevine!" I called out. We both started grapevining randomly across her room.

"Disco!" Mona said. We shimmied our shoulders and disco-pointed with our arms.

"Dougie!" I said. We each Dougied across the room and then laughed like crazy because we don't know how to Dougie and there was no one there to teach us.

"Polka!"

"Nae Nae!"

"Macarena!"

"*Oh!*" I blurted as the song reached its end point. "*Dirty Dancing!*"

I scampered to one side of the room. Mona got in front of her bed and crouched low. I ran right at her and jumped in the air, and she tried to catch me and lift me up like the girl with the big nose from the movie. But I crashed onto her face, and we both fell on her bed and burst into giggles all over again.

"Hey, Nik," she said as our laughter died down. "I have a question for you."

"Okay. Shoot."

"You want to go to prom with me? Like as friends?"

I thought about it for a second, but only a second.

"Are you kidding me? I'd love to."

Then, of course, it happened.

The very next day, it happened.

I got asked to prom. Again.

Mona and I were passing through the Greek at lunch. We never eat there anymore. Too many cheer and dance girls and too many pea-brained boys who worship at the altar of the cheer and dance girls. And speaking of, well, you know, brain stuff, now that Brian's come back to campus for special ed, he's usually in the Greek with Allegra Rey, and I really can't bear to face him—I mean him more than anybody. So Mona and I were on our way past the amphitheater and over to the terraces in front of campus—when the trumpeter stood up.

It was like the bugle boy in a boot camp who rises at dawn

and wakes everyone up, because this guy started playing, and everyone else, all the hundreds of people eating lunch on the benches, they shut their mouths and went to attention at once.

Then a trombone player got up, all the way across the Greek from the trumpeter, and he joined in playing. Then a saxophone boy. And another saxophone boy.

I recognized the song at once. From that movie my parents never let me watch. The detention movie. The one where they all smoke pot and dance on bookshelves and everyone except the nerd gets to hook up at the end.

Mona tapped me on the shoulder, like, let's get out of here, but I didn't move. Whatever was happening, I wanted to see who was doing it and who it was for.

A very large tuba player stood up at the top of the benches, and another kid with a silly-looking horn. They played too, and by this point the sound was very full, like it filled the amphitheater, and no one was saying a word. Everyone had their phones up, to record the scene.

And just when the music swelled, right as the song was about to end, that was when I got this split-second chill, this sudden surge of fear—

Oh my Lord.

Please no.

Anyone but him.

Wiley was in the marching band with these same boys. Wiley had used these boys before, and this exact song, to try to confess his love to Allegra. Wiley had been creeping on me for weeks, spying on me from afar. I knew he and Cole had been up to no good that whole time. I just knew it. Wiley the stalker was getting revenge for what happened between us in detention. He was trying to corner and shame me in front of the entire school.

Just as the music ended, I saw him.

Standing there, at the bottom of the Greek, right in the middle of the stage. He had a megaphone in one hand, a bouquet of roses in the other.

DeSean Weems.

"Hey," he said into the megaphone.

"Why is he pointing at you?" Mona whispered.

He *was* pointing at me. D motioned to the stage, like, *Come on down; it'll be okay.* I looked at Mon like, Is *this okay?* She shrugged like, *Who the hell knows?*

I made my way down the steps, into the belly of the Greek, every pair of eyes on me.

"Hey, Nik," DeSean said as I met him, his voice amplified for all to hear.

"I regret how I acted before. I try to be a good guy, you know, and, like, all I was to you was a bad boyfriend. You know what I'm saying? But I want to do better by you. I want to be a better man. So listen, baby, I got something I need to ask. . . .

"Nikki, will you go to prom with me?"

• • •

In so many ways, it felt like a mistake.

I thought I didn't care what the cool girls thought. I thought I didn't worry about my status. I thought I didn't need a guy anymore. DeSean hasn't spoken to me in months, so how could I trust that? I couldn't tell if he was being genuine, not with so many people watching us. And the last time we dated, all he wanted was one thing from me, and one thing alone.

On top of everything, I didn't want to leave Mona in the lurch.

And yet, as I stood there, weighing my options in the center of the spotlight, I thought about something else too. Something buried way down deep. A certain thing I've dreamed about ever since I was a toddler in Texas:

The fairy tale.

The girl in the storybook doesn't find her love immediately. She has to kiss a few frogs. She has to deal with dragons. But at the end of the story, after all the hardships and heartache, there comes that magical moment. Cinderella puts on the glass slipper. Snow White is awoken by true love's kiss. The maiden has suffered enough. She is ready for the hero in her life. She lets fate save the day.

So which one was it?

Who did I want to be?

The sun beat down. The folks in the stands held their

breath. The band players held their instruments right to their lips. DeSean held my hand in his, looking as sweet and vulnerable as I've ever seen him. I couldn't feel the tips of my fingers.

My head said no. My heart said yes. I had to make my choice. But there was no time to think.

14. COLE MARTIN-HAMMER

We crouched in position, high atop our sniper's perch. I alternated between scanning the hallways below and entering new search terms on my phone. Every few seconds, Wiley poked his head out of the bunker and readjusted his binoculars. Yes, he has actually started bringing binoculars on our after-school stakeouts. Gerd, I love that kid.

"Type in 'Allegra Rey boob job,'" Wiley whispered. "Or 'Allegra Rey boob reduction.' Ooh, ooh, or 'Allegra Rey nip slip.'"

"Come on," I said. "Let's take this a little serious. Why would any of that stuff be on the Internet?"

Wiley put his binoculars down. "Why would *anything* be on the Internet?"

He lowered his voice. "I mean, we've found worse."

I whistled. "Fair enough," I said. "Poor Ms. Foxworth. I almost feel sorry for the girl."

"She deserves everything coming her way," Wiley said.

"You open the Ark of the Covenant without permission, you deserve to get your Nazi face melted off."

"You know, I'm not sure that's the perfect analogy—"

"Besides," Wiley continued. "That one's over and done with. We got our Nikki revenge out of the way. It's Allie's life we need to ruin now."

I took a moment. I let the words wash over me. I covered my mouth to keep from grinning too wide. "Well, well, well . . . ," I said. "The bumbling sidekick becomes the diabolical master."

"Thanks," Wiley said, beaming.

I held up my screen. "But it's been weeks now, and we still haven't found a shred of incriminating evidence against the girl. And as you might guess, that's a first for me. So I'm all for crushing her dippy, drippy dreams, but good gerd I have no friggin' idea how we're supposed to do it."

"Shh," Wiley said, gazing down at the ground. "There they are."

The theater class had been let out for the afternoon. And fresh off last weekend's final performance of *Seussical*, our old friends looked positively triumphant. There they were indeed. Frumpy Butt and the Whale.

Brian was giving Allegra one of his bucking bronco piggyback gallops. She was laughing hysterically, imploring him to put her down, but at the same time loving the ride. The two of them looked like a sickeningly sweet Hallmark card. A carefully crafted piece of barf.

Right at that moment, Wiley twitched.

I spun around. The boy's whole body was convulsing. His mouth was practically frothing.

"Sidekick," I said. "Are you okay—?"

He stopped on the spot. He held up a finger. I shut my mouth.

"I've got it," he said.

"Got what?"

"Revenge," he said simply. He leaned toward me, cupped his hand, and whispered in my ear.

"I don't get it," I said. "What do you mean, 'make a movie'?"

He whispered. He whispered more. He whispered the entire thing.

"Oh," I said. "Oh, good God."

My whole drive home, I couldn't get my mind off Wiley's scheme.

It was good, to be sure. If executed properly, the plot would accomplish everything I ever wanted. It would wipe the smirk off Allegra's face. It would sully her name in this town forever. It would punish her for stealing my spot at Stanford, the life that should have been mine.

More importantly, and my personal vendettas aside, the plan would help Wiley. It would allow him to claim his redemption, perhaps even find his inner peace. That's the whole reason I took the boy under my wing to begin with. Because he seemed lost. Because I wanted him to find himself, the way I've found myself. This plan could accomplish all of that in one fell swoop. It is that powerful.

Honestly, maybe it's too good. I'm a longtime rumormonger, and proud of it, but damn, when push comes to shove, I do question whether I truly want to be a life destroyer. We are getting into unprecedentedly heavy territory here. Moral-turpitude-level shit. I mean, I already feel twisted about the stuff we found on Nikki. I wonder if I've created a monster in Wiley.

I needed to lie down.

I parked in front of my house. I bypassed the usual home cigarette. I went inside, up to my room. I opened the door.

It was there that I discovered an unexpected, unwanted visitor.

"Cole," he said. "It is so good to see you."

My father was sitting at the foot of my bed. He looked scraggly yet somehow not disheveled. His eyes were puffy but weirdly calm. He looked like he'd just found Jesus, or had aliens stick something up his butt.

"No," I said.

I shook my head no, and I shook my hands no, and I

backed away. I had to get out of there as right now as possible. But my pops sprang off the bed and rushed up to me, seizing me from behind. He wrapped me in the hardest hug, and though I tried to squirm free, he had that old-man strength. He wouldn't let go.

"Sit down," he said.

I sat on the corner of the bed, as far away from Earl as I could.

"The ward agreed to let me out early," he said. "So I could be there to see you graduate. At the top of your class, no less," he added, his eyes flashing.

"Second in my class," I said. "To Allegra Rey."

"Oh, right," he said. "Didn't your mother say she's going to Stanford?"

"No," I said. "She's not. She chickened out of an amazing opportunity. An incredible life. Does that ring any bells?"

My dad ignored that.

"Well," he said. "Second in your class. Still pretty good."

"If only I'd had someone to teach me math."

My dad forced a broad smile. "Regardless," he said. "Graduation day. What do you think?"

"I think you can come watch me wear a dopey hat for three hours, but it doesn't make you my father."

Earl shook his head. "Come on," he said. "I'm trying."

"No," I said. "You're not."

"I'm here," he said. "I'm trying."

"Yeah," I said. "Still *trying* to be proud of me after eighteen years, but the fact that you haven't exactly pulled it off, that should say something."

"Come on," he said. "Let this be a happy moment. At least try."

"Why don't you try?" I said. "Instead of slicing your wrists or jamming your gullet with pills every time you get the chance?"

"Hey, Cole—"

"Seriously. Stop faking this shit. Why don't you leave? This room, this life—your call."

"Come on, now."

"I can't believe you'd use that word: 'try.' As if you've *ever* tried with me. The only thing you tried in your life, you failed, and now I have to deal with this insufferable nonsense."

"Son—"

"I'm *not* your son, okay? You could have been a real father, but you weren't. All you did was *try*, allegedly. And I already know what's coming next. You're going to try all over again, the love part, and the proud papa part, and inevitably, you'll go crazy again, and you'll try you-know-what again, and maybe you'll even succeed this time, so do me a solid and shut your mouth, because none of it is good enough. You hear me? None of your empty bullshit is worth it—"

"YES. IT. *IS*."

He leaped off the bed, his arms flexed, both hands in fists. He stared right at me, his nostrils flaring.

"YES, ALL THIS BULLSHIT *IS* WORTH IT."

He sat back down, his breathing heavy.

"I am a tormented person," he said after several moments. "I am self-destructive. I am broken beyond belief. I wish I were not these things. My moods, my reactions, and even my premeditated actions, I cannot account for any of them. And that is a very scary thing to realize, that you are a ticking time bomb. Especially when you do not value life, as I have not for so long."

I resisted the urge to roll my eyes. My mind flashed back to when I was a little kid, when I dreamed of going to Stanford because that's where my parents had met, that's where they'd been happiest. I used to watch my dad as he watched the football games. I listened as he talked about how connected he felt to the place. I wanted to be just like him.

"I admit that I've taken too much out on you. I desperately wish it weren't true, but I know it is. I am jealous of you, Cole. You were born into a very different body than me. A superior vessel, no question about it. And for so long, I've held on to that resentment, that unshakeable feeling of inadequacy. For so many years, I've felt there was no way I could father you, not the way you deserve. You are capable of so much. I feel power over nothing.

"So yes, I tried to take a way out. You might think of it

as the easy way. I want you to know there was nothing easy about it."

Right after I learned of my dad's attempt, one of the first things that hit me was how he tried to do it the summer before my senior year, before I applied to college. He didn't want to see me go to Stanford. I was sure of it. That's why he never helped me with math, as much as I needed him. He never wanted me to be better than him, even though I indisputably was.

"Fortunately, Cole, I did just try that day. I did not succeed. And I am so happy to have failed. To be sitting here right now. Because I can tell you this: There is nothing I can do about what led me to this point. I cannot change my brain, my DNA, everything I've done to hurt you, every painful memory from the past. All I can do now is attempt to be a decent person. All I'm trying to do is good.

"You cannot control what happens to you. Not really, not ever. Even if you've got life ninety-nine percent figured out, there is still that one percent that will come back to haunt you, that will bring you to your knees. And that's not fair. But it's the truth."

But he was lying. Even though I never managed to ace the math, Stanford still wasn't out of my control. I could have gotten in. I would have, if I'd done what I wanted to do. But I got rejected because I succumbed to the system.

Because I tried to do "good." Because I was another stupid cog, just like my father.

"Luckily, thankfully, mercifully, you retain power over who you are. If you want to be good, even if everything is bad, then you can be good. And in the end, you just have to hope that you will create more good than bad."

No. My dad had no right to be saying this. He didn't deserve the chance to try to fix me. He's failed me. I've gotten used to life without him. I don't need him anymore. I don't need him.

"I never wanted to leave you. I have always wanted to be there for you. And I'm here now, trying the best I can. I'm here now."

With that he exhaled, like he was letting go of every pent-up breath, every lingering bit of tension in his body. He leaned over slightly and took a corner of my comforter, which he used to dab his eyes. Then he sat up, all the way up. He took me in his arms. He held me close. As he clutched me, he said one final thing.

"I'm sorry, son. I am so sorry."

As for me, I just sat there for endless minutes. I just sat there and took it. I felt his heart pound, and I listened to him weep, and I closed my eyes tight, all the while thinking, *Oh my God, what has just happened? How can I forgive him? How can I not forgive him? What does this mean? What does it mean for me? What in hell am I supposed to do now?*

15. ALLEGRA REY

"Allegra," my father said. "Would you review this bill for me? I want to make sure I didn't miss anything."

"Allegra," Augusto said. "Watch me do a cartwheel!"

"Allegra," Alejandro said. "Watch me turn my eyelids inside out!"

"Allegra," my *abuela* said. "Not so much rice pudding, *gordita*."

"*Mija*," Mama said. "My tea."

I looked all around me. The voices, they were coming from everywhere. The incessant requests, the ubiquitous stress. There was no relief coming, no escape in sight.

I glanced down at my hands. They were shaking. "I'm sorry," I said under my breath, to no one in particular. "I can't."

I went straight to my room, my head down, shutting out the noise, blocking out the world. I stuffed my bag full of books and fled the house.

I left for the one place I can relax.

• • •

"Allie!" Brian said when I poked my head in the doorway. "You're early!"

I pointed at him and grinned. "What can I say? I missed you."

He double patted the mattress spot next to him. "My bed missed your butt."

"Well, then," I said in a whimsical tone, "let's get them reacquainted."

I hoisted the bulky bag onto the bed before hopping up myself.

"Whadja bring me?"

I unzipped the bag and removed several books. "Well, I'm quite proud of how well we've been doing with our chapter books lately, so I was thinking we could continue on that track. Let's see here, I've got some Matt Christophers, a couple Goosebumps, these Oz novels I used to adore when I was younger, and perhaps, if we're feeling particularly confident, we can move on to something relatively advanced, like maybe *The Hobbit*—"

"Munsch," Brian said.

"Oh, no, Brian. We read that one every day. Besides, I thought we'd progressed past picture books. Let's try to take a break from that particular—"

"MUNSCH, GODDAMMIT."

His face was burning red. His forehead was popping a vein. His mouth was spittly.

I sighed and smiled. "Great. We'll do Munsch."

I took it out, the sky-blue book with the potty-training boy on the cover, the singular item that Brian has forbidden me from ever removing from the bag:

Love You Forever by Robert Munsch.

"A mother held her new baby," I began to read. "And very slowly rocked him back and forth, back and forth, back and forth. . . ."

We went through it, seemingly for the quadrillionth time, the story of the little boy and his mother, who every night takes him in her arms and sings him the same lullaby, all the way through his childhood and adolescent years and into adulthood, up until the day she is so old and frail she cannot hold him and sing anymore, at which point the fully grown boy picks her up and sings to his mother himself before then going home to his newborn daughter and singing it again, the very same song.

"I like that book," Brian said.

"Believe me," I said. "I know."

"I like that book," he repeated. "I like the mom."

"Right," I said. "But there's a whole wealth of superior literature out there—"

"She's like you."

I stopped cold.

"The mom reminds me of you," Brian said.

My skin prickled. My fingers clenched. "Why is that,

Brian?" I said. "Is it because you think *I'm* like *your* mom?"

Brian blinked. He blinked again. He stuck his hand underneath his shirt and scratched. "No," he said. "It's because I love you forever."

He looked me in the eye. I tried looking at him, tried smiling, but I couldn't hold it. I stared at my feet instead.

"Anyway," I said. "Anyway, I was thinking—"

"I love you forever," Brian repeated.

He scooted toward me. He raised his massive hands. He brought them to my shoulders.

"Brian," I stammered. "You know, you know, maybe we could—"

Before I knew what was happening, Brian took my face. He held it ever so delicately. He smiled, as wide as his face would let him. He leaned in, and he kissed me.

And it wasn't just a kiss—it was a perfect kiss. It was the stuff of once upon a time, of eternal girlish fantasies. It was as if his body had remembered everything his brain had forgotten, as if he had been the world's single most excellent kisser in a previous life. His mouth was so warm and loving that I had to kiss it back, and he pressed his fingers into my cheeks, but not too firmly, and he touched his tongue to mine, but not too intently. He kissed me, and I kissed him, and he loved me, and I loved him, and all I wanted to do for the rest of my life was kiss him, and read to him, and make a home with him, and build a family with him, and share the world with him, forever, for always, as long as I'm living, my Brian, my Brian—

And then I realized.

No.

Of course not.

Of course I couldn't do that.

"I'm sorry," I said, pulling my face out of his. "I'm sorry. I can't."

Before he could protest or try to kiss me again, I sprang off of the bed. He flailed at me, but I ignored it. I turned around. I did not take my bag. I left everything there.

I left his house and I got in my car. I turned the key and I drove.

I got on the freeway. Northbound, up the 101. Past Pismo Beach, past San Luis Obispo, past the missions that span the length of this great state, each a day's travel apart, each established as a way station for lost and wandering souls. Past Atascadero, past Paso Robles, past the farmland once tilled by my grandparents, past the berries, fruit, and nuts that are still grown and picked by so many others just like me, only without the papers, without the diploma, without the myriad opportunities I have at my disposal. Past Salinas, where Steinbeck chronicled the sputtering hopes and crushing disappointments of a bygone era. Past San Jose and Mountain View, where tomorrow's code is being written, for better or for worse.

Past all these places, for hundreds of miles, I drove, I drove, I drove.

It's not all about me, is it?

I am not the only one making these decisions. I am not the sole author of my story. Before me came my ancestors, who toiled in neglect, who never could have dreamed that someday one of their own would be able to make this particular drive. Now I have my parents and brothers, who are willing to sacrifice everything for me, even if that thing is me. I had Wiley, who promised to uproot his life in order to make mine happy. I even have Brian, who cannot have wanted me to leave, but who without knowing it has given me the final, crucial push to do the right thing.

All of these people want the same thing for me, even if I've been afraid to take it all year. Even if taking makes me feel like a bad person. I have to shut out my inner critic. I have to let my loved ones in. I need to drive for them, for myself. I cannot go backward when life wants me to speed. I am compelled to embark on this journey. I must take it.

I pulled onto the Stanford campus sometime after midnight. I found an out-of-the-way parking lot, off a palm tree–lined promenade. I crawled into the backseat, my sleeping place for the night.

The plan is to go to the admissions office first thing in the morning, bleary-faced and teary-eyed, and tell them I've made a catastrophic mistake, that I checked "no" on my decision form when all the while I should have checked "yes": Yes, of course I'll come to Stanford; yes, of course I'll leave home.

The plan is to get myself admitted back here and to be here the next four years and to return to Dos Caminos as infrequently as possible. I can think of one reason why I'd have to go back, but only one.

The plan is to become the person I know I'm meant to be. That means wearing pink, and rocking beads, and ironing my hair, and taking hip-hop, and meeting girlfriends, and maybe even a boy.

And my plan, as always, is to be a good person and to give unto others and to act as selflessly toward the world as I possibly can.

But my mother was right. In order to achieve all that, there's really something I must do first.

It's the most selfless thing I can do.

I need to put myself first.

ROAD ONE: GRADUATION

16. WILEY OTIS

In detention that afternoon, I did what I've done every day since spring break, since Nikki stopped showing up. I sat at a table by myself. I didn't touch my homework. I doodled pictures of melted Nazis. I doodled orgy people from *Eyes Wide Shut.* I doodled Dustin Hoffman in his scuba suit, floating in the swimming pool, in that famous shot from *The Graduate.* I thought about my film festival with Nikki and how it ended. I wondered how she was doing. I waited for nothing to happen.

Suddenly, the Bear.

"Grgfff."

"Huh?"

"Grgff, chughh," the Bear said as she slammed a pink piece of paper onto the table. It was a call slip. Apparently I had to go meet with the vice principal.

"Oh, should I—do you want me to—now?"

"Chughh, Wiley. Chughh."

I wasn't sure what to expect as I crossed campus from

the library over to the office. Probably this was going to be a meeting about my grades. Maybe I was getting one last chance. More likely, I was getting no more chances. I was going to find out I have to repeat senior year. I was going to discover that I have no future at all. Not exactly a twist ending.

So I walked into the office, where Ms. Fawcett was waiting for me. But when I got inside, I saw she wasn't alone.

It was like something out of *Indiana Jones and the Temple of Doom*, like that part where the scary high priest dude goes "kali ma, kali ma, KALI MAAAAAA."

Because I felt my throbbing, pulsating heart get seized from my chest.

"Hi, Wiley. Please take a seat. I called you in because I was recently reviewing the academic calendar, and it occurred to me that if we want to make any headway in raising your grades so that you can graduate, then the moment is now. I'd been mulling over what to do, when what do you know, into my office walks Allegra Rey. She informs me that the two of you haven't been as close as usual lately, but she said what I was hoping she'd say, and what I'm sure you're grateful to hear, which is that she wants to help you. So starting now, if you'll put in the effort, Allegra is willing to tutor you in bio, math, and econ. And if you work at it every day, I think you have a genuine chance at improving your grades, enough to possibly—Wiley? What's that? Please sit down. Wiley, come back. No, you may not leave this office. Come back, young man. Wiley. Wiley. Wiley—"

"Wiley, wait!"

I kept my head down as I walked out of the office, down the hill, into the neighborhoods.

"Wiley, come back! I'm trying to help!"

All those times, whenever I did something that offended her even the teensiest bit, she'd storm off; she'd refuse to talk to me. Now she knew how it felt.

"Wiley, listen. Please, listen—"

All those months she was with Brian. Touching him. Loving him. Doing God knows what with him. All those years she was my best friend, and then it was over, just like that. The moment she met someone else. Right before I could make my move. Sure, whatever, she tried to talk to me about it. She shouted my name in the hallway. She joked around like we used to. She attempted to explain. But words are bullshit. Actions are what matter. She couldn't have actually thought we'd still be friends, right? What did she expect, after she'd already made her choice? What did she expect now?

"Would you mind waiting super-quick? I left a few of my belongings at school. We could go back for them, then walk home together, like old times."

I didn't respond to that. As if old times ever meant anything to her. Screw her.

"I didn't mean to offend you just now, with the tutoring. I just want to help you, Wiley."

I made a huffing sound, sort of a snort, almost a cackle. I kept walking.

"Look, you have every right to be cross, but surely you'll admit, you haven't been the most compassionate with me, either. The way you've shut me out. That's not what friends do."

Seriously? That's what she wanted to focus on? That was her way of breaking the ice after all that's come between us, after half a year of silence?

I turned onto our street. I picked up the pace.

"I'm sorry, okay? I'm sorry I picked Brian. I should have known that meant losing you."

Of course she was resorting to apology. Like she hasn't done that a thousand million times before. Like it's ever meant anything.

"I forgot who I am. I lost myself. So many good and bad things happened to me, all simultaneously, and I didn't know what to do. So I detached myself from my past. I cut you out. I didn't want you reminding me of the person I've always been. I wanted to start anew."

She sounded out of breath. I glanced back at her. She was struggling. Her little legs really had to churn to keep up with mine. I eased up. I kept on walking, but I eased up.

"I realize now I've made a catastrophic mistake. By losing you, I've lost a piece of myself. And that's why I haven't felt right these past many months. Of course it's been stressful dealing with Mama, and with my college decision, but those things shouldn't compel me to abandon you. They're why I need you."

We pulled into view of our houses. There they were, side by side, just as they've been for so long.

"I really, sincerely, want to help you with school. I want to help you, and I want you to help me. I want to be friends again. I want to be us again. I want . . . I want . . ."

I finally came to a stop. I turned around. I stood facing her, in the place where we grew up, my oldest friend in the world.

"I want to go to prom with you."

I'd seen Nikki earlier that same day.

It was lunchtime. I'd been searching for her. I was walking past the Greek and there she was, smack-dab in the middle of the bleachers, sitting all alone. I barely recognized her in the gray sweatshirt. She seemed like just another rando among hundreds of others.

I tried to talk to her. I tried like I've done every other time I've seen her since break. "Nik," I said. "I'm sorry."

She pulled the hood up over her head.

I hadn't realized it at first, why she'd stopped coming to detentions. What I used to assume was that she'd been forced to go. Like, the administration made me attend detention for possessing drugs, so I figured maybe she'd had to do the same, as punishment for her sex tape.

Then she stopped showing up, and it seemed like she hadn't gotten in trouble at all. That's when I realized, duh, of course the school never penalized her for a video from well over a year ago. And that's when it hit me—the only reason she had ever come to the library in the first place was to be with me.

What I had to know now was why she never came back.

"I'm sorry," I repeated. "I'm sorry."

Nikki peeked out through the hole in her hood. She narrowed her eyes at me. "Why," she said, "are you sorry?"

"I . . . ," I said.

I took a big breath in. I let it all out. "I'm just sorry, okay? That's all I can say. I'm sorry."

Nikki shook her head. That was it. She pulled her messenger bag over her shoulder. She stood up and walked out of my world.

As she left, she mumbled one final thing. "You really don't remember, do you?"

Nikki was with me on my street this afternoon. I wanted it to be just Allegra and me, but Nikki was with me too.

“Wiley,” Allie said, uttering words I’d been dreaming of for literally my entire life, “will you go to prom with me?”

It was all I could do in that moment not to grab her hands with mine, not to kiss her right on the cheek, not to shout “hallelujah” to the entire universe.

But I couldn’t get that image out of my head. That sad little picture, like one of my movie doodles. The poor girl with her hood up, all alone in the crowd.

No one tried to help her until it was too late. She didn’t make a mistake. She never did anything wrong. But the world punished her regardless. It changed her. And now she’s all alone, on her own path. She won’t accept directions from anybody else.

I had to try to do the right thing.

“Wait,” I said. “I’m not just a replacement, am I?”

Allegra’s forehead furrowed. “What? Wiley, don’t you dare insinuate that you’re, that you’re some sort of *rebound*—”

I shook my head. “I didn’t say ‘rebound.’ I said ‘replacement.’ ”

“What’s the difference?”

“I’m not talking about the past. You shouldn’t apologize for picking Brian. You had every right to do what you wanted in that moment. That’s none of my business. But when I ask if I’m a replacement, I mean . . . are you asking me to fill a certain role? Am I becoming some kind of obligation? Basically, I’m asking about your future.”

Allegra looked lost. "What do you mean?"

"What about Stanford?"

Her eyes glazed over. "I didn't ask you about Stanford, Wiley. I asked about prom."

I stood up a little straighter. "I'm not just an excuse, am I?"

"What?"

"Am I an excuse to stay home?"

"*What?*"

"You don't have to hang around town, you know. You don't have to give up on your dreams just to make sure I'm doing okay. Please don't feel sorry for me."

Allie closed her mouth. She took her hair and tossed it over her shoulder. She stared me down. She stared me down hard.

Then she held out her hands. Her perfect little hands. They were right there, right in front of me, like they've never been before.

"Wiley," she said quietly. "Do you want to fumble this thing at the one-yard line, or do you want to be my prom date?"

17. COLE MARTIN-HAMMER

I'm trying, man.

I'm trying.

Everywhere I go. Everyone I've wronged.

I get it now. I do.

The dreams I've demolished.

The paths I've scorched.

The friends I could have had.

I own my sins. I must atone for them. Each and every one.

I'm trying.

"Sofia," Margot said. "You are my *girl crush*. Like, I want to *be* you. Like, I seriously think you could make it on Broadway, and not just the Broadway of New York, but, like, the Broadway of *life*."

"Rashan," Sofia said. "There were times when no one understood what I was going through, and you would just come up and give me a hug . . . and you have *no idea* how much that meant to me. . . . *You saved my life with those hugs.*"

"Steph," Rashan said. "Thank you for restoring my sense of play this year. I was missing it, and you brought it back. You made me feel like a kid again. *You made me feel like I could fly again.*"

"Margot . . . ," Steph said. "You raised me, okay? My mom and dad, they put food on the table, they put clothes on my back . . . but you *raised* me, you know? You RAISED me. You'll never know how much you mean to the individuals in this room. We are your children. You RAISED US."

These were but a few of the choice snippets from last Friday's theater class end-of-year praise circle. It's the same thing every year. Person A compliments Person B for some inane reason, Person B reaches for the big box of tissues, and everyone else snaps their fingers in robotic agreement, heads nodding, smiles forced. Typically the tradition is referred to as the "cry circle," because that's all it really is. Speaking of Kleenex boxes, I call it the "circle jerk," because that's all it *really* is.

But you know what? Not this year.

This year had to be different. This time I had to be sincere. Even when my fellow actors refused to give me a single morsel of praise beyond "cool hair; I like your little Afro," and "you're good at portraying a jerk," I had to keep my blood from boiling. I had to slap a grin on my face.

Phase one of my rebrand: initiated.

"Neil," I said when it was my turn to speak. "It's hard for me to have people, especially guys, who I can feel close to, feel myself around. The assholes growing up, they rejected me. My parents, they're disappointed in me. But you, dude? You're the one. The last two years, you've let me be fully *me*. And I love you for that. I just never found the right way to say it.

"I've always treated you like an orphan, like street scum. But you're so much better than that. You're better than me, Neil, that's for damn sure. You're the best guy I know, the best buddy a fool like me could ever ask for.

"I'm sorry about the thing that drove us apart. I regret cheating the system. I regret taking advantage of you. I respect that you put me in my place. I accept whatever happens to me moving forward. I am so sorry. I just want to be better. . . .

"Please forgive me."

No one spoke. No one moved. It was like being out in the dead of night, in the middle of nature. It was that quiet on the stage, in our circle. And that's because I was doing the right thing. Nature was taking its course.

Right then, Neil responded:

He yawned.

And everyone else, they did something too.

They snapped their fingers.

Snap, snap.

Snap, snap, snap, snap, snap.

Snap.

They snapped for Neil's yawn.

Like they were all beatniks with berets and bongos. Like they all knew the meaning of life and wouldn't let me in on the secret.

Like I wasn't in the room at all.

Like I didn't freaking exist.

Okay.

So be it.

Phase one: failure.

On to phase two.

I rolled in late to prom.

Normally I'm mad early to school dances. I show up first thing and I nab the latest goss, and I fashion police the shit out of uggos, and I get all Fosse-sexual on the dance floor. But not last night. Last night I was later than a God-fearing girl with an abstinence-only education and a suspicious craving for choco tacos. I said bye to my mom around ten, nicked a tux from my dad's cobwebby closet, and got to the Hyatt ballroom during the last few songs, well after the drunkards and sex fiends had already left for their motels.

All I wanted was to talk. I just needed to find that one girl.

Well, actually two girls, but I couldn't locate Nikki Foxworth no matter where I looked. Which makes sense. After the year she's been through—after what I've put her through—I wouldn't be surprised if she straight up ditched prom entirely. Poor thing.

Lucky for me, I was in fact able to track down the other *chica* whose *vida* I ruined this *año*. There she was, on the periphery of the dance floor, grooving and bopping and looking not that heinous, actually. Her hair was up in sort of a Greek goddess way, and from the looks of her magenta scoop neck, she must have finally discovered she has a bust. After all this time, Allegra seemed like she was at peace with herself, at last having a fun, carefree night with her date, her sneakily cute date with the clean shave, the handsome tan suit, and the duct-tape bow tie, and, what the—duct-tape bow tie—was that—was that really—Christ in a cat tree—was that *Wiley*?

"Damn, y'all," I said, walking toward them, my arms outstretched. "And the award for Most Aesthetically Improved Couple goes to . . ."

Allegra stopped her dancing cold. "What," she said, "are you doing here?"

I snapped my fingers. I grinned. "Something I should have done a long time ago."

Her face didn't move. I thought she hadn't heard me, what with the loud music and all.

"Something I should have done a long—"

"I don't care," she shouted over the hip-hop. "Just go away."

"You don't understand," I said. "This is a new me—"

"I don't care."

"Come on," I said. "Don't Boy-Who-Cried-Wolf my ass. Give me a minute. Let me open my heart here."

Wiley put a hand on Allegra's shoulder. She jerked away.

"We're set to graduate in a few weeks," she said, enunciating clearly, letting me hear every word. "After which point I never have to lay eyes on you again. But I'd like to start early, if you don't mind. So leave, Cole. Now."

I took a step forward, into her bubble. Wiley stood and watched.

"That's exactly why I'm here, girl! Graduation. And beyond. It's fine if you want to stop speaking to me. I totally get it, and most of humanity agrees with you. But if that's truly the case, then I've got to leave you with this:

"You must go to Stanford. For all of us, you have to."

Allegra pointed sideways, at Wiley. "Did *he* put you up to this?"

"I've never spoken to that boy in my life," I said. "And I'm sure he's a good guy, but I'm sorry, dude, he doesn't have the same prospects as you. And neither do I, not after what I did. So he and I, we'll still be here next year, stuck in town, going to city college. We'll be grinding, working our way toward the kind of opportunity that's in front of you right *now.*"

"Stop it," she said.

"I know I'm not the most credible source. But Allie baby, let bygones be bygones for a hot sec. Let me be your fairy godmother here."

"Shut up," she said. "Just shut up."

"I know. I know. Your mom and all. And that's a pretty good reason to stay. But guess what? There *is* no good reason to stay. Not your family, and not your fears, and not because I was a dick to you, and especially not—"

I glanced at Wiley. His hands were in his pockets. His head was down.

"No offense, but especially not Wiley. And again, I'm sure he's a sweet boy, reminds you of your past and all that. But I'm also sure he'll agree with me on this, because you really shouldn't give up—"

"*SHUT UP!!!*" Allegra exploded. "SHUT UP, YOU ASSHOLE! GO AWAY! GO AWAY! *FUCK OFF!!!*"

Okay.

Fair enough.

At least I tried.

"Of course," I said, spinning around, straight out of her life, just as she explicitly requested.

Phase two of Operation Cole Is a Good Person: also a failure.

There is no stage three.

• • •

My hand reached up. It knocked my phone off the bedside table. It fell past the lamp and loose change. Eventually it grabbed ahold of the little cardboard box, my fresh pack of Parliaments.

Over the past few days, I seriously considered quitting. It struck me as the perfect way to cap off my big rebrand. I was going to right all my previous wrongs. I was going to become a trusted friend to Neil and Allegra and countless others in the process. As a result, I wouldn't deserve to die of lung cancer anymore. Yay!

Obviously, my grand plan didn't exactly work out.

So obviously, the first thing I needed this morning was a smoke.

I hadn't even opened my eyes. I had the cigarette in one hand, my lighter in the other, and smoke alarm be damned, I was going to enjoy this thing in bed, even if it was the last thing I'd ever enjoy. My thumb was on the lighter when I blinked an eye open.

"Your mother told me you'd started with those. Terrible habit."

My father was wearing one of his old ratty cardigans. His hair was more grown out than usual, but his mustache was completely shaved. His hands were folded in front of him, perfectly still, like some kind of wax figure.

"No," I said.

“I am so happy to see you,” my dad said. “Just in time for graduation, eh?”

I flopped on my bed, squeezed my eyes shut, and yanked the comforter over my head. I buried my head in my pillow and prayed he would leave. I wished him dead like I did the night he first attempted. I wished him gone the way so many others have wished me gone over the years, wished I would just go away, just leave them be. I kept on wishing my dark violent dream for an eternity, for a lifetime, until he finally stopped saying my name, finally stopped trying to shake me out of it, until the moment when he mercifully gave up and left me alone in my room, when I finally relaxed and passed out again.

18. NIKKI FOXWORTH

My mother tucked some hair behind my ear. She refreshed her Texas-size smile.

"You have to go to, baby," she said. "Prom is the best night you'll ever have, at least until you get married."

She rustled the back of my head like a mama bird, like someone who actually loves her daughter. That woman is faker than her lips and tits put together.

"Mom, just so you know, I can't give anyone my 'special gift' on prom night. I already gave the milk away for free. You know. You saw."

Her smile wavered just the tiniest bit when I said that.

"Well, it's important to me that you go, Nicole. It's the kind of night that can change your life."

"Oh, you mean because I might use my demonic powers to murder everyone there?"

"No, because, well, you know . . . I met your father at my prom."

"I know," I said. "But you had the good decency to wait until God was ready before you let Daddy defile your secret lady place, and as a reward, your life turned out perfect. Well, perfect till I showed up."

Without warning, my mother slammed her hands on my bed. She did it so hard the mattress shook. Her eyes lit on fire. I bounced.

"Look," she said. "I regret how your dad and I have treated you this year. I truly do. We wanted to help put the past behind you. We wanted to let you forget. Instead, it's like we've turned our backs on you. We've shut you out. We screwed up, and it breaks my heart.

"But we're still your parents, and until the day you leave this house, it's our job to parent you. Which means I can't let you skip tonight. You did nothing wrong—absolutely nothing, sweetheart—so you shouldn't have anything to hide.

"Please go. You know how important it is to me. Please try, if only for a few minutes. If I'm wrong, you can leave whenever you want. I'm sorry, Nicole. I am so sorry, sweets.

"Please don't turn your back on life."

Back in Dallas, I used to wear the most extravagant dresses to dances: this Marilyn Monroe white halter with a skirt that only just covered my bottom; a gold sequiny gown that gave me the glow of an Oscar statuette; an almost completely see-through dress with embroidered flowers that covered my pasties and my thong and nothing else, because I wanted them all to notice, because I wanted them to stare, because I wasn't afraid of anybody. . . .

Those days, obviously, are long over.

So sure, after Mama Bird's legitimately kind words, I decided to put in a token appearance at prom. But that didn't mean I had to look the part. I refused to play a role in some Barbie Dream Girl Fantasy. I decided I'd rather be a homeless soccer mom.

Ripped-up, holey jeans. My hoodie I've worn six weeks straight. The least makeup I've put on since the day I turned eleven.

I didn't want to run away from life or anything, but I didn't exactly feel like standing out either. I wanted to blend into the walls. I wanted to be furniture. My plan was to arrive at the ballroom, stay for ten minutes or so, realize just how wrong my mother was, then go back home and tell her I tried, I tried, I really did.

It didn't take ten minutes. Within about zero point zero seconds, I realized just how insane my plan actually was.

As I walked down the red carpet and into the dance itself, Scrotes made finger-fist sex motions at me. Still, I kept my head high.

Brooklyn and Channing strutted past me, very obviously checking their phones and maybe even watching a certain video. But I couldn't let them win, so I waved all excitedly at them, like I was simply tickled to see my best bitches.

DeSean came into the ballroom wearing a magnificent white tux and a cheerleader on each arm. I wanted to hide from him, more than anything, but I didn't. I ran up to D and said how strapping he looked. I told the girls how lucky they were.

But that wasn't all.

Brian Mack came up behind me near the bathroom lines. At first I thought he was going to try to apologize like he did a few weeks ago, and I don't know how I would have felt about that. Yet in that moment, I realized he wasn't talking . . . just staring. Just standing by himself and staring at my ass. So I hurried away.

The chaperones, they stared too. All of my teachers, especially the men—Mr. Pargo, Mr. Aspell, Señor Gomez—they eyed me the entire night. I'm sure they had their so-called reasons. Of course, they could always claim to be protecting me, looking out for trouble. But how many times have I heard that excuse? How many times has my savior turned out to be my biggest shamer of all? So I had to avoid them, too. I disappeared into the masses.

Which is when I saw the happy couple.

They were on the edge of the dance floor, rocking back and forth to the night's first slow song. They were holding hands, with fingers interlaced. They were together forever, like they were always meant to be.

Wiley and Allegra.

I just couldn't.

Everyone was watching. Watching me, judging me, remembering. They all knew. They had to know. They knew in their bones, not just what I'd done on the video, but what I did in the basement, too, what I did with Wiley. They knew what I'd let myself become, even after I'd promised myself not this time, not again. They knew. They would never forget.

I had to get out. I zipped my sweatshirt all the way, I threw my hood up, and I booked it straight for the door. I was leaving the ballroom, leaving the dance, leaving these goddamn people, leaving this goddamn world forever—

When I saw her.

"Sweetheart?" I said. "Sweetheart, what's wrong?"

She was sitting alone, in the corner. She was at a table by the door, the last one I passed as I was about to flee the building. Her head was in her hands. Her entire body was shaking.

"Sweetheart? Talk to me, okay?"

I couldn't believe no one was with this poor girl. I threw one last look at the exit, but I walked toward her instead. I put my hand on her back. I sat down next to her.

"You've got to look at me. Look at me. Talk to me, sweets."

She was darn near having an epileptic fit, what with all the shivers and tears. She stank of so much alcohol.

"Mona, what's wrong?"

After minutes of sniffling and shaking, Mona Omidi finally took her head out of her hands, which were all covered in bleeding makeup. When she saw me, she did kind of a double take and frowned.

"Oh God . . . ," she said in a slurry, growly voice. "What are *you* doing here?"

"I . . ."

I wanted to run again, right then. I wanted to get in the car and rush home and find Mom's antidepressants and just . . .

But I had to help her first.

"Come on, girl," I said, pointing to my hideous outfit. "Isn't it obvious? I'm having the night of my life at prom!"

Mona didn't laugh at that. She cried even harder.

"Shhh, honey," I said, running my hand up and down her back and neck. "Shh, shh . . . Why don't you tell me everything?"

Mona looked up at me, her eyes wide and wet and so, so drunk. "Really?"

"Really," I said. "Tell me everything."

She took some tablecloth and blew her nose with it. "Well . . . I'm here with Cody, right? And we're in love, like, we've been dating all year, but, like . . . there were a couple weeks, way back in the fall, when we took a break, and I was with Liam—and yeah, like, it was so quick with Liam, and it's been good with Cody, but I'm . . . I'm such a bad . . ."

She burst into tears again.

"No, you're not," I said. "Keep going."

"And . . . with prom coming up, Cody and I were really excited, and he booked a hotel, and, you know, we've been keeping it slow on the physical side, first because of football season, and then because I wasn't ready, and Cody thought I was . . . The other night he asked me . . ."

"What happened?"

"I couldn't lie to him. I told him I wasn't a virgin, that I'd slept with Liam during our autumn break, that that had been my first time, and Cody, well, he took it okay . . . or he pretended to."

"But tonight . . ."

"We were pregaming—me, him, a couple of his friends, and they asked about the hotel, and like, he just *said* it. He blurted out what I'd done with Liam. He said it to them, and they stared at me like it was so funny, and he called me 'loose,' and he called me 'the Moaner' to my face, and he called me . . . he called . . ."

"What? What did he say?"

Mona looked at me with her huge, hysterical eyes, and her scrunched-up nose, and her drunk, half-open mouth. She stared at me, scanned me, judged me, like despite all the stuff she was saying about herself, she knew she was still better than me. The girl looked positively hateful.

"Cody called me . . . ," Mona said. "The second-biggest slut at school. Behind only you."

That moment wanted to hit me so hard. It wanted to punch me and cut me and make me gag. That moment wanted to make me wail and scream and run on home and do horrible, unthinkable shit to myself. Right then, in that moment, the universe wanted me to die.

But you know what?

The universe can suck a fat one.

I wanted to do something else.

"Hey, lady," I said. I was smiling. "I've got an idea."

Mona's mouth was hanging open. Her eyes were puddles of goop. I wondered if I could even get her to stand up.

"What?" she said. "What do you mean? Leave me alone."

I wrapped my fingers around her wrists. I squeezed them tight. "It'll make you feel better. It'll make *me* feel better."

"What do you want?"

I leaned in closer, crazy close. My eyes were inches from hers. "Just *promise*," I said, leaning all the way in, pressing my forehead up against hers, so close I was darn near kissing her mouth-to-mouth.

Mona blinked. She closed her lips. She nodded. "Okay," she said.

As soon as she said it, my smile exploded. "All right, girl. Let's dance."

There was real fast electronica playing, like a rave-type song, and once I felt that beat, I couldn't sit still any longer. I wouldn't let my homegirl sit, either. I stood her up, and two shakes later I was dancing right next to her, right in our own little corner of the room.

She was barely moving at first. She was standing, bobbing her head and kind of dangling her arms, but it wasn't enough for me.

I showed her how it was done.

I unzipped my sweatshirt and flung it off, into the corner of the room. I hurled my hair back and forth, side to side, all around. I jumped up and down like a kid on a hotel bed. I punched the air. I kicked it. I head-butted my cares away, and I was so off beat, I was such a terrible dancer, all my years of training were for shit. I grabbed Mona's arm and pulled her with me. We jerked and twerked from the table to the center of the floor. I shook. She shimmied. We shouted as loud as we possibly could. I'm sure people were watching us, whispering to each other, maybe even recording us, but I didn't look because I didn't care, and Mona didn't care because I didn't care. We held out our hands. We locked fingers. We began spinning. We twirled together, in epically dizzying circles. We shrieked and cursed and spun, we spun, we spun. It was ridiculous how uncoordinated we were. It was hilarious how much better this was than sex. We spun and fell and stood up again, and we sweat and panted, and we spun until the floor emptied out, until prom night was through. And we left the dance together, and we stayed together, and we danced forever till the sun came up.

I am a person. I am a wonderful person. My new friend Mona, she's a wonderful person too. We are wonderful people, and we get to do the things that wonderful people do, which means that whenever we want to, whenever the fancy strikes us, we get to dance.

19. ALLEGRA REY

"You nervous?"

I shook my head. The tassel on my cap came loose and fell over the front brim. I shook my head again to make it go away. "Not nervous," I said. "Just ready."

"Ready for your speech?" Wiley asked.

"Sure," I said. "But I think it goes beyond that. Of course I'll stand at that podium, try to impart whatever wisdom I can. But truly, what I'm most excited for is what comes after my speech ends."

Wiley grinned. "Grad Nite?"

"Naturally," I said. "I can't wait for tonight. Disneyland with you. The energy, the churros, the stolen moments when no one's looking our way on a dark, quiet ride. But there are so many other things I can't wait for too. This summer, and next year at DCCC, and fun times with my family, and wherever we end up transferring in two years, and . . . well, I guess just life. I'm ready for life, Wiley. I'm ready to spend it with you."

I clutched the front fabric of his robe and pulled him in for a tender kiss.

"You know," I added. "Perhaps 'ready' isn't the right word. Maybe it's more like . . . 'impatient.'"

Wiley blushed. I kissed him again, this time on the cheek.

"I'm ready to hear your speech," he said.

"I wrote it for you," I said.

"Then I'm impatient to hear your speech," he said.

I kissed my hand and pressed it to the top of his mortarboard. "I sure do like you, Wiley Otis."

Not so many minutes later, I stood up from my seat, out on the raised stage, under the blazing sun. I stepped forward to the mic.

"My fellow graduates . . . ," I said. "Whose time is it?"

None of the hundreds of seniors in front of me responded. None of the thousands of parents and supporters surrounding us in the football stadium made a single noise.

"Let's try that again," I said. "Whose time is it?"

Still no sound. Perhaps a cricket or two.

"Our time," I said. "It is 'our time,' as we have been exuberantly chanting at pep rallies and pole-scalings all year. But let me pose a question to you, dear graduates: What is the definition of this nebulous phrase? What, in fact, does 'our time' really mean?"

I snuck a peek at the graduating class. Most of them were whispering in each other's ears, or playing on their phones. There were even a few snorers. I kept going, though. I'd written this speech for them, and some of them especially. They were going to hear me, whether they listened or not.

"To answer this pressing inquiry, I have decided to consult the very same people whom we seem to refer to any time we face a difficult problem in AP Literature. . . .

"That would be old, dead white guys."

This got a couple of laughs, by which I mean two or three out of more than five hundred graduates. At least Wiley showed me some love. He overexaggerated a hearty guffaw and extended a big thumbs-up to the sky. That boy.

"In one of my all-time favorite novels, *Moby-Dick* by Herman Melville, the doomed protagonist Ahab soliloquizes, 'The path to my fixed purpose is laid with iron rails, whereon my soul is grooved to run. Over unsounded gorges, through the rifled hearts of mountains, under torrents' beds, unerringly I rush! Naught's an obstacle, naught's an angle to the iron way!'

"Essentially what the captain declares here is that the future is predetermined, or ironclad if you will, and that to change his fate would be impossible. Thus, he must face it head-on."

Anyone who'd tittered at my earlier joke was now stone silent again. I peeked at Wiley and even he was glassy-eyed. Still, I kept going.

"Yet in our schooling this year, we have also encountered the contradictory worldview. In Mr. Pargo's class, we analyzed the work of Robert Frost, who famously wrote, 'Two roads diverged in a wood, and I—I took the one less traveled by. And that has made all the difference.'"

I glanced momentarily over my shoulder, where Cole was sitting onstage behind me, in the salutatorian's spot. I can still remember his pessimistic interpretation of the Frost poem, back at the beginning of the year. I think about how this year has gone for him. I wonder if he now knows how wrong he was.

"And I can see we have some *Seussical* stars in our midst today, so surely you all know that Theodor Geisel, aka Dr. Seuss, was speaking to graduates everywhere in *Oh, the Places You'll Go!* when he stated, 'You have brains in your head. You have feet in your shoes. You can steer yourself any direction you choose.'"

Part of me wanted to look Brian's way as I referenced Dr. Seuss, part of me wanted to see how Horton would react, but most of me refused. I had a glimmer of a chance with him once, it's true, but that's not my life anymore. I've picked someone else. I can't go back.

"These two men, Frost and Seuss, do not abide by the predetermined future mind-set. They refuse to believe that our choices are made for us. Rather, they contend that each time we face a fork in the road, *we* select which path to take, and thus we control the outcome. We are the masters of our own destinies.

"So, my fellow graduates. We have our dueling perspectives. The Great White Whale versus the Cat in the Hat. God's will versus free will. Now, let me get all dialectic for a minute and put the question to you all . . . fate versus choice . . .

"Which of these views is right?"

Not a single person in the entire stadium was remotely interested in what I had to say. The school administrators behind me fanned themselves with their programs, to keep from both heat and boredom. The graduates before me were zoning out in such large numbers that it felt like we were in a folk tale, the kind in which an entire village is placed underneath a witch's sleeping curse. The silence in the arena completely and paradoxically drowned out my voice. Occasionally it was punctuated by the blasts of a couple of rogue foghorns. On the whole, I think the graduation attendees were more interested in what the foghorns had to say than they were in me.

"I'm going to talk about myself for a moment."

Now, this rhetorical pivot didn't exactly make everyone perk up with curiosity, but you know what? I didn't care.

"My mom became sick this year. Very sick. Cancer. Ovarian. Stage three. And thankfully she's here to see me graduate today, but who knows if she'll be at the next one.

"This year I made the decision to be there for her, to

stay with her, to devote everything I have to healing her, no matter what. Now, you may ask, was that really my choice, or was I preordained to take that route, due to circumstance or some higher power?"

At last a handful of graduates looked up from their phones. The "c" word tends to do that to people.

"This year I was also accepted to Stanford University, my longtime dream school. However, due to a variety of factors, I will not be attending next fall. Again, I ask: Is that the result of fate conspiring against me, or have I made my own proverbial bed?"

Now nearly all eyes were on me, although probably less because of the captivating gravitas of my words and more because my oversharing was turning me into something of a traffic accident, a disaster on display.

"Finally, on a much more affirming note, not so long ago I reconnected, and actually fell in love with, my best friend. And who knows what the future may hold for the two of us, but I intend to devote myself to him for as long as I have time left to love. So, once again, the question must be asked: Is that destiny, or is it my decision?"

Everyone was watching me. Everyone was staring at me. Wiley's cheeks were bright, bashful red. The foghorns were silent.

"Now, this is an age-old debate, one that practically predates time itself. It is the central query that, deep down, informs every piece of literature, every work of philosophy, every scientific experiment, every religious text. And, to be perfectly honest, as far as questions go, it's not exactly answerable.

"There is ample evidence both ways. There is confirmation bias everywhere you look. Reasonable, even brilliant minds, disagree wildly. There is not, strictly speaking, a right answer.

"But you know what? This is my speech. I am the valedictorian. This is my day. So here's what I think. I think that if I get to pick between fate or free will, then the answer is easy. . . .

"I choose having a choice.

"I choose to stay home with my family, because my family needs me, and I need them just as much. I choose to spurn Stanford, because there's more to life than on-paper accomplishments. I choose to love Wiley, because that's what love is; it's a choice, a mutual choice that benefits both parties.

"So why would I ever let that doubt creep in? Why would I leave my future in the hands of some mystical, malevolent force that I don't understand? Why should I constantly second-guess myself, perpetually regret the actions of my past, the things I should have done differently? Why should I live a life that is anything but my own?

"We are eighteen years old. Our futures stretch in front of us with infinite possibilities. We cannot know what's coming next. This, to put it mildly, is terrifying. We have no idea where any of our roads are going. Some will turn out to be dead ends. Others will become U-turns. Some will turn into one-way streets. Others, endless loops.

"But you know what?

"We are eighteen years old. Our futures stretch in front of us with infinite possibilities. We cannot know what's coming next. And this, to put it honestly, is *exhilarating.*

"This is it, graduates. This is our moment. Today is everything. The minute we turn our tassels, the split second we toss our caps into the air, we transform from high school students into adults, into full-fledged members of society. We begin the journey that will span the rest of our lives. So let us navigate that road cheerfully and compassionately, and above all, responsibly. Let us remember that we have brains in our heads and feet in our shoes. Let us never forget that we have exceptional, even divine power over our own choices. Let us glory in the fact that the future is ours.

"And with that, my fellow Bulldogs . . .

"I leave you with one final question . . .

"WHOSE TIME IS IT?"

"OUR TIME!"

"WHOSE TIME IS IT??"

"OUR TIME!!"

"WHOSE TIME IS IT???!!!"

"OUR TIME!!!!!!"

• • •

"That was incredible," Wiley said, jogging up to me.

The ceremony was over. The last bits of confetti were floating through the air. The field was littered with programs and mortarboards. That graduation song, the one about something unpredictable but having the time of your life, was blasting over the loudspeakers. Families were waddling out of their seats and down to the grass to take pictures with sweaty, exultant graduates.

"Do you see my mom and everyone?" I said. "Are they coming this way?"

"Oh," Wiley said. "Uh, probably."

He rubbed his nose. He sniffled once, twice. "There's actually, um, something I need to talk to you about."

"Really?" I said. "Right now?"

"It's important."

"But my family—"

"You have to go to Stanford," Wiley blurted.

It came so suddenly, the catch in my throat.

"What?"

Wiley paused. He took a slow, deep breath. So did I.

"I've wanted you," he said. "For the past ten years. More than anything, I've wanted you. I've dreamed of you every day. And I've gotta be honest. I never really thought this time would come. The day when you'd want me, too.

"But since you asked me to prom, since we got together,

I've had this feeling like, I dunno . . . and especially today, just now, listening to your speech, I couldn't get it out of my head, this nagging feeling, like . . ."

"No," I said. "Please don't say it."

"Like I'm holding you back," Wiley said. "Like I'll always hold you back if you stay back here. And even once . . . even after, you know, stuff happens, you know, with your mom, I mean, I'll continue to be your excuse, the one excuse that never goes away.

"You have to go to Stanford. As soon as possible. I don't know how you'll manage it, but you have to. I'm making you. Go there now. Tell them your mom's dying. Tell them it was your boyfriend's last wish, right before he dumped you."

"You," I said, "are being so condescending."

"I know," Wiley said, covering his mouth, almost smirking. "That's kind of your thing, huh? And in two minutes it can be your thing again. I promise.

"But, Allie, you can't patronize *me* by limiting your own potential, just because you think it'll help me. I won't let you. I'm okay on my own. Don't you worry about me."

"Well, what if . . . ," I tried. "What if you came up north? With me?"

"I've thought about that," he said. "And I wish it could work. But it wouldn't be enough. It wouldn't be fair. We'd just be tethering ourselves to the past. I want more for us."

"But," I said. "But I love you—"

Wiley shook his head.

"I love you too," he said, softly but firmly. "But I can't be with you. That's *my* decision. And as far as your college goes, I mean, you can make whatever choice you want, but like . . ."

He took a step toward me. He lowered his voice to a whisper. "Deep down, you know . . . you were always meant to do this."

With that, he opened his arms. I stepped into them, and he held me in the tightest, warmest hug. We didn't say anything else, not for some time. The two of us simply stood there, among the thousands of revelers, under the broiling sun, waiting for his mom and my family, waiting for whatever comes next, waiting, wondering, waiting.

Goodness.

Didn't see that one coming.

20. BRIAN MACK

It's my last image of high school, my girl, confetti and balloons falling all around her, music and "woooos!" filling the air. Her eyes are closed. Her little fingers are clenched. She's swaying, breathing, just being. She thinks no one is watching. She looks so huggable in her little yellow robe. She's the cutest she's ever been in her entire life.

And she's in the arms of another man.

Goddammit.

"Honey," my mom said. "Turn this way. I want to get a picture of you and Coach."

"Well, dang," my dad said. "Would you look at DeSean's leg? That boy'll be flying down the field in no time."

"Hey, fatface," my brother said. "You look like a potato in a fancy hat."

I shut them out, all of them. I kept my eyes on Allegra and Wiley. I watched those snuggle birds living out my dreams just ten feet away from me. As I watched them, I faced a choice. It was kind of like how Allie put it in her speech. I had two options:

One, I could march up to them. I could punch Wiley in the face and the dick, in that order. I could sweep Allegra into my arms and give her a make-out so sexy it would wipe out the whole past year and transform the next seventy. Then I could stomp on Wiley's d again, just for shits and gigs.

Two, I could implode. I could run away from the happy couple. I could return to my natural habitat, the lawn, where I'd sit in the grass and pick at my ass like a brain-dead cow for the rest of my days, all the way till they sent me to the burger factory.

Love. Loss.

Happiness. Helplessness.

Immortality. Irrelevance.

These were the paths I faced.

I went with door number three.

Everyone was headed for Disneyland.

That's the tradition. After the diploma ceremony comes Grad Nite, where you hop on a bus with all your best pals and cruise down to DLand, where you ride Space Mountain till you yak, and you pop pot brownies on It's a Small World, and you hook up with some freaky girl dressed as Captain Jack Sparrow on Mr. Toad's Wild Ride. Basically you do all the carefree shenanigans that crazy-ass kids with unlimited futures do at the Happiest Place on Earth.

But not me. My happiness was waiting elsewhere.

I found Cole in the student lot, leaning against his car. His robe and grad cap were already off. His parents were nowhere to be found. I wonder if they came today at all. He was smoking a cigarette.

"Hey, bud," I said. "Was hoping I'd find you."

Cole took a long drag. "What do you want?"

I pooched my lips out and crossed my eyes. "Well . . . ," I said all slowly. "I wath hoping . . . you could tell me . . . about the rabbith."

He shook his head. "Go home, Lennie. You're drunk."

I half laughed to myself. "Naw, dude, just playing."

Cole took another puff. "Okay." He blew some smoke into the sky.

I twiddled my fingers. "I . . . ," I said. "Look, I—"

"Just tell me why you're here," Cole said. "So I can tell you why you should leave."

I opened my arms wide. "I want to be buds again. I know I tuned you out. I blamed you for things crumbling between Allegra and me. And I regret that. But I'm over it now. You're the only friend I've got left, dude. I want to do right by you."

Cole made a little upside-down "u" with his mouth. He crushed out his cigarette. "Impossible," he said. "What's done is done."

"Come on, man, you serious? Didn't you hear Allie's speech? We have a choice. We always have a choice."

"Actually," Cole said. "We don't. Believe me, I thought so too. But then I tried to help you, and it ruined your year, not to mention Allie's and Nikki's. After that, I tried to win redemption. I tried to be heroic. But nobody gave two shits. And I know you have no one left, no one besides me, but look, I'm the reason that's the case. I bring out the worst in you, Brian, and I always will. I love what we had, but it's over. High school is over. And not to get all Greek philosopher about it, but all we have left to look forward to is adulthood . . . aka the long, lonely road to death."

Cole turned away from me and stared down the hill, off into town, as far away from here as he could possibly get.

I let out a sigh. "I don't know, man. I just thought there might be somewhere out there where you and me could do a little good. But yeah, that was probably dumb."

I took one last glimpse at my ex-friend. Then it was my turn to fade away. I pulled the stupid hat off my sad potato head. I dropped it to the asphalt. I plodded off, through the parking lot, past the cars, back to the drawing board, back to square one.

Cole whistled. The loud kind, with his fingers.

I spun around.

"Wait," he said. "I know a place."

• • •

The first thing that hit me was that familiar smell. We got inside, and it was like sewage meets tapioca meets Febreze meets Florida. After just half a sec in there, I swear I almost vommed and peaced immediately. I mean, if I was going to throw up anyway, at least I could do it on Space Mountain. And Allegra would be there. . . .

But naw. We couldn't run from this. This was our density. I mean, destiny. I mean—

"Ramon!" Cole shouted at one of the handful of people in the room.

"Maggie!"

"Duke!"

"Tyrone!"

"Inez!"

". . ."

"*Happy Philanthropy Friday!!!!!*"

When those folks saw us, their faces just exploded with joy. Cole jumped into the center of the room, and he was like the stuffed animal from childhood they thought they'd lost forever. He gestured to me, and I was like the brand-new family pet.

"People of Casa de Maria," Cole said. "Meet Brian. Brian, meet my friends."

"I like your cowboy hat, mister cowboy hat guy," I said to Duke. "And your attitude. Can I call you 'Hattitude'?"

"What's the hot goss from the past few months?" Cole said to Maggie. "I heard Noreen said we're not getting clam chowder anymore, so we're stuck with corn tortilla instead. What kind of goat shit is that?"

"I remember you from before," I said to Inez, who had just given me a jowly, lipsticky cheek kiss. "Can I call you 'Girlfriend'? I really need a girlfriend."

"Speaking of girlfriends," Cole said. "Heard it through the grapevine that you just got one, Tyrone! When are we gonna meet her? She too good for us? She at some fancy hospice on the other side of town? Or are you making her up? You can tell me. I can keep a secret."

"Ramon," I said. "That mustache is absolutely incredible. I'm gonna call you 'Porn Lips.' You can thank me later."

We stayed there for hours. We slopped soup, and we played cards and Connect Four, and we listened to their old-people stories, at least some of which I'm sure are true, and we told them about graduation, and we talked about next year, about our hopes and fears but mostly hopes, and the whole thing was honestly, and maybe not-so-surprisingly, a gigantic friggin' blast. It wasn't philanthropy at all. It was just damn good times.

Look at me, Coach. I finally came to play on Friday night.

"I gotta say," I told Cole at the end of the evening, as we washed ladles and put bowls away. "If you'd've asked me a year, or even a few hours ago, where I'd be tonight, I never would have said here."

Cole was admiring his reflection in one of the pots. He adjusted his hairnet. It looked weirdly stylish on him.

"Well," he said, "to quote the late, great Robert Frost: 'The future . . . it be a mysterious bitch.' "

I laughed a little. "Come on," I said. "Be real."

"You know I can't 'be real.' I am an artificial creation, designed by you humans to horrify and arouse the world. Sixty percent murder drone, forty percent glambot."

I plucked his hairnet off his head and tossed it in the sink.

"Seriously, man. Don't you ever think . . . what if things had gone differently, you know?"

Cole paused to think. "Honestly? Nope. I don't."

"Come on. For real? You never think like, what if you made this choice differently, or that one? I mean, what if I never met Allegra? What if I never auditioned for the play with you?"

"Guh," he said. "You humans. Too blind to see that one day the sun will explode and none of this crap's gonna matter anyway."

"I'm not saying there's anything I can *do* about it. I'm just wondering."

Cole widened his eyes, wiggled his fingers, and made a spooky "oooooh" sound. "*Brian* . . . you are now entering the Twilight Zone. . . .

"What if you boned Allegra, and your d was so magical it cured her mom's illness?

"What if Stanford gave me a special scholarship for evil cheaters who feel bad about it later?

"What if there's a parallel universe in which we're all just slaves to our omnipotent overlord Scrotes?

"What if your daddy had pulled out a nanosecond earlier, and you never amounted to anything more than a lil' piece of sperm?

"What if? *What if?* Oooooooh . . ."

Cole laughed sarcastically. I stared down at the bowls. There was a while when we said nothing.

After a few moments, he spoke up again. By this point his face had changed. Before it was a smile. Now it was, I don't know, something pretty different.

"Don't dwell on what could have been," Cole said. "It hurts too much."

"Okay," I said. I nodded. I kept nodding. "Yeah. Fine. Yeah. Okay."

But I don't believe him.

ROAD TWO: GRADUATION

16. NIKKI FOXWORTH

Mona said it was okay.

I told DeSean yes that day in the Greek. I accepted his promposal, because what with everyone staring at me, what with the band about to launch into a happy song, I kind of had to say yes. But I swear I would have taken it back. I absolutely would have rebuffed DeSean if Mona had had any problem at all. But I found her after lunch, and she was so cool with it.

"Of course you should go with the guy who asked you," she said.

"Yeah," I said. "It's a no-brainer, right?"

"You sure you can trust him?"

"Yes," I said. "I really am. How about you? You sure you'll be all right?"

Mona smiled. "Oh my God. Obviously. Forget about me."

"You know I could never do that."

"Just do one thing for me," Mona said. "Have the best prom ever. You deserve it."

"I'll try my best," I said.

It was storybook, the way tonight started off. D wore his father's tux. I wore bridal white. We took pics out on my back patio, and my parents had the proudest expressions as they snapped photos of us, like I was a good little church girl all over again. DeSean got the fanciest stretch Hummer to pick us up, and he joked that he was paying for it with "recruiting violation money." He kept me laughing all the way through dinner with impressions of his coach, goofy Male Ballet moves, and the most inappropriate jokes about groping my breast. At the same time, he was so considerate, too. He took time to apologize for how he behaved toward me this year, the breakup and stuff. He made sure to say that sex wasn't everything to him, that it was the last thing on his mind. I looked into his eyes as he said it. They were perfectly sincere.

We got to the Hyatt. The theme of the dance was "Hollywood Nights." As DeSean walked me down the red carpet and into the ballroom, I really did feel like a movie starlet, only without all the baggage that follows those poor actresses around, everybody reading about their divorces and drug addictions. I felt like the cleanest, most glamorous, most self-assured version of a movie star—the kind you see on the cover of a fashion magazine, or winning an Oscar, and you think, *This woman has it so together.*

"Damn, Nikki!" some guy shouted as we walked past.

"Sexy mama!" another girl chimed in.

"Take it off!"

I rolled my eyes at that. DeSean and I stifled big, dorky grins.

I did see a few things on the walk that made me mildly uncomfortable.

First there was Brooklyn and Channing, and a few other mean girls from dance. I didn't want to run into them for obvious reasons. None of them saw me, though, as I walked past. They were all on their phones.

Then there was Wiley. He was with Cole. They weren't looking my way either as we reached the door, but they were staring a little too pointedly in the other direction, like when the cat's in the litter box and you don't want it to know you know it's doing its business, because otherwise it'll freak out and run away.

Finally, just before we got inside, DeSean and I passed Mona. She looked dazzling in seafoam and bronze. She was standing by herself, though. I felt bad for her.

"Are you okay?" she said.

"Huh?"

"Are you okay?"

"I should be asking you the same thing," I said. "You look kinda lonely, sweetheart."

"Oh no," she said.

"What?"

"You don't know."

"Holy shit," DeSean said, pulling his phone out of his pocket. "The hell is *this*?"

Suddenly everybody on the red carpet was eyeing me. I looked over my shoulder, through the glass doors, into the ballroom. Everybody on the dance floor was staring at me. I looked at everyone's hands. There were dozens of phones everywhere. I glanced at the video on DeSean's screen. I saw the skinny girl with the long brown hair. That's all I needed to see.

"Those bitches," I said, and I got ready to charge at them, even though I didn't know who those bitches were. I mean it could have been Brook and Chan, paying me back for the locker-room episode. But it just as easily could have been Wiley, lashing out at me for whatever twisted reason, trying to make something out of his pathetic life.

In any event, I was going to do it. I was going to bash some skulls together. I was going to make those wicked people screech like slaughtered hogs. Even if I had to take on every damn hater at the dance, I was going to do it.

Then I heard the commotion behind me.

It came from inside. Gasps at first, then *oohs* and whispers. People's phones shot up automatically. The crowd parted as if summoned to by a higher power. The ballroom door swung open, and out walked the last person I expected to see.

He was tall, dark, and unfortunately, very handsome. He had a cleft on his chin and reddish-brown stubble on his cheeks. And of course, of course, of course, he was holding roses.

"Look!" the gawkers whispered all around me.

"Is that *him?*"

"No way—"

"Holy fu—"

"It's the guy from the video!"

I am not letting myself repeat his name. I will not give him the power.

He ambled toward me, holding the bouquet to his chest. People fell over themselves to get out of his way, like he was some kind of royalty. I found myself walking too, walking helplessly toward him, a prisoner headed to her execution.

"Hey, Nik," he said when we reached each other. "You know I've been searching for you all year? I've been missing you something awful."

I stared at the ground.

"Not a day goes by when I don't think about what I did. I've spent all these months reflecting, regretting.

"Lucky for me, some friends of yours found me online. They told me about prom. I found a cheap ticket out. Now here I am. How cool is that?

"I get to tell you how I sorry I am. I get to show you how much I've changed. I'm a new man. I really am."

I couldn't. I couldn't. I kept staring down.

"Come on, Nikki. Smile for me, girl."

Just then—

"RRRRRAAAAAAAHHHHHHHH!!!!!!!!!!!!!"

Like a bullet train, DeSean came hurtling out of the shadows, he shot right to where we were. As all the folks around us lost their minds, D left his feet and flew at my tormentor, knocking him to the ground with a perfect football tackle. With his knees on the asshole's chest, DeSean started throwing punches, one at the ribs, another at the throat, like he was the one who deserved the right to apologize to me, not my ex, and I didn't even have time to consider whether that was true. That's because the guy who destroyed my life, he fought back. He took his hands and flung them at DeSean's neck, and he took his legs and wrapped them around D's body. In one motion he swung himself up and slammed DeSean to the ground, and he pinned all his weight on top of my prom date, and then he started punching and kneeing, and slapping too, and he got body blows in for, like, ten solid seconds. DeSean looked down for the count, completely spent, practically unconscious, until *he* battled back. He kicked the asshole square in the groin. He sprang back up, and everybody around them was gasping and cheering, taping the drama and watching me squirm, living and dying with my every reaction as these two men fought for my honor, fought for my virtue, fought for the right to call me theirs.

And I was trapped all over again, in the room with two doors.

No matter what happened tonight, I was the loser.

Obviously, if my ex won, then that would be humiliating. I'd be seen as the enemy, the *femme fatale*. The seductress who put the hero in a spell for just long enough to weaken him, who through her own careless promiscuity let the big boss strike the final blow, after which he could take her away to his lair and do whatever he wanted with her.

Then again, if DeSean was the victor, if my Trojan warrior in shining armor was able to slay my demon, then the result would be just as, if not even more, shameful. I would be the hooker who got saved despite herself. I'd be Mary Magdalene. DeSean would try to reform me, and everyone else would avoid me, and no would ever know me, not a single soul would ever think of me as anything but that poor, misguided wretch.

It's a funny feeling to watch the end of your story be determined right in front of your eyes and you don't even care.

And—

Wait.

I *didn't* care, did I?

I didn't care.

Oh my God. I really didn't care.

The longer I watched them scuffle, the louder the masses got, the more my reputation was at stake . . . the less invested I felt.

I wasn't regretful. I wasn't anxious. I wasn't depressed. I wasn't afraid.

I was just bored.

"Hey," I said under my breath as the two overgrown boys continued to beat the living tar out of each other. I knew I didn't have to speak up, or move at all. The person I was saying "hey" to, I knew she'd be right behind me.

"You wanna get out of here?"

Mona and I spent prom night at the spot. From ten or so until darn near breakfast, it was just the two of us, hanging on a blanket beneath the night sky, like it always should have been. Now, it wasn't your typical night at the spot—there obviously wasn't any kissing or feeling up, and there certainly wasn't any sex—but there was absolutely everything else, all the things a prom night actually needs:

Laughter. Great conversation. Milk shakes.

Stargazing. Spooning. Pizza.

And dancing, of course. So much terrible dancing.

There are no bad girls. There are no good girls. It's all made-up. It's just a fairy tale.

17. BRIAN MACK

Allie was by herself. Everyone else was in the middle of the dance floor. They were shouting "woo!" and sex-grinding. But she was alone at a table, staring into space. She looked hot as balls in a sparkly gold dress. I asked my teacher if I could go talk to her. He said yes.

"Hey," I said.

"Oh," she said. "Hi, Brian."

"Are you okay?"

Her face didn't move. Her eyes budged a little but not really.

"Are you having fun at prom?"

She kind of shook her head. "I think I'm just tired."

"How was Stanford?"

She twisted in her chair. She wiggled her body. It seemed like she had ants in her bra.

"I'm happy you get to go there next year," I said. "That's so tight."

She didn't say anything to that.

"Hey. You wanna dance?"

Allie pointed at the door. "It's so loud in here," she said. "I'm feeling overstimulated. I think I need some time outside."

"Okay," I said. "Can I come?"

"No," she said. "No, Brian."

"Okay," I said. "I get it."

I think I get it.

Allie wants what we all want. She wants to be happy. I don't blame her for that. Next year, she needs to go away to be happy. Right now, she needs to be by herself. That makes sense. I want her to feel good.

I don't have a problem being by myself. I kind of like it sometimes. It's nice how no one's around who feels like they have to help you. Also you get to think about stuff.

Today after school, I went to my lawn. I sat and I plucked. I plucked and I thought. I thought about Allie. I think about her a lot. I hope not too much.

I'm happy Allie gets to go away next year. It makes me so stoked, thinking about her playing in the band at football games, imagining her hanging out with her smart new friends. I want it for her. I want her to have that life.

But I want it for me, too. That's what messes me up. Because I had it before. I had a great life with Allie. She read to me. She talked to me. She even kissed me back. And then she left, just like that, wham bam. She picked somewhere else. I wonder if I'm the reason why. I don't want to be alone anymore.

A loud sound snapped me out of my thoughts. It jingled in my ears, like coins in my pocket. It sounded like Allie used to, back when I gave her piggyback rides. Someone was laughing.

Two people were laughing. I looked up and saw them across the lawn from me. There were two pretty girls. They were having some kind of picnic. One of them had tan brown skin and eyes like a cat. The other had crazy shiny hair and eyes like a baby.

Maybe I could talk to them.

"There you are!" I yelled. "I've been looking all year for you!"

Nikki stopped laughing. She looked at Mona. Mona looked at me. She smiled and waved. I ran up to where they were.

"I've been missing you," I said. "It's great to see you again, Nikki."

Nikki's eyes got bigger than normal. She looked down at the grass.

"Cool if I sit with you guys?"

Mona nodded. She patted the ground. I sat down. She handed me a stick of licorice.

"So," I said in between bites. "You guys go to prom?"

"Look," Nikki said, still staring down. "I feel sick to my stomach, Brian. I realize I never came back to visit you. I want you to know I've been thinking of you all year. I know it's no consolation, everything I'm saying now, but I so deeply regret not being a better friend. I've punished myself for it plenty."

She sighed real soft. I smooshed some grass in my fingers. I pulled a handful out of the dirt and crushed it down to nubbins, till I got the green bits all up in my hand skin.

"That's okay," I said. "I understand."

Nikki and Mona looked at each other.

"Really?" Nikki said.

"Duh," I said. "We all have our own stuff to deal with. You shouldn't punish yourself one bit. I'm just happy to see you now."

"Good man," Mona said.

"Lord," Nikki said. "What a relief."

"Yeah," I said. "Plus, you were right to take a break from me. Didn't I grab your boob? That was hella creepy."

The second I said it, Nikki, Mona, and I all exploded into laughter. Theirs sounded like little Christmas bells. Mine sounded like a moose farting out of its face.

We laughed about lots of things. They told me why DeSean and that guy fought each other at prom, how it was all about Nikki. I said I had no idea; I thought it was just a big penis contest. Mona said that's the real reason they fought. Then Mona started talking about her mom, like how strict she is. I guess her mom judges her for every little thing she eats. I said we should trade moms, because mine's been trying to fatten me up like the witch from Hansel and Gretel. After that, I told them I'm actually trying to get fit again, because Coach asked me about playing football next year, and I said I told him that sounds amazing, because all I want is to be a Bulldog again. Mona and Nikki both looked so freaked when I said it. Their skin went pale. Their smiles went away. But then I said, "Just kidding. Oh man, got you so good," and the three of us just laughed. We laughed like little kids for the longest time.

"This is fun," I said. "I'll miss this."

"Us too," Nikki said.

"I wish you weren't leaving," I said.

"I know," Mona said. "You should get to graduate with us. It sucks they're not letting you. But don't worry. We'll come back and visit a bunch."

"And for what it's worth," Nikki said, "it's not like we're particularly jazzed about next year, either."

Mona nodded. "Yeah, I'm sure city college will be fine and all, but you won't be missing anything special, Brian."

"So true," Nikki said. "I'm actually kind of dreading it, to be honest."

I grabbed at some grass. I shook my head. "Well, that's no good."

Nikki and Mona looked at each other.

"What do you mean?" Mona said.

"I don't want you guys to have a bad time."

"No one does," Nikki said. "But maybe that's just what adulthood is. Slogging through life, letting the bad times stack up and hoping you'll reach that one lucky moment when you have at least a sliver of a chance at happiness."

I said it quiet. "No."

Nikki's eyes got narrow. "What do you mean, 'no'?"

"You should make your happiness," I said.

"Sweetheart," she said. "It's all well and good when you say it like that, but I'm not exactly sure how we're supposed to 'make' our own—"

"You should help people."

Nikki smiled, like she still thought I was dumb. "Brian, if you want us to come over next year and read stories to you, then all you need to do is ask."

I made a fart noise with my mouth. "No," I said. "You're not listening. It's not about me. I don't need any more help."

Nikki shook her head. "I don't understand. Then who would we be helping?"

"I don't care," I said. "Anyone. Old people. Sad people. Girls with bad boyfriends. Boys who have no friends. Dogs. Like, fat ones that can't walk. You'll know who they are. You'll know when you see them. But if you're ever feeling stuck, then the best way out is to help someone else, someone who feels stuck too. Jeez. I thought that was obvious."

Mona looked at Nikki. Nikki looked at the ground. We all sat quiet for a sec. Then Nikki reached her hand out. She touched her hand to mine. She wrapped her fingers around it. She gave my hand a big ol' squeeze.

"It can be easy to forget these things," she said. "But you have a funny way of making me remember. You're very clever, you know that, Brian?"

"Yeah," I said. "I am."

We stayed on the terraces for the longest time, me and my friends. It was the best. I loved helping them, the way Allie used to help me. Not by doing too much, just by being there. All I did was listen. I tried to make them feel important. I think it worked. I can't wait to see who they'll help next.

After a while, Nikki and Mona had to go home, but we made plans to hang again soon. I'm going to give them dance lessons.

I stayed on the grass for a little longer after they left. Like I said, I like being by myself. I like sitting. It's good to think about my life.

But I wasn't alone for even a minute. Before I realized it, someone else showed up on the lawn. Another friend for me.

"Hey, Big Mack. You wanna make a movie . . . ?"

18. WILEY OTIS

It's official: I'm not graduating.

Ms. Fawcett told me today. She said she couldn't figure out why I'd completely quit on my schoolwork, that she was shocked and disappointed in my effort. I didn't react. She mentioned that I could still take summer school classes, but that I seriously need to get my act together. I zoned her out. She told me about the college opportunities that might one day be available to me. I didn't care. I'm not supposed to be some scholar or whatever. I'm supposed to be a filmmaker.

After school, I waited in the library. I waited for Cole, but he never came by. Screw it. I didn't need him. He wasn't essential to the plan anyway. I made the final preparations. I checked my backpack. I poked around the hallways to make sure they were empty. I walked through the campus, maybe for the final time. I made my way to the front lawn.

Brian was sitting there, all by himself, just as I'd expected. He had the emptiest expression on his face, like a zombie. His mouth was hanging open, like a fish.

"Hey, Big Mack," I said. "You wanna make a movie . . . ?"

He squinted at me. The wheels seemed to turn in his head. After a few seconds, something clicked.

"Wiley," he said. "Wiley Otis."

"Wow," I said. "How'd you know my name?"

"You were in my econ class."

"How'd you remember, though?"

"Because I'm very clever."

I couldn't help but smile at that. "Indeed you are, Brian. Indeed you are."

I walked over to where he was sitting. I dropped my backpack and sat across from him.

"I know you're smart," I said. "As a matter of fact, that's why I came to talk to you, buddy. Because I need your help."

"Help with what?"

I unzipped my backpack and took out the nice HD camera I recently bought. "I'm making a movie," I said. "A documentary, actually. And I want to interview you for it. How would you like that?"

Brian scratched his chest. "I dunno," he said. "What's the movie about?"

I held the camera to his face. I hit record. "Allegra Rey."

"About Allie? Why?"

"Because she's our friend. This is a surprise for her. Do you want to be in the movie?"

He shrugged. "Okay."

I held out my fist. Without thinking, he held his out too. We bumped fists. We blew them up.

"I happened to notice you and Allie chatting it up at prom," I said. "I've seen you two a lot together lately."

"Oh yeah," Brian said. "She's my best friend."

"Best friends. Exactly. And most of this year she's eaten lunch with you every day, yes?"

"Yes."

"And she helped you with rehearsals for the spring show, yeah?"

"Yeah."

"And for several months she's been coming to your house each night for your rehabilitation, right?"

"I don't know what that means."

"Does she come to your house or not?"

"Oh. Yeah. She comes over. We play games. We read books. I mean, we used to read books."

I looked up from the camera. "Used to?"

"Well," Brian said. "Allie doesn't hang out with me anymore."

I steadied my hand to keep it from shaking. I spoke again, in a softer voice. "May I ask, ah . . . what happened?"

Brian picked a clod of dirt out of the ground. He threw it away. "I don't wanna talk about it."

"No. Of course. I didn't mean to pry. . . ."

"Things just got weird is all."

I nodded. "Totally, totally. It's your business. We can leave it at that."

"Yeah," Brian said. "Allie told me she got 'overstimulated.'"

I repeated the word. "'Overstimulated.'"

"Yeah," he said. "But I don't wanna talk about it."

"For sure, for sure. I can respect that."

Both of us sat. Neither of us spoke. I just let the camera do its thing.

Then I said something, in the lowest possible whisper. "Brian, would you say that you and Allie . . . became close?"

"What? Well, duh. We were best friends."

"Did she ever share her deepest feelings with you?"

"What do you mean? Like did she talk about how she used to be friends with you? Only a little. She doesn't like you that much anymore, but she's over it. That's what she said."

I tried not to dwell on those words.

"No, no. What I'm saying is, did she ever reach out to you in a way that felt . . . above and beyond?"

"I don't know what that means."

"Brian, did she ever kiss you?"

"Well, uh . . ."

"Brian?"

"I don't know. Um, I don't know if I should—"

"Tell the truth, Brian."

"Yeah, she did, but it was, like, normal I guess. Normal kissing."

"Did she make out with you?"

"Yeah, yeah, she did, but that's not the reason we stopped hanging out, you know, and like, why is this in your movie, because I don't know why people would want to know about that, and like, why are you making a movie about her anyway—?"

"Did she ever . . . sleep with you?"

"WILEY!

"WILEY OTIS!

"STOP!!!"

Cole burst into view, rushing from the student lot. He sprinted like mad, his finger jabbing at my face. Brian beamed when he saw his old costar. I felt myself become small.

"Wiley," Cole said, huffing as he reached us. "What the *hell* are you doing here?"

I crossed my arms. "What the hell *weren't* you doing here?"

"Hey," Brian said. "What's going on?"

"Shut up," I said.

"Shame on you," Cole said. "I specifically said Operation Forest and Jenny was a *no go.*"

I couldn't help but scoff. "You're kidding me, right?"

"Turn that thing off," Cole said, lunging for my hand.

"Screw you," I said, jerking the camera away. "Whatever happened to 'Don't get sad; get even'?"

"Wiley, this isn't the way—"

"Who are you, Obi-Wan from the prequels?"

"There's more to life than petty revenge."

"Since when are you some noble saint?"

"Since five minutes ago, but you know the drill with Jesus; you can convert anytime."

I let out a laugh. "I don't believe it. I do not believe it. All this gossip stuff was your freaking idea to begin with, remember? What about Nikki?"

"Nikki?" Brian said. "Where?"

"Goddammit," I said. "Shut up."

"*Be nice,*" Cole said. "And you're absolutely right. We made a mistake with Nikki, but now we can—"

"So we ruined her life, but now we get to walk away whistling?"

"Look, I regret what befell Nikki. We can't ever let something like that happen again. And we'll atone for it in time, but first we must change. Turn the camera off."

"Make me."

"Allegra has a future."

"What about my future?"

"Let's talk about your future."

"You're full of it, asshole."

"Look, I'm not saying I'm one hundred percent reformed. But I can help you."

I laughed again. I snorted. "This is all about your father, isn't it?"

"So what if it is?"

"You're still hung up on that stupid little pep talk, aren't you?"

"Well, actually, he made some excellent points."

"I don't believe this. A few bullshit words from your deadbeat dad and suddenly you're a goddamn guardian angel. Suddenly *you* of all people get to tell *me* how to live *my* life."

"Just turn that camera off."

"You can't just change. You know that, right?"

"Turn that camera *off.*"

Cole dove at me and slapped the camera out of my hand. It bounced on the ground. It broke. The memory card popped out. Cole fell on the grass to claim it. I lunged at him. Cole tried to stick the card in his pocket. I seized his hand. I clutched his fingers. I bent his arm back. Cole wriggled free, but the card slipped out. I threw myself at it. So did he. We dove at the same time. Neither of us grabbed it. We were both on the ground, wrestling over control, fighting for the future.

I couldn't believe what Cole was doing. This was the

same guy who promised he could solve my problems. He swore to me that he knew the way. He was the one who *made* me this way. And now *he* gets to act all rehabilitated? He gets to wash his hands of Nikki, of Allegra, and pretend like those sins are mine alone? He gets to leave me here in the darkness? No way.

Suddenly, I couldn't move.

The Big Mack was squatting on me. Brian had me pinned, all his weight on top of my body. I couldn't budge. I could barely think. I tore an arm free and elbowed him—*whabam*—right in the face.

"Ow!" Brian yelled, burying his nose in his hands.

"Monster," Cole said, barrel-rolling out of my reach.

"It hurts," Brian said, blubbering at the top of his lungs.

"How dare you," Cole spat, a man possessed. He knelt above me. I couldn't get up. Brian was still on top of me, still crushing my spine. I caught sight of Cole. I couldn't believe what he was doing to me, how swiftly he had betrayed me. He stared me down, not blinking at all. Without warning, he drew his hand back and slapped me, down and across the face. With just one move, without a second thought, Cole finished our friendship, with everything he had.

Cole helped Brian to his feet. He collected the memory card. He checked to make sure Big Mack was okay.

And they left me. As I lay there, my head whirring, my

face throbbing, the two of them walked away. Cole put his arm around his new best friend's back.

Before he left, though, he turned around. He said one final thing to me. A series of words I couldn't possibly forget.

"You fucking loser. Why did I even bother with you?"

Twenty minutes later, I pressed the doorbell.

Allie opened it on the first ring. She was wearing a red hoodie with STANFORD across the chest. Her hair looked different from normal. It was more up than I've ever seen it, pulled back and shimmery. She looked really great.

"Wiley?" she said, her hands on her hips. "My goodness, what an unanticipated and yet not altogether unpleasant surprise. You know—"

I stuck my hand up quick.

Like any good musician, she went quiet immediately.

I coughed to clear my throat. "You've made all the right choices," I said. "Congratulations on your success."

Without adding another word, and before she could say any of her own, I walked away. I went back through her mother's garden, right onto the sidewalk, down my front pathway, and into my house, where my whole life awaits me.

19. ALLEGRA REY

We milled about the softball field, like wildlife around a watering hole, waiting to graduate. Much like on the savannah, it was sweltering in the hour leading up to the ceremony, easily ninety-five degrees, plus even stickier inside our church clothes and polyester gowns. Also maintaining the circle of lifeness of it all were the creatures themselves, the soon-to-be-graduates, so reductively animalistic in the predictability of their rituals.

There were the big cats, the prides of lionesses and coalitions of cheetahs, checking their phones for gossip on prey and promising to hunt together all summer and into college. There was the crash of rhinos, smashing into each other for sport and boasting about the size of their horns. There was the cackle of hyenas, snickering at the other beasts from their Hacky-Sack circle and scavenging on whatever munchies someone happened to leave behind. And of course, there were those without groups, there were the free birds like me, who mostly try to stay above the fray, who look forward to migrating hundreds and hundreds of miles away as soon as all this is over.

As the sun blazed on, and as diploma time drew near, I watched and waited, and there were but two animals that I could not for the life of me locate.

One was Wiley, my erstwhile friend, the erratic baboon. I haven't seen him much at all lately, save for this past week, when he came to my front door and cryptically fled just as quickly. I did hear from a frustrated Ms. Fawcett that he hasn't earned enough credits to graduate, which explained why he wasn't out on the field, sweating through his cap and gown like the rest of us. Still, I hoped he'd at least be in attendance at the ceremony, watching from the bleachers or something. Obviously it's been tough between the two of us these past several months, but one weird year shouldn't define the rest of our lives. I miss that boy. I wanted him to hear my speech.

Just as I finished having that thought, I saw him.

Not Wiley.

The other lost animal.

Horton the elephant.

Brian wasn't wearing a mortarboard. He doesn't get to graduate either, not after he missed the better part of the whole fall semester. Still, he was out on the field, and he seemed jubilant to be playing with his old friends, who appeared to have rediscovered him just in time for today. There he was, choreographing a multistep handshake with

DeSean. There he was, accepting a noogie from Tua and giving a wet willie to Scrotes. There he was, flirting with Nikki and Mona, like this was nine months ago, like he was the Big Mack on campus all over again.

I haven't talked to Brian but for a few fleeting moments on prom night, and before then, not since the night in his bedroom. It's the complete inverse of my situation with Wiley. With Wiley, I felt betrayed, but now that I'm on the brink of leaving forever, I'd love to get back in touch, as long as he can muster the maturity. Alas, I can't seem to find him anywhere. Whereas with Brian, he and I had a phenomenal year. I mean in so many ways I think it was the best year I've ever had—

Which is why I can't bear to face him again.

Which is why I retreated from the sun-beaten graduates and into the shadows.

Brian has his other friends now. I don't think he needs me anymore. I had to get away. I had to be alone. I'm not trying to betray him.

I just had to practice my speech.

"Fellow Bulldogs," I said minutes later, up at the podium, all eyes on me.

"I stand before you, in keeping with tradition, as your valedictorian and commencement speaker. Now, I'm not sure what exactly entitles me to be up here. Presumably the logic goes that if I was able to amass a 4.8 GPA, more than one thousand community service hours, and a 'Most Likely to Study Through the Birth of Her Own Child' senior superlative, then so too must I be able to impart some sagacious advice as we convene on this field in the final moments of our collective adolescence.

"And yet . . . am I so qualified to be giving advice? After all, look at the decisions I've made over the past year:

"I turned my back on my neighbor. I let my relationship with my lifetime best friend go dormant, to the degree where I don't know if I will ever get to speak to him again."

I glanced up from the lectern and into the stands, in the vain hope of spotting Wiley. But there were too many people. The glare was too bright. There was no sign of him anywhere.

"Following this, I made a new closest friend, a new companion, but I left him in the lurch as well, right at the moment when he needed me most."

I caught a peek at Brian, sitting on the sideline in a place of honor with his parents. He looked bored, expressionless. He had zero notion that he'd just been referenced.

"And now I am on the brink of straying from my family. I am going to leave them for intellectual paradise. I am about to abandon them for good—which I know is the right thing to do—but still, it feels unfair; it will always feel so selfish and beyond wrong."

I knew precisely where my family was sitting, but I couldn't bear to lay eyes on them, not unless I wanted to be wiping mascara off my cheeks through the remainder of my speech.

"I have made these choices. I do not take pride in any of them. And, dwelling on these dubious decisions, I can honestly say that I'm sorry, but I have no idea why I deserve to be up here. I refuse to believe that you all should listen to a word I say.

"And yet . . ." I lifted my hands from the podium. I raised my voice. I looked out at the graduates. They needed to hear this.

"What if the most selfish thing of all is my assumption that these choices are mine alone to make?

"When it comes to forecasting our futures, we get caught up in this familiar debate: destiny or decision? Fate or free will? It's the oldest question in the world, not to mention the least answerable. Life feels like a series of independent choices with rational outcomes, right until the moment when everything goes wrong, when suddenly it becomes so tempting to believe the exact opposite, that life is nothing more than a relentless barrage of arbitrary punishments and unearned rewards.

"But, graduates, I stand before you today, as your valedictorian, to tell you that this debate, irresistible as it is, is made-up. It's thoroughly fictional. There is no fate. There is no free will. There is no 'deserve.' There is no 'unfair.' To quote the Book of Jeremiah, and a cannibalistic robot girl from a novel I once read, 'Our lives are *not* our own.'

"We do not live in our own, separate, completely isolated bubbles. Of course we do not. We are here together. We are interconnected, all of us. We are tied together, to our family members, to our friends, to the random kid in econ to whom we've never once spoken.

"Each and every choice we make exists not in its own universe, but as the end result of all others that have been made before. And no matter which course we take in a given moment, we cannot help but be at the mercy of those other decisions, all of which have led to this point.

"I am going to college not just because I want to, but because my parents couldn't. I am leaving my new friend behind, but who is to say if we ever would have become close if not for a random, tragic accident, one that happened on this very field. I played a role in letting things slip with my neighbor, but there were so many other factors too, far beyond my control.

"This truth is overwhelming. It's terrifying, to realize how powerless each of us is in the grand scheme of things. It so easy to gaze up at a colossal skyscraper, or at billions of stars in the midnight sky, and to feel impossibly intimidated, to know you are so, so small.

"But it's empowering, too! It's exhilarating! Just because

our lives are not our own does not mean we sit here and do nothing. We cannot stay sitting on our hands, taking life on the chin, waiting to expire. Screw that. We get to be here. We get to be heroes. We get to bear witness to the awesome and perplexing ways of the world. We get to play a part in this madness, an integral role, and that shouldn't be paralyzing, because it's freaking freeing!

"We may be pawns within our own lives, but when it comes to shaping the paths of those around us, we are grandmasters. We are each other's green lights. We are the speed bumps, the detours, the stop signs, the fast lanes. We are gravity. We are godlike.

"So what does this require of us? This realization that every choice we make will have a profound impact on everyone we will someday encounter? How do we account for the part we play in this butterfly effect, this chain reaction? What are we supposed to do now?

"Not much, really. We just have to stay the course. Try to be good people. That's really it. Not every kind deed will be reciprocated. Not every cruel act will be punished. But that's not the point. The idea is to follow the golden rule, to perform the occasional mitzvah, to maintain a steady karma, and to do all this, well, just because. Do what you think is right, even if your own future remains in doubt. You don't get to know why. You just have to keep on trying.

"Imagine yourself as the middle man on a Grease Pole

team. There is someone beneath you, whose shoulders you are teetering on and whom you must put all of your trust into, but at the same time, there is someone else too, that guy on top, and his entire fate is in your hands.

"So, fellow Bulldogs, even though you've worked unbelievably hard to get to today, try to forget about yourself. Remember those beneath you. Remember those you must hold up. And remember that all of those people, and not you, never ever you, determine whether you fall to your doom or reach the very top. Remember that, graduates. Remember that always.

"It might make all the difference.

"Thank you."

I searched for my family. I scanned the thousands of spectators cascading down the bleachers and onto the field. I saw the mothers placing leis around their daughters' necks. I watched the fathers blasting foghorns in their sons' ears. In that moment, I didn't feel I deserved to be among them. I realize this runs counter to the speech I had just delivered, in which I endeavored to eliminate the concept of "deserve" entirely. But still. I watched all of my classmates, none of whom could accurately be described as my friends, and I felt guilty. If life is a Grease Pole, then I can't help but feel as if I stomped on all of their backs in order to make my ascent.

Right then, without warning, my body got crushed. I was seized from behind—*whoomp!*—and squeezed like a tube of toothpaste. The boy I'd been avoiding for weeks was suddenly here, and naturally he was wrapping me in the Guinness Book of World Records's most suffocating hug.

"Allie!" he breathed into my ear. "I missed you!"

"Hi, Brian," I said, extracting myself from his boa constrictor grip.

"Great speech," he said.

"Thanks."

His smile was wide. His forehead was glistening. His eyes were far too trusting.

I shifted back and forth.

"Look," I said, feeling nauseous, feeling ashamed, feeling filled to the brim with pity, feeling supremely condescending, trying to formulate any words to say, simply convinced I needed to apologize, utterly positive I was about to throw up.

"I'm sorry," I said. "You know, I didn't mean to abandon you. I didn't—"

Brian didn't seem to comprehend. "What?" he said.

"I—I'm leaving you. I chose myself. I—"

Brian scratched the top of his head. "Oh," he said. "Yeah. I don't care."

Just then, he looked past me. He peered over my shoulder. He saw something. His eyes lit up.

"ABUELA!" he cried.

"Mr. Rey!" he shouted.

"Mrs. Rey!" he hollered.

"Alejandro!"

"Augusto!"

"GUYS!!!!!"

Brian bounded past me to meet my family. They clapped and cheered like he had just graduated magna cum laude. My mom placed a lei around his neck as though he were her son. Abuela plied him with as many Goldfish crackers as he wanted. My dad took pictures of him with me, dozens and dozens of them. My brothers insisted on a game of impromptu two-hand touch, scrambling onto the Big Mack's body, screeching in ecstasy as they dragged him to the ground.

I stood and watched them, my family and my friend. All the people I will be leaving behind next year. All of these vital parts of my being.

My loves are in good hands. They are. Of course they are. Of course they are.

I've done what I can.

20. COLE MARTIN-HAMMER

"Fellow Bulldogs . . ."

I sat there, up onstage, in the salutatorian spot. Random vice principals and school board members were seated to my left and right, fanning themselves like racist jury members in a Southern courtroom. A sea of my former victims lay out in front of me, sweating like ball sacks and dreaming of Disneyland. Somewhere in the stands were my parents, waving a blue and gold sign that read, PROUD OF OUR BOY.

"I stand before you, in keeping with tradition, as your valedictorian and commencement speaker. . . ."

Ooh, shocker. Allegra was using the opening paragraphs of her speech to remind us of her lofty scholastic achievements and the selfless volunteer work she did with deaf tsunami victim street babies.

I know, I know, that's gratuitous. I need to remember what my pops said. I'm supposed to be nice now. But come on, I'm allowed to hold on to this one grudge if I say I am.

"And yet . . . am I so qualified to be giving advice . . . ?

"I turned my back on my neighbor. I let my relationship with my lifetime best friend go dormant, to the degree where I don't know if I will ever get to speak to him again."

Damn. A Wiley mention. First one of those we've gotten from her since maybe the Ming dynasty. When she said it, I scanned the crowd for him, almost as a reflex. I couldn't find him, but it was hard to see from the stage.

"I'm sorry, but I have no idea why I deserve to be up here. I refuse to believe that you all should listen to a word I say. . . ."

Ha. Crocodile tears. Like I'm supposed to believe a smidge of that nonsense. Everyone knows what you're about to do there, girl. You pretend to apologize, and you project mad humility, but then you pivot and you talk about how secretly you were right all along and how everyone needs to follow your genius Stanford example.

"Life feels like a series of independent choices with rational outcomes, right until the moment when everything goes wrong, when suddenly it becomes so tempting to believe the exact opposite, that life is nothing more than a relentless barrage of arbitrary punishments and unearned rewards."

You know, that's actually Wiley's problem. He's got this idea, this fixation, that certain things are supposed to happen for him. Whether it's moving up north with Allegra, making a pass at Nikki, going all out on the revenge plot with me, he recklessly puts it all on the line for these other people, and when it inevitably doesn't pan out, he just falls so far.

"Each and every choice we make exists not in its own universe, but as the end result of all others that have been made before. . . . I played a role in letting things slip with my neighbor, but there were so many other factors too, far beyond my control. . . ."

Where *was* Wiley, anyway? I wanted to make sure he heard this speech. I wanted to find him after the ceremony, so I could make up for the camera incident, for how I treated him that day. I had to apologize for how I've used and abused him. I needed to convince him that none of it was his fault, that I'm dealing with tons of other stuff. Of course he's not a bad person. He's my best buddy, for crying out loud.

"So what does this require of us . . . ? What are we supposed to do now . . . ? Not much, really. We just have to stay the course. Try to be good people. That's really it. . . ."

And that's where I've utterly failed. I've had infinite opportunities to clean up my act, to change my stripes, to be a good dude for once in my existence. Each time, though, I took the vengeful route. Even when my dad gave me that pep talk, the come-to-Jesus that I thought would change my life, even when I tried to do the right thing by stopping Wiley from making that video, it only lasted, like, ten seconds. The moment I felt like he was trying to undermine me, I snapped right back to my truest self. I breathed fire at him. That's what monsters do.

"Imagine yourself as the middle man on a Grease Pole team. There is someone beneath you, whose shoulders you are teetering on . . . but at the same time, there is someone else too, that guy on top, and his entire fate is in your hands. . . ."

Wait.

Hold up.

What did she just say?

"And remember that all of those people, and not you, never ever you, determine whether you fall to your doom . . .

Whether you fall to your doom . . .

Whether you fall to your doom . . .

Holy shit. Holy shit.

I knew where Wiley was.

Oh my God.

With all eyes on Allie, I leaped out of my chair. I dashed past the principal and superintendent. I flew off the stage. As the applause for the speech poured in, I rushed as fast as I could down that field. I know how ridiculous I must have looked—still in my Harry Potter robes, still in my mortarboard, rushing the wrong way down the sideline like some football idiot—but I kept running, running like the fate of the world was at stake. I got there just as it was about to happen. I skidded and screamed without stopping to breathe—

"DO!!!

"NOT!!!

"JUMP!!!!!"

There Wiley stood, at the very peak of that behemoth of a theater, some forty or fifty feet up in the air. He was standing on the farthest edge of the roof, same as he had months ago. The only difference was he was even closer to the drop this time. I mean I could see his feet. They were balanced halfway off the ledge, like they were hanging ten on a surfboard, nothing below them but the ground.

"Wiley! Wiley! Look at me! *Listen* to me!"

"No," he said, more to himself than to me. He stared ahead as he said it, off in the direction of the field. "Didn't you hear Allie's speech?"

He said it in the lowest, slurriest voice. I could barely make out his words. My heart was thumping too damn loudly.

"I heard it," Wiley said. "From up here. I heard what she said. She admitted it. She gave up on me."

"YES, BUT SHE ALSO SAID DO GOOD—"

"I am doing good. This is the best thing I can think of. All I've done all year is torment the people around me. It's all I've ever done, you know? I get close to you people, too close, and eventually you run away. Shouldn't I take the hint by now?"

"BE GOOD TO *YOURSELF.* YOU'VE GOT TO BE GOOD TO YOURSELF, WILEY."

"I am, though. I'm not going to repeat senior year. I refuse to stay here forever while you all leave me behind. I won't live in purgatory. I can't let it come to that."

He sounded so creepily calm as he spoke, so premeditated, like he'd been thinking about this all year, secretly plotting his nuclear option in case all else failed.

"YOU'RE A GREAT GUY. PEOPLE LIKE YOU. THEY LOVE YOU, WILEY. YOU'RE THE BEST."

One of his mouth corners twitched, like it was as close as he could get to a sarcastic laugh. Beyond that, the rest of him remained exactly the same. His shoulders were slumped. His eyes were vacant. His toes were inching off the roof's edge. His body would not stop wavering. I think he was drunk.

Just then, he lifted one foot in the air. He extended it in front of him the slightest bit. His entire body shifted when he did that, like, a lot. He held his arms out for balance. He looked so unsteady as he did it, like the slightest gust of wind would send him toppling over. I prayed silently to a God I don't think I believe in.

"WHAT IF THE FALL DOESN'T END YOU? WHAT ABOUT THAT? DID YOU THINK ABOUT THAT? I

MEAN, HOW HIGH IS THIS BUILDING, REALLY?"

"Actually, I have thought about it," Wiley said, placing his foot down. "Honestly, Cole? It doesn't matter what happens. I accept either result. Either this ends up working, and you all won't have to deal with me anymore . . . or it doesn't work. But in a way it still works. Maybe I hurt myself. Maybe I'm damaged so badly it makes me different. You know, more like Brian. I wouldn't mind that, actually. Having that routine. That mind, that life. I could find the happiness he's found."

"BRIAN'S GETTING BETTER! AND YOU CAN TOO!"

"It's too late," Wiley said. "I'm a failure, okay? I failed high school. I don't want to fail at life, too."

"THIS IS JUST THE BEGINNING! YOU HAVEN'T FAILED AT ANYTHING."

"You don't know me."

"I DO. AND I BELIEVE IN YOU."

"Fuck you."

"NO, FUCK *YOU* FOR DOING THIS."

"Don't say 'fuck you' to a guy who's about to jump off a roof."

"I CAN'T HELP IT. IT'S WHO I AM."

"This is who I am."

"NO, IT'S NOT."

"I'm worthless."

"YOU ARE MY FRIEND."

"Shut up," Wiley said, his tone flatter than ever, his eyes at their deadest. "Shut up, Cole. Fuck you. Just leave me the fuck alone. Fuck you. I'm a loser. I'm a fucking loser. I'm a loser."

He lifted his foot again, and this time it was real, like he lifted it, and he didn't hold his arms out, and he leaned his body forward, and he still wouldn't look me in the eye, and he tipped his head down, the whole long way down, down toward his endpoint, and he unbent his knee, and he stretched his foot forward, and it was like he was about to take the most casual step on the most ordinary day. Only he wasn't; he was walking into nothing, right into nothing forever—

And I don't know what possessed me to do this. I mean I'll never know what in heaven's name led me to do what I did, but before he could move another millimeter, I threw my hand up, and I yanked my mortarboard off my head, and I did what so many before me have done. I cocked back and flung the thing high in the air, like way high, like ten feet up, twenty feet, thirty feet, forty, and I belted as loud as I could—

"YOU!

"ARE!

"A!

"GRADUATE!!!"

And it flew, it flew, end over end, through the air, right on target, like it had somewhere it needed to be.

And Wiley got so distracted by the random flying hat suddenly entering his field of vision that he went and did the automatic thing, the thing any person would do in that situation:

He reached out and caught it.

He looked down at it, this graduation cap in his hand. He looked down at me.

Then back at the cap.

Then back at me.

Back at the cap. Back at me.

The cap. Me. The cap. Me. The cap.

He returned his outstretched foot to the ledge. He held his arms out for balance, and he took a step down and a couple back, until he was all the way safe on the roof.

And then he did something else:

He started giggling.

It shook his whole body, the laughter. He seized so hard and he wouldn't stop. He laughed for the longest-ass time, and only after his entire body was completely spent from spasms did he finally die down.

"Wow," Wiley said.

"Yeah," I said.

"That shouldn't have worked," he said. "That really shouldn't have worked."

I just dropped my head in my hands. I let out the breath to end all breaths.

Then I stuck a hand in the air. A finger, to be specific.

"Okay, little birdie," I said. "Time to fly home."

We made it back to the field in time for the tail end of post-ceremony pictures and congratulations. When my parents asked why I'd run off like that at the end of the speech, I said "Hey, sometimes nature calls," and we all laughed like fools. My pops pulled me aside and asked if everything was okay. I said I'd had to help my friend Wiley and that we'd need to get him professional help as soon as possible. My dad patted me on the head and said, "Good man." The four of us agreed to have dinner together that night. I said first we had to stop at the gas station for some Nutter Butters.

Wiley's family wasn't there, of course, since he wasn't graduating, and also because, well, I don't want to think about why he hadn't invited them. But even though his folks didn't show, Allegra's family spotted him from across the field. They looked overjoyed to see him, like he was one of their own. Papa Rey made Wiley and Allegra take a BFFs-for-life pic. She looked legitimately cute in the photos, her arm around Wiley, clutching him close. He still had his same smile from the roof.

I didn't get a chance to see Nikki or Mona on the field. I'm guessing they hustled out with their parents as soon as the ceremony ended. Given what they went through at prom, and really all year, I honestly don't blame them. I know I'll never truly be able to make amends with those ladies, but I hope I find a way to try. I guess that's something I'll have to deal with moving forward.

Brian Mack was the most boisterous kid out there. He scampered around, giving ginormous hugs to every Bulldog in a robe he could find. He even hugged me. He hoisted me up and squeezed my body till my ribs crackled. Everyone took pictures of us and cheered.

And it made me happy, seeing my old friend so happy like that. At the same time, though, I have to admit, as I watched Brian dance and play, as I felt the brute force of his embrace, I felt something else, too. More bitter than sweet. You could even say I got a little depressed.

I wonder how it should have been.

EPILOGUE:
HOMECOMING WEEK

BRIAN

I stepped forward to take my bow.

I didn't expect lots of cheers. I mean I'd only been onstage for the last five minutes. My part didn't even have lines. The little girl who played Scout had to memorize, like, three hours of stuff. And Cole was mind-blowing as Tom Robinson—he actually cried during the trial scene, like, legit tears down his cheeks. That's real acting, right there. All I had to do as Boo Radley was walk onstage and stand there like a dumbass.

But I'm not any ordinary dumbass, am I?

I'm the Big Mack, bitches.

The second I stepped forward, everyone in the audience, all the people in the city college performing arts center, they got on their feet. They whooped like wild monkeys. They stomped like Polynesian football dudes. They chanted my name, again and again.

So come on, of course I had to give them a show.

I held out both my hands. I slapped them on my gut. And I jiggled.

I jiggled *hard.*

My mom and dad covered their eyes. My brother cheered, "Hell yeah," and so did my old teammates and *Seuss* friends, the ones who haven't left for college. Nikki and Mona giggled their butts off. Coach just smiled.

I thought I spotted someone else in the very last row. She was all by herself. She was wearing a red sweatshirt. Her hair was straighter than normal, but still a few curls. I couldn't see her face. Her hands were in her face. Maybe she was crying.

But Allie couldn't have come to my show. She's up at school now. She can't be back in town. There's no reason for her to be here.

So I didn't worry about her. I danced for myself. I boogied the night away.

Jiggle, jiggle, jiggle.

ALLEGRA

As the pews emptied out yesterday afternoon, I made my rounds. I stopped by each cluster of family members and friends to thank them for coming.

I thanked Pam Otis for bringing all of the food. I told my band friends how lovely their rendition of "Amazing Grace" had been. I thanked my dad and Abuela for being so emotionally open, and I thanked my brothers for being so brave. I thanked the priest for his exceptional eulogy.

Wiley thanked me. He told me how much it had meant to him, getting the opportunity to compile and edit the footage for my mom's tribute video. I told him no thanks were necessary, that we simply chose the best man for the job. He said he appreciated it all the same. I hugged him and said, "See you this Christmas. I can't wait for your birthday film festival."

After the service and reception, I escorted my family back home. We gathered on the living room couch, said a brief prayer, and ate a quick dinner. We shed a few final tears and headed to bed.

By five this morning, I was off.

I'm never quite comfortable leaving my family behind, especially under such trying circumstances. But all the same, they understand. They really do.

There is much to get done.

I have my chem 31 midterm on Monday, not to mention a paper due for my gender and sexuality class. The marching band is meeting after lunch to walk through the halftime show for USC, but I'll have to leave early for improv, and I'll have to jet out of there in order to make it to Wilbur Dining in time for faculty night, at which I'll be hosting my linguistics professor, who I'm crossing my fingers will write my letter of rec for this summer program I've been looking at in Ecuador. On top of all that, I owe Chloe a boba date, and Pooja and Alexis want to try fountain hopping with me, and David invited me over to watch a foreign film in his room, and I'd really like to see where that goes.

So I drive.

So I head north, through the blue-orange dawn, hands ten and two, eyes fixed ahead. I ride on, up the 101, refusing to relinquish my past, yet eager to take hold of all tomorrow brings.

Thank you, Mama. Thank you for letting me go. Thanks for making me.

You've let me be a freshman again.

WILEY

I held for lighting. I checked for sound. I hit record. I told my subject we were rolling. I waited a beat, for her to get ready. I called out, "Action."

She walked down the hallway, pausing to stop at various classrooms. At each window, I told her to place her hand on the glass and look pensive. When she wasn't being pensive enough, I told her look more pensive, like you have regrets. Eventually, after five or six times of this, she turned to me. She opened her jaws and snarled.

You know what they say the number one rule of filmmaking is:

Don't work with animals.

The Bear asked why we needed so many takes of this exact same shot. I explained that in any good documentary, you want lots of random footage of the subject looking thoughtful. She said she was starting to have doubts about this whole documentary thing. I said, "Do you want to be in the Dos Caminos Film Festival or not? Do you want to help my career or not? Do you want to be a star or not?"

The Bear grunted and nodded.

Just then, the door closest to us opened.

Dozens of girls streamed out. All different kinds of girls. Hot girls breaking dress code. Wide-eyed freshmen with braces. Religious girls in Jesus shirts. Jock girls who could destroy me. AP girls clutching textbooks. Bad girls who smell like smoke.

I kept my camera trained on all of them, for stock footage purposes.

In the end, two girls were left. They were chatting and laughing. One had strikingly shiny hair. I recognized them both:

Nikki Foxworth and Mona Omidi.

Nikki looked flustered to see me. She gripped Mona's shoulder and almost moved behind her. I asked what they were up to. Nikki said volunteering. Mona explained that it was a peer mentorship group they'd started, to talk with girls about their self-image. I said that sounds awesome. Nikki asked what I was doing here. I explained that I've founded my own production company, and that I did the video tribute for Magdalena Rey's memorial, and a docuseries about stoner culture post-graduation, and now I'm making my magnum opus, *Ursa Major: Thirty Years of Maude Behrman at Dos Caminos High.*

Right then, I got an idea. I snapped my fingers. I smiled.

I asked Nikki if she ever wanted to be in a movie.

Mona's jaw fell open. Nikki's hand shot to her cheek.

It didn't hit me at first.

Then it did. I realized what I'd just said. My whole body went numb. There were one, two, three beats of silence.

And then Nikki . . .

She burst into laughter. She bit down on her fist and died of ridiculous snickers. Mona did too. And I did too. I doubled over, nearly in pain. I cracked up hardest of all.

The Bear swiped her paw. She shushed us repeatedly. She yelled at us to shut up.

Just like old times.

NIKKI

Peer group was amazing.

Mona and I had planned on keeping the meeting short and the focus narrow. What with homecoming this weekend, we wanted to discuss dance-related anxiety and lead a group dialogue about just that. After I shared my experiences from last year, though, Lindsey raised her hand and said she felt like she was being pressured into having sex with her boyfriend, and Dominique shared the same. Kyndall said her boyfriend had been making comments about how she was going to look in her new dress, and that she'd been stress-eating as a result. Mikayla admitted she was concerned because her best friend hasn't been eating nearly enough, and Andrea said it wasn't her boyfriend she was scared of not pleasing; it was her mom.

The afternoon was pretty heavy overall. I mean it wasn't exactly nonstop fun, but at the same time, for me it weirdly kind of was. Not to be boastful, but Mon and I really are great listeners, and I know we're making those ladies feel actually valued, and even important, and yeah, the session just flew by today, like so quickly I completely lost track of the hour, so by the time I finally looked, I realized—whoops—I was late for class.

I rushed out the door. I laughed my way through an awkward run-in. I jammed over to DCCC. A few minutes later, I sprinted into the beginning stats lecture hall. I grabbed the only free chair I could find.

Yet in my haste, there was something I didn't notice.

That one free seat, it happened to be located directly next to a certain someone.

Professor Martin's favorite student. Professor Martin's only child.

I plopped down right beside Cole Martin-Hammer.

Of course I did.

I could have buried my face in my palms. I could have raised my hand and demanded a seat transfer. I could have spat at that boy, or punched him, or screamed.

But you know what?

Why give him the power?

I stuck my hand out and said this moment was long overdue. I told him I look forward to getting to know the real Cole. I promise not to judge. And if he, or anyone else, should judge me?

Then hell, I vow not to care.

COLE

My pops asked if I wanted to go with him to the homecoming game.

I said sure. Sounds like fun.

I'd never in my life attended a football game before tonight, but I have to say, it was kind of how I'd always imagined it. The air was brisk. The smell was corn doggy. The boys stared at the field. The girls stared at their phones. The smart boys talked to the girls. Wiley was in the very top row, videotaping the action. Brian was in the Bulldog Ring of Honor, surrounded by his family and a bunch of drunks.

There was one thing that surprised me tonight. Something I truly didn't expect.

My sudden irrelevance.

Apart from Wiley and Big Mack, and the occasional Scrotes sighting, I barely knew a soul at the game. For reals.

I'm a thing of the past. I don't know these new seniors. I don't know their faces, don't know their names. And, more than anything, I don't know their gossip.

Where's the big party tonight? Who's bringing the good stuff? Who's gonna get lit? Who's gonna get liver failure? Who's gonna hook up? Who's gonna bump uglies? Who's gonna make babies? Who in this stadium is about to make a mistake so monumentally moronic that it will fundamentally change who they are as a human being forever?

Who just sucks?

I watched these strangers. I studied them closely. Obviously Earl is never going to get me to care one bit about football, so I spent the night fixated on these kids' faces. I tried to learn their stories.

The homecoming queen, receiving her tiara and sash, bursting with joy as her so-called princesses give her the side eye.

The slacker in the stands, drooling after the girl two rows up, failing to realize that all that stands between him and her love is a simple shave of the 'stache.

The band nerd in the college beanie, playing her heart out but playing too hard, not understanding that sometimes she needs to take a breath.

The big boy on the field, the one with the paunch, who Coach won't stop yelling at: "Get your head in the game. Get your head in the game."

Huh. Maybe I do know these kids.

I don't know everything about them. I don't know the intimate details of their actual lives. I don't know their dilemmas, don't know their dreams. But I know these seniors. I understand their world. I can see it from the bleachers, from my bird's-eye-view. I see the interconnections, the invisible strings.

And, just as I think that, I hear something.

Swwst. Psswt.

It's beneath me. Underneath my feet.

Pswpsst. Spwst.

I peer between my legs, below the stands. I can see two people. Two boys. One is tall, dark-skinned, and rocking turquoise pants. The other is as puny as a rat.

The tall kid says something. The little boy's eyes go wide and white. The older one smirks. He leans in, cups his hand, and whispers another scandalous secret. Then he pulls something out from his back pocket. It's a long, tubelike snack, and—

Oh my Gerd.

That kid. The lanky kid with the bright-ass pants.

That's—

No way.

Neil?

Half of me knows I have to run down there right now. I've got to command Neil to cease with the slander, to stop corrupting that poor tiny frosh. I need to beg and plead him not to repeat my mistakes. I must definitively declare that this isn't the way.

The other half of me knows there's really no point. It's out of my hands. I can't change the changeling. That's not how things work.

To tell him who to be, or to let him be?

That is my question. That's always the question. . . .

I've never been good at making decisions.

ACKNOWLEDGMENTS

This book would not have been possible without the following people and one cat:

To Alex Glass, whose instincts I trust more than my own. Thank you for the otherworldly agenting, and for letting me ride shotgun as you embarked on your own road. I'll be the Renée Zellweger to your Jerry Maguire any day.

On a related note, thank you to Christian Trimmer, for performing endless plastic surgeries on this book until it was finally beautiful. You pushed me to my absolute artistic limits, and I'm terrified of knowing what happens in the alternate universe in which our paths never intersect (answer: my life is immeasurably worse, but you do win that one tennis match).

Thank you to Krista Vitola, for merging into my lane at the last possible second. Additional thanks to the entire visionary team at Simon & Schuster: Justin Chanda, Krista Vossen (like I always say, one Krista V. isn't enough, you gotta have two Krista V's), Hilary Zarycky, Katrina Groover, Chava Wolin, Penina Lopez, and a special thank-you to Catherine Laudone. Thanks also to Francesco Bongiorni, for the mind-altering cover art.

Thanks to Jason Richman, Josh Adler, and Julian Rosenberg, for all the showbiz support, and for being so alliterative.

Thank you to Sylvie Greenberg, Jordan Carr, and Andrew "Andrea" Molina, for the middle draft reads. No Jordan, Big Mack isn't based on you. Yes Molina, Nikki is based on you.

Thanks to Channing, for casually strolling across the keyboard every single time I was about to write an important sentence. You nearly prevented this horrible book from ever existing. Thank you for your service.

An unfathomably huge thank-you to my magic feathers and best friends, Team Steinkellner: Kit, for the fashion descriptions and unreal sense of story, Emma, for the alcove lunches and boundless inspiration, Brian, for the, uh, stuff, Dad, for the joke-writing genes and also the sensitive crybaby genes, and Mom, for every last nugget of advice, whether unwanted or yearned for, whether pragmatic or woo woo. Many thanks also to Team Khademi: Monib, Julie, Casey, and all seven rodent-dogs.

Finally, thank you times infinity plus one to the love of my life, Court/Raj. When I first conceived of the idea that became this novel, we were fighting our way through the darkest year imaginable. Days into my work on the final draft, I happened upon your engagement ring. Now, three short months after the book's release, we'll be married. And all this time, you've been lifting me, listening to me, leading me down the road, one arm around my waist, the other thrust to the sky. Thank you for the enduring companionship and the daily joy. I love you. I love you. Caught it.

Teddy Steinkellner